Mr. Bob Stoddard
8446 Cranford Way
Citrus Hts, CA 95610

MW00582540

TIME FALL

A Novel

BY

TIMOTHY ASHBY

Copyright © 2013 Timothy Ashby
All rights reserved.

ISBN: 1939990157
ISBN-13: 978-1939990150

"The separation between past, present, and future is only an illusion, although a persistent one."

Albert Einstein

"Ashby's blissfully concise prose makes this 350-pager feel half the length. History buffs will delight in the World War II backdrop, but the book's action, style and unremitting pace make it a triumph across-the-board."

Kirkus Reviews

Also by Timothy Ashby
Devil's Den

PROLOGUE

Berlin, April 20, 1945

The boy stood in the shell-cratered Reich Chancellery garden, eyes swollen from smoke and sleeplessness. He swayed in his rotting boots, listening to explosions and the ratcheting noise of automatic weapons fire a few blocks away.

At that moment the biggest worry of 12-year-old Hanno Kasper was not death or maiming, but stench. His own, to be exact. He knew that the Führer, whom he was waiting to meet, was a stickler for personal hygiene. Hanno had not bathed or changed his clothes in over three weeks, and when he wasn't concentrating on survival, the reek of his body made him gag.

Eight other boys between the ages of eleven and sixteen waited with him. They wore soiled and torn Hitler Youth uniforms and *Einheitsfeldmütze* caps. One of them, the smallest and thinnest, had his sleeve cut away from a bandage-swathed arm. Fresh blood seeped through the dirty white of the bandage. Hanno watched the smaller boy's pained expression, wondering if he'd be able to hold his tears until the audience with the Führer was over.

There was movement at the far end of the *Reichskanzlei* garden. The SS guards around the boys stiffened. The haggard lieutenant responsible for them muttered *"Achtung,"* and the youths came to attention. Hanno couldn't suppress the trembling of his exhausted body.

Hitler shuffled towards them, accompanied by Artur Axmann, the Hitler Youth leader, and several Nazi functionaries that Hanno didn't recognize. He stood fifth in line, watching from the corner of his eye as Hitler stopped in front of each boy. The Führer walked in a stoop, limbs shaking as if palsied. A Russian shell screamed over the shattered Chancellery walls and the Party officials ducked instinctively. Hitler seemed oblivious to it and continued to move down the rank like an automaton.

Then he was in front of Hanno. Hitler's face was white and puffy, his eyes feverish. Dandruff flecked the turned up collar of his overcoat. Hanno felt a lump in his throat as big as his fist. Axmann gave the Führer a medal from a velvet-lined box, smiled at the boy, and introduced him as a hero who had knocked out a Russian tank. Hitler paused with the decoration in his quivering hands. For an instant, his eyes locked with the boy's. He nodded and pinned the Iron Cross first class on Hanno Kasper's stinking jacket.

In the days that followed, as the boy slept in concrete drains next to corpses, as he roamed the burning city with a band of Hitler Youth and SS troopers, ambushing Russians and executing German deserters – even when he was caught by a Russian patrol whose Mongol soldiers cuffed and kicked him - he hid the Iron Cross in his cheek.

Nobody was going to take away his most cherished possession. And nothing was going to make him forget what Hitler had said as he pinned the Iron Cross on his jacket. The Führer's voice had been reduced to a thin rasp, but

Hanno had heard the words like thunder in his head and heart: "You are the guarantor of the future."

Berlin, Present Day

"....guarantor of the future," the old man whispered.

Hanno Kasper opened his eyes and gazed out the floor-to-ceiling window of his penthouse office in the Treptowers building. The Berlin spread out below was almost unimaginably different from the ruined city where he had fought and survived as a feral child seven decades earlier. He sneered at the huge "Molecule Man" sculpture in the River Spree, shaking his head at the irony of its seemingly bullet-riddled figures rising from a spot where he had seen dozens of drifting corpses after the fall of Berlin. And adding insult to the injury of his German pride, the sculptor was both an American *and* a Jew!

Kasper's eyes returned to the *Bild* tabloid spread on his desk. "Fire Terror!" the headline screamed, describing a wave of car burnings by young anarchists that was convulsing Berlin. His jaw clenched as he read the newspaper's interview with him in which he had called the arson "a precursor to terrorism." The reporter had described Kasper as national security advisor to Germany's chancellor, a retired

Brigadegeneral of the *Kommando Spezialkräfte* – the elite military special forces unit known as the KSK – and current Chairman of Deutscher Sicherheits und Hilfdienst GmbH Berlin (DSH), Europe's largest private security company.

Well, at least those yellow journalists got that *right!* He glanced at an article about yet another attempt to get good German taxpayers to bail out lazy Greeks and Spaniards, then angrily wadded up the paper and threw it at a credenza, where it knocked over a recent photo of Kasper with the Chancellor and the American President. *A female Ossi and a neger leading two of the world's greatest nations!* Kasper snorted in disgust.

He reached across the desk, opened a little walnut case, and took out the Iron Cross. The talisman was showing its age - like him he thought wryly - its edges tarnished and the swastika's blacking nearly worn away. Yet the connection was still profound, a direct link to a better time when Germany's great destiny had been unblemished and young Hanno had believed in his Führer and the Reich. He closed his fist around the medal and heard Adolf Hitler's words again across the decades.

"I *am* the guarantor," he vowed. *"Zu Befehl!"*

Over Europe, April 21, 1945

"The poor sods. Their odds of returning alive are about the same as playing Russian Roulette with five loaded chambers – one in six."

Lieutenant Arthur Sutton, aboard the C-47 transport carrying him to the drop zone halfway across Europe, remembered the words of his instructor. The pub in the village of Achnacarry had been crowded and noisy after their last day of training at the Scottish commando school. Sutton had been standing behind two of the British training sergeants, trying to attract the attention of the barmaid so he could order a glass of ale. The tough Welsh instructor was on his second pint, and his voice was loud and ragged with sorrow as he spoke to his companion.

Sutton pretended not to have overheard as he pushed to the bar. The instructor greeted him with a grin and raised his tankard in salute, but Sutton saw the bleakness in his eyes, as if he were toasting the deceased at a wake.

Now, as the C-47 shuddered, Sutton tried not to dwell on what awaited him and the five US Rangers he commanded. His battle experience just made the fear worse. He remembered corpses littering the rocks beneath Pointe du Hoc. Two hundred and twenty-five Rangers had climbed those cliffs; Sutton had been among the ninety survivors. However, compared to this new mission, D-Day had been a cakewalk.

His eyes closed as he conjured an image of his girlfriend, Elaine, to replace the horrors of Normandy and the mournful eyes of his instructor. He smiled as he remembered their last evening together before he shipped out in the fall of 1943. Sutton had scrounged some gasoline coupons so they could drive his '32 Ford coupe from Lee's Summit into Kansas City. The USO dance band was a third-rate imitation of Woody Herman's, the Spam sandwiches were stale, and Elaine's feet hurt. But on the way back, he had parked in a cemetery and the Ford's windows soon fogged. Elaine let him unhook her bra. Her carmine lipstick smeared his face, and her nipples hardened under his fingertips. He had groaned and reached for her garter belt.

"No," she gasped, stopping his delving hands. "I'm not that kinda girl, Art."

"C'mon, baby. Who knows how long I'm gonna be away fighting for our country? Could be years and we'll be getting married anyway when I come back ho–"

The aircraft dropped in an air pocket, jolting Sutton back to the present. He peered up the row of men in canvas bucket seats. The Rangers' faces bore a variety of grimaces as the transport bucked through the turbulence. At the end of the bench, an Alabama farm boy named Holcombe nervously transferred grenades from a canvas pouch to cargo pockets in his jump trousers. Holcombe's lips moved in prayer while perspiration streaked his cheeks. Sutton knew from his own damp hair and armpits that sweat got cold fast in the cabin's thirty-eight degree Fahrenheit temperature.

Sergeant Hugo Roth sat beside Sutton, scowling at Holcombe. Roth unsnapped his safety belt and staggered up the aircraft's pitching deck. He thrust his face at Holcombe's.

"Leave the grenades alone!" he barked. "You could blow us up!"

Holcombe gulped and nodded. Roth returned to his seat and buckled himself in. He looked at Sutton with frosty blue eyes, mouth twisted in disapproval.

"How are we expected to carry out this mission with sad sacks like that?" Roth asked in his strong German accent. "I don't know how he got into the Rangers."

"Can it, Sergeant," Sutton said wearily to his second-in-command.

"The kid sets a bad example! I could see that weeks ago when he—"

"I said *can* it, Sergeant! That's an order!"

Roth's eyes blazed defiantly before he turned his glare back to Private Holcombe.

The Rangers' transport was named *Bouncing Betty*. Like the men she carried, the airplane bore a combat veteran's scars. Shrapnel from anti-aircraft batteries across Europe had pierced its wings and pitted its fuselage. Scottish sleet and Sicilian sun had weathered the cartoon of *Betty Boop* on the transport's nose, fading the letters of her name.

Bouncing Betty was part of a formation of ten C-47's from the US IX Troop Carrier Command based near the Essex village of Boreham. At 8:51 P.M. British Double Summer Time, they had rendezvoused with ten British transports over Shoeburyness and formed into a staggered pattern to give German radar and ground observers the impression of an aerial armada.

A squadron of P-51 Mustang fighters joined the formation over Dunkirk, pacing the lumbering transports above and alongside to protect them from the Luftwaffe's new jet ME-262 night fighters. *Betty's* pilots grinned as the Mustang jockeys filled their headphones with wisecracks.

The transport's teenaged flight engineer ducked inside the cockpit. "Radio operator just picked up a weather report," he said. "Severe electrical storms northern France, southern Germany. Low cloud ceiling."

"It might screw up the Kraut radar a bit," the copilot remarked, "but it's going to be hell dropping those boys at low altitude."

"No shit," said the pilot, frowning.

Sutton kept looking at his Hamilton wristwatch, a gift from his grandparents after he graduated from the University of Missouri. His grandparents had raised him since he was six years old after being orphaned by a tornado. Grandpa, a retired dentist, had grumbled when Sutton chose to study history and German instead of re-opening the little office on Market Street in Lee's Summit. Still, he had shared Grandma's happiness when Sutton strode across the stage in his spanking new US Army uniform to accept his college diploma. After the ceremony, Grandpa had joked that Art would be "catnip to the ladies" – thinly disguised pride from an old man who still had a twinkle in his eye.

Sutton hoped he wouldn't be catnip to the Germans.

He looked around the dimly lit cabin, wondering if his men had written "just in case" letters and left them with the chaplain, as he had. Sergeant Roth appeared to be asleep. Another Ranger talked with the jumpmaster. The remaining men rubbed black camouflage greasepaint on their faces and checked equipment.

The aircraft lived up to its nickname as it bounced through patches of disturbed atmosphere from the storm front. Sutton touched the breast pocket of his tunic, feeling the outline of a folded letter from Elaine. It had arrived the day before he left Achnacarry. He had read it a dozen times already, trying to extract nuances from her bland sentences. Elaine was working in the big ordnance factory at Lake City, making more money than she had ever dreamed of, but complained that rationing provided little opportunity for her to spend it.

He sighed and again withdrew the letter, imagining her fingers folding it, tongue licking the envelope. A tiny round object fell from the envelope onto the aircraft's metal deck. It rolled towards the tail as he desperately fumbled with his safety belt. *Bouncing Betty's* flight engineer picked it up and walked toward Sutton.

"This belong to you, Lieutenant?"

The flight engineer opened his palm, displaying a button with President Franklin Roosevelt's image surrounded by the red, white and blue words "Carry On With Roosevelt." Sutton grinned, feeling sheepish, and plucked it from the young sergeant's hand.

"Yeah, thanks. It's, ah, my good luck charm. I've had it for nine years now and this would be a hell of a time to lose it."

The flight engineer nodded. "Know what you mean. Had me a rabbit's foot up until I got drafted." He pushed a fatigue cap back on his crew-cut head. "Name's Jim Ward. Home's back in Springfield, Missouri."

Sutton introduced himself as a fellow Missourian and held up the campaign button so Ward could see.

"Would you believe old FDR himself gave this to me."

The flight engineer's eyebrows rose. "No shit?"

"Bet your life. The President came to Kansas City in '36 to give a speech. A bunch of us kids from the high school got to shake his hand afterwards. He had this box of buttons on his lap and he pinned one on each of us. When my turn came, I wished him good luck, and he said he hoped the same for me."

Ward squatted beside him. "Did you have good luck after that?"

Sutton laughed. "Hell yes! The next night I got laid for the first time and I've had nothing but good luck since."

"Can't believe he's gone."

"Yeah," Sutton shook his head. "He was president for more than half my life."

Sutton and Ward exchanged anecdotes about Missouri childhoods and marveled that a one-armed man had been signed to play major league baseball for the St. Louis Browns. Sutton sensed Roth listening as they talked; from the corner of his eye he saw the sergeant sit up as they began discussing the Rangers' mission.

"I knew you guys was Rangers from your badges." Ward pointed to the blue lozenge-shaped insignia on Sutton's left shoulder. "So I figured this was some kind of special mission. What are you guys called? 'Fox' team?"

"Yeah, we're trained to operate behind enemy lines. Jumping into Germany to—"

"*Lieutenant Sutton!*" Roth's agitation thickened his accent. "Must I remind you that our mission is of the utmost secrecy! For all we know this man may be a Nazi spy!"

Sutton clenched his fists. He never intended to tell Ward any more than basic facts about their mission.

"Talk about Nazi spies!" Ward stared at Roth. "Where the hell you from, Fritz, the Gestapo?"

Roth paled. He loosened his safety belt with trembling fingers and moved to the far end of the row of seats.

"Is that guy for real?" Ward asked. "Does he really talk like that?"

"Sergeant Roth is a German Jew. A refugee. The Nazis killed most of his family."

Ward cleared his throat and slumped into Roth's vacated seat. "Guess he's right about your mission being secret and all, Lieutenant. I shouldn't have asked."

"So what could you do even if you were an enemy agent? I don't think it makes any difference now that we're airborne. Besides, you know too much about the old Missouri State Fair to be a spy."

"Just curious," Ward replied.

"We're part of what the brass calls Operation Bandstand," Sutton said. "A German resistance group called Freedom Action Bavaria is planning to take over Bavaria from the Nazis, but they want the Allies to help them out with an airborne assault."

Sutton paused, remembering the words of the intelligence officer who had prepared them for the mission. "Our side doesn't want to risk too much helping those Resistance guys kick out the Nazis, but they didn't tell the Germans that. Instead, we've leaked word to both Freedom Action

Bavaria *and* the Nazis that a major Allied air assault will take place."

Sutton grinned. "Buddy, we're part of that gigantic airborne army of exactly one hundred and twenty-two British Commandos and American Rangers."

"Only a hundred and twenty-two?"

"Yup. It's a con. Rumor is, Churchill came up with the idea. See, we're jumping into Bavaria to raise hell so the Krauts will think a big-time attack *is* taking place. The brass hopes the Wehrmacht will pull out some of its divisions along the Rhine to reinforce Bavaria. They also hope that our little diversion will cause the Resistance fighters to come out of the woodwork and tie down the Nazis."

Ward sucked a breath deep into his lungs, shaking his head. "And to think I wanted to be a Ranger!" His intent gaze made Sutton feel that the young sergeant was imprinting his face on his memory. He wondered if Ward saw that beneath his attempt to look tough, he was struggling to contain his fear.

Ward touched Sutton's shoulder. "Better keep a tight grip on that good luck charm, Lieutenant."

At 10:31, five minutes after crossing the Rhine south of Rastatt, the P-51 fighters withdrew, hurtling off to refuel at a forward base near Metz. Two minutes later a red flare burst from the Bandstand formation leader and the code word "Gangbusters" was repeated three times over the radio, signaling the transports to scatter and seek their individual drop zones. Eleven thousand feet below, an artillery duel stabbed the night with dozens of tiny flashes like fireflies in a field on a Midwestern summer's night.

Bouncing Betty descended, her copilot balancing slide rule, navigational charts, and stopwatch on his knees as he snapped course changes. Sergeant Ward shone a flashlight over his shoulder.

"I just can't be one hundred percent sure without a visual," the copilot said nervously. "Shit, Cal, an error of a few degrees and we'll hit the Alps."

"You're doing okay, Woody," the pilot soothed. "I reckon we'll drop 'em right on the nose." He glanced at the instrument panel clock, then checked it against his wristwatch. "Tell the jumpmaster to give 'em the warning," he told the flight engineer.

Sutton saw Ward come aft and speak to the jumpmaster. The man nodded and stood.

"Twenty minutes, guys!" he bellowed, pointing at his wristwatch.

A Ranger named Sarnoff gazed at Sutton with wide eyes, looking like a minstrel show actor with his blackened face. "Oh jeez," he said. He fished a packet of D-ration Wrigley's gum from his musette bag and offered a stick to Sutton before cramming three into his mouth. He chewed furiously, wiping sweaty palms on his baggy trousers. "Oh jeez," he repeated.

Private Holcombe lurched towards the toilet bucket in the aircraft's tail, but didn't make it. Kneeling on the metal deck, he spewed the remnants of what the Rangers termed "The Last Supper." He rose and tottered to his seat, hands shaking so badly he barely managed to fasten the safety belt. He blinked at the man next to him.

"Airsickness," he gasped in his Alabama twang. "Happens to a lot of guys, I hear tell."

"Looks dirty," the pilot remarked. He pointed ahead where the half moon illuminated a vast wall of thunderheads streaked with lightning.

Stress aged the copilot's twenty-year-old face. "That's the storm front we were warned about."

The pilot checked the clock and airspeed indicator. "Yeah, we'll be inside it in a couple of minutes. Wish we could drop those guys over it."

An updraft buffeted the aircraft, shoving it several degrees off course. The pilot swore and corrected the compass bearing.

"We could abort if it gets too bad," the copilot said.

Cal shook his head. "And get our asses in a sling? This is a priority mission, Woody. Naw, we'll give it a try."

Violent gusts hammered *Bouncing Betty* as she sank into the seething clouds. The pilots fought the controls, relying on their few instruments as the aircraft flew blindly. Woody's gaze alternated between his scribbled computations and stopwatch. "Approach pattern!" he barked. Cal jerked a nod at the hovering flight engineer and eased back the throttles.

Sutton felt the aircraft's wings vibrate as the engines slowed and the C-47 tilted downwards. Then the jumpmaster was beside him.

"Five minutes, Lieutenant."

Sutton rose, swallowing to free his voice. "Action stations!"

The men fastened helmet straps and tightened harnesses as the flight engineer and jumpmaster moved towards the cargo door.

"What the hell?" Woody yelled. Cal's eyes swept the windshield, widening at a kaleidoscope of sparks flecking the glass. Beyond, the aircraft's nose was bathed in an eerie glow. He glanced out a side window, seeing the same bluish flame flickering along the port wing.

"It-it's only St. Elmo's Fire," he said, quavering voice betraying his doubt. "Happens when you're flying through a charged atmosphere like this thunderstorm. Nothing to worry about."

Woody continued to watch, mesmerized by the ghostly display.

"Glad *you* think so," he said hoarsely.

"Stick up, hook up!" the jumpmaster boomed.

Sutton steadied himself and clipped the hook of his parachute strop to the steel cable running the length of the ceiling. The cargo door was open now, the engine noise almost drowning the jumpmaster's shouted commands.

"Check equipment!"

Sutton, as leader of the stick, faced the doorway. The jumpmaster moved past them, checking the fastenings of the strops to the cable by pulling at the "D" hooks. The Rangers swayed, gripping the aluminum safety bars to keep their balance as the storm-tossed aircraft yawed and shook. Sutton saw sparks shooting past the black maw of the doorway.

All eyes watched the light panel over the door. Although he was expecting the two minute red warning light, Sutton tensed when it came on.

"Stand in the doorway!" the jumpmaster yelled.

Heart pounding, Sutton shuffled forward, the bulky parachute pack jouncing against his thighs. Then he was at the doorway, fingers hooked into the perforated jambs, hunched against the shrieking gale outside. He could see the tip of the aircraft's horizontal stabilizer shimmering with phosphorescent light. The metal skin of the aircraft hummed ethereally, rising in volume like a celestial chorus.

An uncanny prickling raised the hairs on the back of Sutton's neck. He wondered if it was a premonition of death.

"Knots one-oh-eight," Cal called. "Twelve hundred feet!"

"Roger!" Woody released the supply canisters from racks on the transport's belly, then punched a button turning the jump light to green.

An enormous thunderclap shook the aircraft. At that moment the electric blue glow shrouding *Bouncing Betty* intensified along with the humming sound. Sparks crackled throughout the cockpit. The aircraft's radio went dead and the compass spun like a demented top. Cal's jaw fell open, fingers tightening on the control yoke as the airplane seemed to plummet into a void. Ears ringing, he frantically scanned the instrument panel, watching its gauges fluctuate. A spasm of nausea wrenched his gut.

"Woody!" he gasped, glancing at the copilot before returning to the instrument panel. His eyes widened. The banks of red-lighted instruments were now functioning perfectly, every needle steady. "Wh-what the fuck was that?"

Woody bit his lower lip to control its trembling. "Felt like we took a direct hit!"

Cal shook his head, feeling vertigo like oxygen deprivation. He figured that the phenomenon had lasted several seconds, roughly the length of time it took for the parachutists to leave the aircraft.

"Dunno," he said, "but that weird St. Elmo's Fire is gone."

Ward stuck his head between the pilots' seats. "Everything okay?"

"Yeah," Cal replied. "What about our passengers?"

"They've jumped. Out as clean as a whistle."

"God bless 'em," Woody said. "Let's get the hell out of here and back home where we belong."

Cal banked *Bouncing Betty* into a turn and climbed out of the storm. From the corner of his eye, he saw Woody shake his left wrist, then lean forward and rap on the instrument panel clock. "Hey," the copilot said, "let me borrow your watch. Both mine and the aircraft's have stopped."

Cal pushed up his sleeve. Surprise tightened his features. "Mine's stopped too."

"Hey," added Ward, "so's mine."

Two days later, *Bouncing Betty's* crew gathered in a country pub. Cal rambled drunkenly about the strange phenomena and instrument failure while Woody watched a trio of WAAFs at the bar. But Jim Ward drank quietly, wondering what had caused every timepiece aboard the aircraft on the Bandstand mission to irreparably stop at 11:08 P.M.

Bandstand proved to be a failure, one of history's footnotes. Nearly three-quarters of the 122 British and American commandos involved were killed or captured, the bedraggled survivors eventually linking up with General Patch's Seventh Army as it rolled through Bavaria. The Bandstand commando attacks were too sporadic to convince the Germans that they were part of a major Allied airborne assault. No *Wehrmacht* units were withdrawn from the German divisions along the Rhine and the resistance fighters remained underground. The anti-Nazi movement called Freedom Action Bavaria failed to wrest Munich from the Nazis.

The war ended weeks later. Prisoner of War camp records and Graves Registration investigations provided information on those members of the Bandstand operation listed as Missing in Action. By September 1945, all but six of the commandos were accounted for.

Those six men were the members of the US 2nd Ranger Battalion's "Fox" team, commanded by First Lieutenant Arthur Sutton.

On April 22, 1946, one year and one day after the six Fox team members were last seen, the US Army declared the men legally dead.

In West Kankakee, Illinois; Loachapoka, Alabama; Philadelphia and Brooklyn, families acknowledged the end of a year's desperate hope and placed the customary gold stars in their windows.

In Fair Lawn, New Jersey, the uncle and brothers of Staff Sergeant Hugo Roth recited *Yizkor* for him and the twenty-seven other members of their family who had perished at the hands of the Nazis.

On a humid June day in 1946, a pre-war Chevy pickup bounced along a rutted farm track in Jackson County, Missouri. The driver, a recently demobbed sailor named Merle, glanced at the young woman beside him.

"Perfect day for a picnic, ain't it?"

"I guess," Elaine replied, flapping a paper fan while her jaw gyrated on a wad of chewing gum.

They parked by an isolated pond. Leaving on the truck's radio, Merle lifted a picnic basket out of the pickup's bed while Elaine spread a GI surplus blanket on the ground. Merle uncapped a thermos and poured a generous measure into a pair of metal cups, wondering if Elaine would notice that the lemonade was spiked with gin.

Before long they were lying on the blanket with Elaine's Montgomery Ward blouse undone and Merle's hand creeping up her thigh. Just as his fingers snagged the elastic band of her panties, Elaine heard a song on the radio, a hit by a young singer named Perry Como.

Till the End of Time. The song's title caused a twinge of sadness as an image of Art Sutton surfaced behind her closed eyes. She briefly wondered what had happened to him after his letters stopped coming over a year before.

"Well, life goes on," she thought, arching her hips to help Merle remove her underwear.

While Elaine was relinquishing her virginity, a memorial service was being held at the First Baptist Church in Lee's Summit.

The old church was crowded. The scent of cheap colognes mixed with the aroma of mothballs. Tears mingled with sweat to saturate handkerchiefs. Little boys in choking collars fidgeted. Little girls tried to catch the eyes of the little boys. The town's last surviving Civil War veteran fainted. Yet all eyes turned in sympathy to the elderly couple weeping in the front pew as the preacher begged repose for the immortal soul of their only grandson, Arthur Sutton.

Decades passed. Other wars flared and were extinguished. Young Americans disappeared into freezing Korean mud, fertilized Vietnamese rice paddies, and expired in Afghan valleys. Aging World War II veterans forgot the boredom and fear of their youth, wistful for the camaraderie and sense of purpose. Memories faded like photographs of lost soldiers gathering dust in attics and closets.

1

Lt. Arthur Sutton hit the ground like a sack of corn dropped from a silo. Breathless and disoriented, he lay on the cold earth and watched lightning vein the sky. He whispered a prayer of thankfulness to be alive. The jump had been the most harrowing he had experienced, like being sucked into a Kansas twister, pummeled by shrieking winds. He seemed to have fallen for miles with his senses numbed, even though he knew that the low altitude drop could only have taken seconds.

Now I know what Dorothy felt like. Except I'm somewhere a lot more dangerous than Munchkinland.

Dizziness hit him and he sat with his head between his knees. Wind billowed his parachute, jerking him backwards. Stark fear galvanized him. He climbed unsteadily to his feet, collapsing the canopy and fumbling for its harness coupling.

Thunder clapped as the storm moved east into Czechoslovakia. A dog howled in the distance. Sutton

1

stiffened, remembering Grandma's tales about dogs howling when spirits walked. *Goddamit, I'm alive and mean to stay so!*

He unclipped his Thompson submachine gun and slung it over a shoulder then wadded the parachute into a ball and tucked it under his arm. Sutton revolved slowly on his heel, pushing his senses to overcome the muzziness. He wondered where his men were. In such conditions, it would be a miracle if they had landed in their drop zone.

A breeze brushed his face, bringing with it the tang of cow dung. Cattle lowed, their bells tinkling. He heard another sound in the mist, the faint jangle of military equipment. Sutton flung himself flat, wet grass tickling his nostrils. More noises, muttering voices. Then the sharp *click-clack* of a tin cricket. Repeated.

Sutton felt for the tin cricket taped to the stock of his Thompson and answered the recognition signal. Four figures materialized from the darkness.

"Here!" Sutton thrust himself up. A face pushed close to his.

"Lieutenant?" asked Roth.

"Yeah." Sutton squinted at the four figures. "Who's missing?"

"Sarnoff. He was behind you in the stick, so he should be nearby."

Sutton expelled a breath and peered at the luminous dial of his wristwatch.

"23:08. Let's find those supply canisters before we start hunting for Sarnoff." He swung around, pointing. "You men landed up there, so the supplies should be back that way. Okay, line abreast. Move out."

They felt their way across the pasture. Sutton halted the men to check his compass, then swung the line on a tangent. Seconds later they found the first supply canister. Sitting astride it was a helmeted figure. The man jerked up his head as Roth snapped his toy cricket. A mouthful of white teeth shone in the blackened face.

"Why didn't you answer the signal?" Roth hissed. "You're lucky we didn't cut your throat!"

"Shit, Sarge," Sarnoff replied groggily, "ever since I jumped I've felt like I was concussed by a near miss from an eighty-eight. Head's spinning, ears ringing like crazy."

"Cut the chatter," Sutton ordered, wondering why Sarnoff had experienced the same strange symptoms that he had. The thought was quelled by the activity of lugging the metal cylinder into the pine forest bordering the field.

Roth took three men to sweep the pasture for the second canister. Sutton and Holcombe unfolded their shovels and dug a shallow trench beneath a tall evergreen that could serve as a landmark. They dragged the cylinder into the hole. Holcombe held a GI elbowed flashlight while Sutton unbuckled the straps securing the lid, revealing packets of food, explosives, medical supplies, and pre-loaded clips of .45 caliber ammunition.

Sutton finished packing C3 plastic explosives and detonators into backpacks as Roth and the others trudged into the clearing. They lowered the other heavy canister into the trench.

"Okay, cover the supplies." Sutton checked his watch. "Just be sure we can find 'em again when we need to." He led Roth aside. They crouched as Sutton took a waterproof packet of maps from his jacket. He spread a map across the ground and laid his compass on it.

"If we landed on target we should be here" - Sutton's finger stabbed a tiny rectangle labeled DZ - "four miles south-southeast of Kötzting." He aligned the compass along the drop zone mark, using the ruler to measure the distance to a red square marked with a numeral one. "The panzer depot should be a mile and a half due south."

Sutton glanced up as the four other men appeared from the darkness.

"Any questions?" he asked as he refolded the map.

"What if we landed in the wrong place?" Roth said.

"Then we figure out where we are and choose the next closest target with an "A" rating. There are supposed to be thirty targets within a ten-mile radius."

Roth grunted, intent on screwing a silencer onto the barrel of a Walther P-38 pistol. Sutton set off through the pine trees, the other men following with Roth bringing up the rear.

Tension had robbed Sutton of sleep for the past two nights, but at that moment, tramping through the German forest, he had never felt more alert, so much a warrior. Adrenaline fired his blood, burning off the last traces of dizziness from the parachute jump, heightening his senses so sight, sound, and smell took on new dimensions. He remembered childhood war games in the familiar woods of Missouri. Now the game was real: a special mission for his country from which he would return a hero.

A fantasy picture flashed across his mind: a *Movietone* newsreel of himself standing at attention as President Truman - another fellow Missourian - looped the Medal of

Honor over his head and Elaine watched, eyes shining, smiling the way she would when he returned to Lee's Summit and swept her into his arms again. His chest swelled, and for a moment he forgot his fear.

The men skidded and clutched at branches as the dank pine forest sloped downwards. Then the trees ended. Sutton ran down an embankment and onto a narrow road. He glanced left and right as his team hurried across to him.

"Looks like we hit the right place," Roth whispered. "This road was on the map."

"We'll know for sure in a minute." Sutton trotted up the road.

He halted after a few hundred yards. The others bunched around him, squinting at a Bavarian religious shrine marking a crossroads. Christ's pink-painted toes peeked from a bouquet of wilted flowers. Sutton pointed to a nearby post with yellow signs sprouting from its side: Kötzting 8 km, Arnbruck 17 km, Cham 39 km.

"Guess those flyboys really know their stuff." Sutton's voice betrayed his relief. "Dropped us right on the button. The panzer depot is just a quarter mile up that road." He thrust an arm towards a field stretching away into the darkness. "We'll cut across there. I want everyone crawling the moment we see the compound. Move it."

They started across the field at a lumbering run. The heavy canvas sack of explosives chafed Sutton's shoulder through his wool shirt and jacket. Soil balled on his boots, hampering his progress. The field ended and they struggled up a knoll crowded with spruce trees. Sutton reached the crest first, flinging himself to the ground.

"Down!" he rasped.

Fifty yards away, across a denuded firing zone, a ten-foot steel mesh fence ran diagonally. Triple-strand barbed wire jutted from the barrier's top, lit at hundred-yard intervals by arc lamps. Beyond the fence loomed the shadowy outlines of buildings, some showing light at their windows.

"Haven't the Krauts heard of blackouts?" Sarnoff muttered. "Shit, with them lights this place is a sitting duck for bombers."

Sutton had his binoculars out, a frown creasing his forehead.

"Those intel officers said there'd be a strict blackout here," he whispered. "This is going to be a bitch to get into without any cover."

Sutton traversed the cleared ground in front of them, checking for the humps of mines before raising the binoculars to the military buildings beyond the wire. A sentry appeared, patrolling at the farthest reaches of his vision, a dark figure in a distinctive *Wehrmacht* helmet, the barrel of his rifle a line above his shoulder.

"You think that ground is mined?" asked Roth.

"Looks okay. Can't see any humps. The bright boys in Scotland seem to have been right about that at least."

The sweep of Sutton's field glasses stopped at the camp's main gate, a white concrete blockhouse dividing the access road, with black and white striped barrier poles on either side. An empty flagpole was planted in front of the building with a large sign beside it. Sutton strained to read the sign's black letters, managing, at that distance, to only pick out the enlarged words at the top.

"Höhenbogen Kaserne," he said, lowering the binoculars.

"Maintenance depot for the Eleventh Panzer Division," added Roth.

"We still goin' in?" asked Sarnoff.

"You bet." Sutton pointed. "The darkest part of the fence is dead center between those lights. We'll go through the wire there."

He glanced around the grim faces, then began divesting himself of webbing belts and equipment. The others did likewise, retaining only their weapons. Sutton slipped a pair of wire cutters into a pocket and checked his watch while Roth distributed explosives from a canvas backpack. "Only seven minutes past midnight, so we're doing great." He wondered if the others could hear his pounding heart. "Okay, you guys know the drill." He settled his helmet on his head and began slithering on his belly towards the fence.

Stones and roots tugged at his clothing, grinding into his chest and groin. His breath came in spurts and he blinked his eyes, expecting the flash and agony of an exploding mine. Then he was at the fence, its heavy gauge mesh rearing above him. He felt naked under the arc lamps, cursing the blinding brightness that prevented him from seeing the sentry patrol path that ran along the perimeter fence.

He dragged the wire cutters from his pocket and opened the tungsten steel clippers to bite the first wire strand. Roth was beside him, his own cutters snipping a neat line up the mesh.

They finished together. Roth pulled out the rectangular piece of cut wire and laid it aside. Sutton hugged his submachine gun to his chest, rolled onto his back, and poked his head into the narrow opening, shoulder blades undulating to wriggle his body inside.

Roth clasped his arm, strong fingers restraining him. Sutton froze, ears and eyes straining.

Boots crunched on gravel, approaching from the right.

2

Roth gripped Sutton's jacket to drag him from the aperture in the fence.

As Sutton cleared the wire, he rolled onto his belly. Roth's helmet tapped against his, the elongated barrel of the sergeant's silenced pistol inches from Sutton's face.

"I will take care of him," Roth whispered.

"Only if he sees the hole," hissed Sutton. "You can't risk a shot from this position."

The footsteps came closer, scuffing the gravel. Sutton pressed into the ground, trying, as the commando instructors had taught him, to imagine himself part of the landscape. Roth lay so close that the hot air from his lungs warmed Sutton's face.

Sutton allowed only his eyes to move, flicking between the tread of the sentry's boots to Roth's pistol. He noticed the sergeant's hand trembling.

Boots less than two yards away. The sentry trudged nearer, steps erratic, scattering gravel chips. A pebble clinked against Sutton's steel helmet.

The sentry was almost in front of them now, tan boots and camouflage trousers in sharp detail, face shadowed by the Nazi helmet's rim. The boots dragged again, then halted directly in front of the hole cut through the fence.

Sutton saw Roth's hand steady as he took aim at the sentry's head. They heard the click of what sounded like a lighter. The pungent odor of cigarette smoke filled the air. Sutton thought it seemed impossible that the sentry would risk possible intruders seeing the red glow of his cigarette, but then the entire camp was supposed to be under blackout.

The sentry suddenly began speaking. Roth's tightening trigger finger froze. He and Sutton glanced at each other in disbelief as they heard the man softly recite what sounded like an incoherent poem in fractured English while shuffling in a strange dance routine:

Yo, I'm runnin' through these ho's like Drano
I got that devilish flow, rock 'n' roll, no halo
We party rock, yeah, that's the crew that I'm reppin'
On the rise to the top, no lead in our zeppelin, hey

The sentry made some whooshing noises, nodded his head, then threw the butt of his cigarette to the ground and mashed it with his boot. He yawned, seemed to adjust something on his ears under the helmet, then bobbed away.

Sutton realized that he had been holding his breath. He expelled it as the tread of the sentry's boots faded. There was no time to consider the man's odd behavior now. He slithered back up to the opening in the wire and propelled himself through, rising without breaking motion into a crouching run that brought him to the deep shadows under the wall of a building. The Rangers behind him hurled themselves against the wall at five-second intervals.

Sutton visualized the panzer depot's layout from among the two dozen target plans he had memorized over the past weeks. Followed by the others, he sidled to the end of the building and peered around the corner. The terrain was like the plan said it would be: an unlighted alley running past vehicle maintenance sheds until it ended at a parking lot for repaired vehicles at the far end.

Sutton darted from the sheltering wall. The vehicle park was surrounded by a rusted mesh fence - an unnecessary precaution, as the huge double gate yawned wide, one side crumpled as if a careless driver had collided with it. The repaired vehicles were segregated into columns of tanks, trucks and personnel carriers. Lampposts cast ineffectual pools of light at wide intervals, illuminating olive drab paint, white stars, and the large, stenciled letters *US ARMY*.

Sutton skidded to a halt, wondering if his eyes were deceiving him. He heard the gasping breaths of the other men as they slid against the wall beside him.

"What is it?" Roth asked. He saw the vehicles. So did the other four men.

"Holy shit!" someone hissed.

"What the fuck do you think–"

"Silence!" Roth snapped. He moved closer to Sutton.

"What gives, Lieutenant? These are all American vehicles."

"Don't know," Sutton said. "The briefing officers said nothing about this."

He studied the ranks of machines, bafflement growing. He pointed at a row of tanks, their cannon barrels raised like a lancer's salute.

"Never seen tanks like those before. They can't be ours, or British for that matter."

Roth grunted an assent. "They look more like German King Tigers – the *Panzerkampfwagen* Six. Must be a new type that our intelligence doesn't know about yet." Roth thrust his jaw towards the parking area. "Most of the other vehicles are unknown to me also. But why are they all painted to look like Americans?"

Something nagged at Sutton's mind, a memory of an article in *Stars and Stripes,* a story given substance by conversations with men who had served in the Battle of the Bulge five months earlier.

"It's a Kraut trick. Armored columns painted to look like they're Americans. They used that trick at the Bulge last Christmas. Really fooled our guys. Even had English-speaking Krauts in our uniforms."

"I'll be damned," Sarnoff muttered. "I remember hearing about that from a guy who was at Bastogne. Dirty motherfuckers!"

"Our fighter pilots will sure think twice before attacking 'em," Sutton added. "Let's make sure they never get out of here! Rendezvous where we left our gear in fifteen minutes."

They separated at the vehicle park gate, each man intent on his assigned task and the few minutes allotted him. Sutton ran down a lane between a row of tanks and a mixed column of self-propelled guns and armored personnel carriers.

Choosing a tank at random, he knelt beneath the engine carapace at its rear. He took a sausage-shaped piece of plastic explosive from his shoulder bag, stuck it to the armor plating and affixed a pencil detonator. He snatched up the bag of explosives and raced to another vehicle.

Sutton attached the last of his twelve explosive charges to the treads of a self-propelled howitzer, then feverishly checked his watch. Three minutes to the rendezvous. He reached the damaged gate at the same time as Roth and a private named Kemp. They trotted back down the alley, hugging the walls until they reached the barracks. Roth halted, delving into his shoulder bag.

"One last gift for the Nazis." He pressed an explosive charge against the brick wall over his head.

The three other Rangers were waiting for them on the knoll overlooking the camp, buckled into their web harness. Despite the extreme tension, Sutton sensed a feeling of professional satisfaction behind the blackened masks of their faces.

"Nice work, guys," he said.

"Will we hit the Nightfighter base next?" Roth asked.

"It's the next closest target." Sutton squinted at his watch. The time was 00:31 on the morning of April 22. "Wouldn't want the Luftwaffe to feel neglected, would we?"

Sutton felt a surge of pride as he watched his men fall into line. Maybe the Welsh instructor had been wrong — perhaps their chances of returning alive were better than he'd said.

The Rangers set off at a ground-eating trot led by Sutton. After a few minutes he recalled the strange poem of the Germany sentry.

He slowed, allowing the other men to pass him until he could walk beside Roth. "What was up with that sentry?" he asked in a low voice so the others wouldn't hear. "With the guy's mumbo-jumbo?"

Roth didn't look at him.

"*Ein Verrückter* – a madman!" he replied derisively. "The Nazis must be so short of recruits that they are emptying the asylums!" He grunted as he shifted his heavy pack. "If I was his sergeant, I would have him shot for smoking on duty. Of course, he'll be shot tomorrow anyway after they receive our gifts."

3

Höhenbogen Kaserne, Bavaria
April 22, 2011

None of the 197 men and women of the Arkansas Army National Guard's 224th Maintenance Company had any idea that Höhenbogen Kaserne had been a German Panzer base over half a century earlier, and few would have cared anyway. The camp was one of several dozen NATO bases left over from the Cold War. Largely forgotten by the US Defense Department, Höhenbogen was used to store rusting, nearly obsolete military vehicles ostensibly maintained by National Guard troops.

Like his comrades, 19-year-old Private Doug "Beamer" Kimble of Little Rock was grateful to serve his tour of duty in Germany instead of Afghanistan, even if he was nearly bored out of his effin' mind. It was still better than playing video games in the basement of his parents' home or temporary jobs stocking shelves at big box stores. Fortunately, neither the officers nor the NCOs seemed to mind him smoking on sentry duty (as long as it wasn't weed), or listening to his iPod.

Beamer finished his circuit of the camp perimeter and went into a latrine to take a leak. Under his PASGT helmet – still worn by some Army National guard units who called it a "Fritz" for its resemblance to World War II *Wehrmacht* headgear - he adjusted his ear buds, replaying LMFAO's *Party Rock Anthem*. He shuffled in a little Party Rock dance while he relieved himself.

The first explosion tore a five-foot hole into the latrine's wall, scattering bricks and plaster. Although knocked out by the blast, Beamer's urinal was shielded by a row of toilet stalls and his only injuries were concussion, minor lacerations and soiled underwear.

Another blast came seconds later. A team from the US Army's Criminal Investigation Command (CID) later confirmed that the blast originated from approximately 400 grams of plastic explosive. It detonated against the fuel tank of a Humvee, leaving the vehicle a blazing hulk. The next three explosions occurred within less than a minute.

The unit commanding officer, Dean Kozak - a middle-aged major whose real career was as an E-Z Mart produce manager in Texarkana – sat up in bed. A loud WHAM rattled his quarter's windows. Rubbing his eyes, Kozak staggered to the window as more explosions rocked the base. Mouth agape, he incomprehensibly watched mushrooms of flame leaping from the area of the vehicle park.

The general alarm went off as Major Kozak struggled into his pants. The telephone rang and he hopped across the room to answer it.

"D-duty Officer, sir," a panicked young voice gasped. "Are we under attack?"

"Attack?" Kozak gulped. The Standing Orders for Emergency Situations were locked in a safe in his office on the other side of the Kaserne and he couldn't remember what the classified document said to do in such a situation. *Don't want to jump the gun,* he thought. *Could just be a gas main leak.*

A WOOMPH rolled over the camp as a gasoline tanker erupted into a gigantic fireball, galvanizing Kozak into action. He ordered the base evacuated, then opened his government issued Panasonic Toughbook CF-31 and typed an encrypted email with "Emergency Situation – Hőhenbogen Kaserne" in the subject line:

Multiple explosions from unknown cause. Probable extensive damage. Facility being evacuated.

Kozak sent the message to Command Post, US Army Europe (USAREUR) V Corps, Campbell Barracks, Heidelberg, adding the email addresses of his own commanding officer at the nearby Hőhenfels garrison, and the 66th Military Intelligence Group (66th MI) in Wiesbaden. He finished dressing and buckled on his holstered M9 pistol. Taking his Toughbook and smartphone, he scurried out of his quarters as a pair of explosions lifted the turret off an Abrams M1A1 tank and gutted the cab of a recovery vehicle.

In a pasture a mile from Hőhenbogen Kaserne, six young Americans in World War II combat gear paused as explosions awakened the Bavarian countryside. They watched distant flames illuminate the clouds, looked at each other ... and grinned in grim satisfaction.

The final explosion occurred at 01:08 local time. The shaken Major Kozak waited another hour outside the kaserne, spending most of the time taking calls from higher up the command chain.

Major Kozak held his company aside in platoons, where they nervously fingered their M16A2 rifles. He had ordered a communications blackout, but the men and women under his command largely ignored him, tweeting and texting alarming messages that were immediately rebroadcast by their recipients.

Drawn by the explosions, several dozen Germans had gathered from nearby farms and villages. Like the National Guardsmen, some of the German civilians took smartphone photos of the burning vehicles and blasted buildings. Within minutes, the pictures began appearing on social media sites and in email in-boxes around the world. Reuters, UPI and Deutsche Presse Agentur had the story hours before the Pentagon and the German Defense Ministry.

After being told to expect teams from both the German police and the US Army CID, Kozak led his troops cautiously back inside the base, where they were met by the dazed figure of Private Beamer Kimble staggering out of the latrine.

Two miles away, Sutton frowned at Private Sarnoff. "You're sure?"

"Yes sir. Nothing inside that hanger but a funny looking glider, a gas tank on a trolley and a whole lot of junk. And that shitty little lock on the door wouldn't keep a baby out."

Sutton shook his head, gazing at the single hanger and two-story tower building bordering Mühldorf Airfield's grass strip.

"Place is like a ghost town," Private Holcombe added as Roth trotted up.

"Well?" Sutton snapped.

"This can't be a Luftwaffe base," Roth said. "There are no barracks, no tents. Not a sign of any military presence." He gestured towards two aircraft behind them. "And those are certainly not Ju-88 Nightfighters! They are painted in red and white!"

"Maybe they've abandoned it," Holcombe suggested.

"No, it's operational. There is a radio set in the tower and signs that it is in use during the day. I destroyed the radio."

"Somebody in intelligence must have got their wires crossed on this one. I reckon this must be just an emergency field with a couple of spotter planes." Sutton opened a canvas backpack. "Well, we can still give Heinie conniptions."

While Roth and two others placed explosives inside the hanger and tower block, Sutton attached a charge to the fuselage of a Dornier DO-28, then moved to the other aircraft, a Cessna 172. He wondered if the unfamiliar machine was one of the new spotter aircraft produced by

19

the Messerschmitt factory, but was puzzled by the lack of camouflage paint and military markings.

An automobile's headlights bounced through dips in the country road, engine roaring and tires protesting as it took the last curve at 130 kilometers per hour. The sentry at Hőhenbogen Kaserne's main gate tensed as a flashing green and blue light appeared above the vehicle's headlights. He flipped the fire selector switch of his M16 to full automatic and raised the rifle, ready to blow the car off the road if it tried to ram the gate.

The Bavarian *Landespolizei* BMW 521i halted five meters from the gate's lowered barrier. Its *Wachtmeister* driver leaned out his window, scowling as he saw the weapon pointed at him. A black MP sergeant appeared beside the sentry with a raised pistol.

"What you want?" he growled

The car's passenger door opened and a man cautiously moved into the glare of the floodlights, letting the sentries see his peaked cap, green jacket, and the gold rank stars on his epaulettes.

"I am Hauptmann Engelmohr," he said brusquely. "We have been summoned by your *Kommandant.*"

"That so?"

The American sergeant pursed his lips, studying the florid-faced German police officer from the toes of his polished shoes to the crown of his cap. "Hmm," he said, and holstered his pistol.

"Lemme see your ID," he told Engelmohr.

The police driver muttered, but Engelmohr silenced him with a waved hand. He removed the leather case containing his badge and identity card, showing his teeth as he smiled at the MP. Although wearing the uniform of a Bavarian state police captain, Englemohr was an officer of the *Landesämter für Verfassungsschutz* – the regional branch of Germany's secret service. The MP pretended to examine the card. He pondered the German words, wondering what this Kraut's rank would be in American terms.

"Okay." The sergeant handed the case back. "Gotta be careful, you know. You'll find the CO on the southwest quadrant of the perimeter fence. Drive right through the camp and make a right at the vehicle park. Can't miss *that*. And don't get yourselves shot, hear now?"

Engelmohr returned to the BMW as the barrier was raised. His tight-lipped driver drove past the sneering American soldiers.

"*Verdammter Schwarzer!*" the young driver spat.

Engelmohr calmly lighted a Davidoff Gold cigarette and hid his smile. "Ah, Dieter, one would think you are not overly fond of our brave American allies. Remember, they were here to protect us from the Eastern Hordes and now from … God knows what."

"Protect us!" The younger policeman scowled. "They have no right to be here! Their country is bankrupt and Germany can defend itself. These are weekend warriors who would rather watch reality TV and listen to rap music than protect themselves!"

Engelmohr nodded, watching fires inside the American base tingeing the night. "Perhaps someone decided to test the Ami's vulnerability tonight," he said softly.

The driver glanced at him. "*Herr Hauptmann*, I read the BfV alert last week. It said there was 'credible intelligence' about a terrorist attack in Bavaria. Do you think this was the work of—"

"A good policeman assumes nothing until he has examined all the evidence," Engel snapped. "Turn here, *bitte.*"

The driver slowed, eyes widening. *"Mein Gott!"* he whispered.

The repaired vehicle compound looked like a junkyard. Flames licked the blackened skeletons of trucks surrounding the remains of a gasoline tanker. Hoses snaked over the steaming asphalt pavement towards teams in fire-fighting gear. Noncoms screamed commands at men squirting chemical extinguishers into the glowing interiors of tanks. A bulldozer dragged a blistered Humvee aside to clear a path for the base fire truck.

Englemohr watched without expression, then stabbed out his cigarette in the car's ashtray. "Drive on, Dieter," he said mildly. "Down there, where all the lights are."

The German policemen saw flashlight beams bobbing across the cleared firing zone beyond the camp's perimeter wire and up the hill into the pine forest. Heavily armed MPs with guard dogs patrolled the fence. Engelmohr tapped the driver's shoulder, indicating that he should stop near a knot of American soldiers huddled near portable spotlights. Lighting another cigarette, he left the car and approached the group, noting gold oak leaves on the collar of a man in helmet and body armor.

Engelmohr introduced himself in passable English and shook hands with Major Kozak. They moved apart from the group.

"Thanks for coming so quickly," said Kozak. "CID ordered me to cooperate with your authorities, so I thought we should get an early start."

Engelmohr nodded. "So you do not believe this to be internal sabotage?"

The major shook his head. "Outside job, no doubt about it. Take a look at this."

Kozak led the German through the circle of American soldiers and squatted by the opening cut through the mesh. Engelmohr hunkered beside him, trained eyes narrowing.

"Six sets of footprints lead from the woods out there, into the Kaserne and back out again," said the major. "I've warned my men to mark them and stay clear."

Engelmohr sucked thoughtfully at his cigarette and shook his head.

"Our Jihadist friends have been suspiciously quiet lately," he mused. "Since the murders of your personnel at the Frankfort airport I have been wondering when they would return to haunt us."

Kozak's jaw hardened. "Then you think ...?"

Engelmohr remembered the alert that his driver had referred to, a top secret report from Germany's version of the FBI, the *Bundesamt für Verfassungsschutz* or BfV.

"Yes," he replied curtly. "*Terrorists.*"

4

"What's wrong with 'em?" Sarnoff said impatiently. "It's been twenty minutes since we set the first one. "

"Any second now," Sutton replied.

A flash bloomed on the airfield in the valley below. Fire engulfed the Dornier. The explosion's sound reached them seconds later. Then the other charges destroyed the hanger and tower. Sutton turned away as the Cessna flipped onto its back and burst into flame.

The Rangers returned to their cached supplies. The Bandstand mission planners had envisaged a pattern of targets lying on concentric rings around the teams' drop zones. Using the buried canisters as a base, the commando units could strike a series of targets, then quickly replenish munitions. Sutton handed out extra clips of .45 caliber ammunition, hand grenades, and K- and D-rations.

Sutton's vigor was still high, the eight miles covered since the team's landing nothing compared to their twenty-five-mile training marches over the Scottish Highlands in the dead of winter. He found a dry spot on the ground and took out his map, target list and flashlight. The other Rangers hovered over him, cheeks bulging with D-ration Hershey's chocolate and candy Charms.

"Where we going next, Lieutenant?" Sarnoff asked.

Sutton consulted the coordinates on his list and ran a finger down the map's surface.

"This is going to be one of the toughest nuts to crack," he answered. "It's an SS *Werewolf* training camp."

"Werewolf?" Sarnoff joked. "You telling me they got guys dressed up like Lon Chaney over here?"

Sarnoff's flippancy infuriated Roth.

"The *Werwölfen* are the most fanatical of the Nazi killers," he snapped. "The Germans realize that they will soon be beaten, so they are training SS and Hitler Youth volunteers to serve in special commando units called Werewolves. These beasts have vowed never to surrender, so when the war is over they will continue guerrilla operations to harass the Allied occupation forces."

Sarnoff looked around the huddle of men. "So the six of us are going to take on a whole SS training camp? What they got there, a battalion?"

"We're not going to make a suicidal assault," Sutton replied. "Remember, this is a decoy operation. We've got to keep up the act and make it hard for the Nazis to tell our bullshit from the real McCoy."

Sutton's eyes swept the five men hovering over him.

"You can be damned sure that every Kraut installation in Bavaria will be on alert by now, so these werewolf bastards will be waiting for something to happen. All we want to do is pick out a guardhouse or something small and hit it fast with grenades and tommy-gun fire. Make as big a ruckus as possible so they'll think a larger force *is* assaulting them. Those briefing officers back in Scotland said we should give the Krauts a glimpse of our American uniforms to panic them even more, but as far as I'm concerned they can stuff that idea. We're getting in and out of that place as fast as we can."

"If you don't mind my asking, sir," said Private Holcombe, "where're we going after we hit the werewolf camp?"

Sutton checked his watch. "It's nearly 02:45. The Werewolf base is three miles from here, so by the time we finish it should be getting close to dawn. We'll trek as far as we can from there, then hole up for the day. Tomorrow night we'll cross the border into Czechoslovakia. Roth and I have been given names of contacts in the Czech underground, so maybe we can give them a hand until the Red Army reaches us, which should be pretty soon."

"Wait," said Roth. "Why will we leave our target area so soon? You said there are many other Nazi targets we could attack!"

"Be practical, Roth," Sutton said. "All of Bavaria is going to be in such an uproar that we'll never get anywhere near those other targets. We can accomplish more by helping the Czech underground keep the Krauts pinned down. We're Rangers, not kamikazes."

The other men nodded. Roth scowled.

"But we can at least hit one more of our targets tonight," he said stubbornly. "Every blow we strike against the Nazis helps to bring the end of the war closer!"

"You're beginning to sound like a goddam war bond salesman, Sergeant."

Roth ignored Sutton's retort. He kneeled to reopen the map.

"This square marks the *Werwölfen* camp, yes?"

"Yeah," Sutton snapped, angered at Roth's persistence yet feeling guilt from his decision to disregard orders and end the mission so soon. He wondered if his motive was to protect his men, or whether it stemmed from what the Army called "lack of intestinal fortitude" – cowardice. *Get a grip!* he told himself fiercely. Any guy who won a Silver Star for climbing the cliffs on D-Day wasn't a coward. He was just tired of the war, as tired as the other GIs were ... except Roth.

"Look," Roth continued. "Here is a target which would be right in our path if we head directly from the *Werwölfen* camp to the Czech border. Do you know what this one is?"

Sutton tossed him the list of map coordinates and target descriptions. "Look it up yourself. We're pulling out of here in five minutes, Sergeant."

Roth grunted, eyes darting across the typescript and back to the map.

"Excellent," he said. "A very easy target. We should have time to finish the job before dawn. It is one of the assassination assignments – the Nazi Luftwaffe hero von Scheller."

"Fuck that," one of the other men muttered.

Sutton felt the four privates watching him, waiting for that nebulous thing called leadership that gave him the right to wear silver bars on his shoulders and send trusting men to their deaths. He suddenly felt old beyond his twenty-four years, weary and homesick. Did all officers feel this way or just him? He squared his shoulders, resorting to a leadership technique taught by one of his OCS instructors - imitating movie tough guys like Jimmy Cagney or George Raft.

"No fucking way, Roth. The Limeys wanted assassinations on this mission, not us. I'd pop Adolf or one of their generals if I had 'em in my sights, but not a wounded pilot."

"Yeah, it stinks," Sarnoff said.

"The Nazis stink!" Roth replied savagely. "Von Scheller is a national hero. We will hurt the Germans' morale greatly if we kill him!"

"Forget it, Sergeant," Sutton said. "Let's get our gear toge—"

Roth sprang up, fists clenched.

"You Americans would think differently about soiling your Snow White little hands if *your* parents and sisters were shipped off in the cattle cars!"

"I'm sick of your fucking insubordination, Roth!" Sutton quivered with rage. "Now get your goddam gear and prepare to move out!"

"Yeah, save your energy for your werewolf pals ... *hymie,*" Sarnoff sneered. "You can call Americans names later."

Sutton watched Roth stalk toward the supply canisters, then turned to Sarnoff. "Shut your trap! Another crack like that and you'll be cleaning latrines when we get back."

It never ends, Hugo Roth thought, teeth clenched so tightly that he was surprised they didn't crack under the pressure. They all hate us – scratch an American and you'll find a Nazi underneath. We've been pariahs for two thousand years and Jews will never be safe until we have our own nation again and can fend for ourselves. I'll kill as many Germans as I can then join the fight for *Eretz Israel*.

What else do I have to live for?

5

Inside the old SS headquarters building, a man snapped awake. Years spent eluding an alphabet soup of security forces had honed his senses to a fine edge, especially the intuition that had saved his life on numerous occasions.

He strained to separate the night noises. Snores from the men sleeping in the rooms around him, footsteps from the guards on the roof overhead. After a few minutes, he relaxed, but did not return to sleep. He thought of tomorrow's operation, the masterstroke that would convulse the world, and smiled.

His *nom de guerre* was Sebastian. A *terrorist,* he thought, staring into the darkness. A German citizen born in Stuttgart of Bosnian immigrant parents, raised as a Muslim.

No, not a terrorist. Not even a jihadist despite what the fools under my command may think. I'm a ... retributionist. No, even that's no longer true. Nihilist? Not really. These days I am simply Bored.

As a teenager, he had become radicalized by the ethnic cleansing committed in 1995 by Serbian Christians in

Srebrenica, his parents' home town. Over 8,000 Muslim men, including a dozen members of his family, had been massacred and bulldozed into mass graves. Tens of thousands of women, children and elderly people were forced to leave the area. Sebastian's aunt and two teenage female cousins were brutally raped and tortured by units of the Army of Republika Srpska under the command of the "Butcher of Bosnia," General Ratko Mladić.

Relatives' letters sent from UN refugee camps documented unimaginable savagery: men and women mutilated and slaughtered, children killed before their mothers' eyes, a grandfather forced to eat the liver of his grandson. Ultimately, the Balkan war claimed the lives of over 65,000 Bosnian Muslims.

Sebastian vowed to his mourning family that he would avenge the genocide. His parents begged him to focus on his studies. A brilliant scholar, he attended a *Europäisches Gymnasium*, mastering four foreign languages. Tall, blue-eyed and fair-complexioned, he excelled at a range of sports and bedded a remarkable number of *fräuleins*.

Ach ja, die fräulein. He smiled, thinking in the language of his youth. Women seemed to have a sixth sense about his dangerous double life that drew them to him like *Bienen* to *honig*.

As a dutiful son, Sebastian contained his wrath, but stealthily developed a network of contacts within the youth wing of the *Islamische Gemeinschaft der Bosniaken*, the Association of Islamic communities of Bosnians in Germany, or IGBD. He began spending weekends at a certain mosque in Berlin whose Imam had taken a special interest in the intense, Aryan looking high school student.

Like many young Germans, Sebastian took a year off between graduation from Gymnasium and entering university. While other graduates backpacked around the world or did volunteer work for the poor, Sebastian had other plans. His Imam sent him to Antibes, where he spent several days aboard a 92 meter yacht owned by a charming Saudi prince. There, he met with several Middle Eastern men who questioned him relentlessly about his background and knowledge of the Koran before asking him to take a polygraph test.

So irksome. Yet necessary.

Sebastian spent the following six months training in an Al-Qaeda camp near the town of Zamzola in Pakistan's South Waziristan region. After becoming proficient in a variety of handguns, he moved on to standard infantry weapons such as the AK-47, T56, G3 and M16. Midway through his course Sebastian was trained on rocket-propelled grenade launchers (RPGs), light anti-tank weapons (LAWs), surface-to-air missiles (SAMs), mortars and other stand-off armaments. His final six weeks at the camp were spent in learning how to improvise low-cost mass-casualty explosive devices.

Sebastian was unsurprised to discover that nearly a third of the terrorist trainees were young Caucasian men and women such as him – other Bosnians, Chechens, an Argentine, a couple of Americans, and an Irishwoman.

The final phase of the program was a SERE (Survive, Evade, Resist, Escape) course taught by an embittered black American – a devout Muslim - who claimed he had been a US Marine.

33

Sebastian and several other European trainees were next sent to Islamabad where they stayed in a safe house disguised as an educational exchange program administered by a Moroccan who passed as French. There, Sebastian toiled for weeks perfecting his linguistic abilities by watching videos and reading popular magazines. By the end of three months he could speak idiomatic English, French, Spanish and Russian. His handlers were astonished at his ability to switch from Mississippi accented American English to a Newcastle Geordie dialect, or from the singsong Spanish of an Argentine *Porteño* to the lisp of an upper class *Madrileño*.

Nothing astonishing about it, he told himself, stretching on the uncomfortable inflatable mattress. *Considering that I tested at the genius level before I entered gymnasium.*

Graduation from the course required each trainee to plan and execute a personal terror operation. Sebastian returned to Germany and sublet a flat in Frankfurt. Adopting the persona of an American student, he became a regular at clubs popular with US servicemen.

On a Saturday night five weeks later, a bomb placed under a table in a club killed three people and injured over two hundred, including forty-six American servicemen. From a doorway down the street, Sebastian savored the screaming until the emergency vehicles arrived, then returned to his apartment and slept soundly.

His mind drifted back to that night. *Beautiful.* Better than sex any day. Fucking gets old after awhile, but the visceral thrill of killing is the ultimate high.

That autumn he entered Heidelberg University to study economics. On his Al-Qaeda handlers' orders, he stopped attending mosque services and avoided contact with any of the numerous left-wing or Muslim university organizations. He chose his *nom-de-guerre* from an eponymous hit single by the English rock band Steve Harley & Cockney Rebel.

In the spring of 2001, Sebastian worked as an intern in New York for Cantor Fitzgerald, an investment bank on the 101st–105th floors of One World Trade Center. Professing an interest in architecture and structural engineering, the personable young German who spoke such flawless English was allowed access to the management offices and all areas of the Twin Towers. A report detailing the vulnerabilities of the structure, including projected casualty numbers, was given to Al-Qaeda in June, earning Sebastian the blessings of Osama Bin Laden. On September 11, safely back in Heidelberg, Sebastian watched the airborne terrorists' attacks with secret glee beneath his feigned horror.

Following graduation, Sebastian was employed in Berlin by a sovereign wealth fund owned by the United Arab Emirates. His job as an international investment banker provided the perfect cover for intelligence activities on behalf of Al-Qaeda. Sebastian became a master at strategizing and coordinating operations, from the 2003 assassination of Serbian Prime Minister Zoran Đinđić, to the 2005 London transport attacks and the 2008 assaults in Mumbai.

Global security forces knew of his existence but not his identity despite state-of-the-art profiling technology. Interpol called him "Geppetto" after Pinocchio's puppet master, and the code name was used by the CIA, MI6, BND, the SVR and other intelligence agencies.

Sebastian narrowly evaded capture on several occasions. In 2010, while scouting the Knesset in Jerusalem, he had aroused the suspicions of security guards who observed him on CCTV taking photos that did not fit the pattern for normal tourists. Detained, he used his American Bible Belt accent and false ID to convince the Israelis that he was a simple-minded Baptist who took pictures indiscriminately. The planned terrorist operation was aborted, and Sebastian never returned to Israel.

Over the years he had grown cynical about the radical Jihadism of Al-Qaeda. Privately, he thought people who believed such dogma were idiots and the Koran was a mind-numbing crock of camel turds. The combined largesse of remuneration from his cover employer and access to unlimited operational funds had given him a taste for a lavish lifestyle. He drove a Bentley Continental GT, owned a 310 square meter penthouse in Berlin Mitte, and alternated holidays between Mustique and Raffles in the Seychelles. A seemingly unlimited number of nubile young women were eager to share his bed and luxurious possessions.

Now, Sebastian heaved an impatient sigh and wished the night would pass quicker. Mere boredom did not adequately describe his mental state. He was jaded, tired of being *Geppetto*, the orchestrator and manipulator. He *needed* to get close to his victims, witness their terror, hear their screams, feel the hot tide of adrenaline surge through his arteries. That's why he had begun planning the operation that would take place the next day, a *coup de main* to eclipse the Mumbai massacre that killed 166 innocents and wounded over 300.

Sebastian's targeting criteria were simple: the attack had to be on a scale that would garner global media coverage, and his personal risk had to be minimal. No 9/11 suicide attacks for him, even though he had sent dozens of foolish young men and women to die as martyrs for the Jihad.

To his delight, he discovered that the World Youth Congress was scheduled to hold its next meeting in Munich. A thousand young leaders from 140 countries would assemble at the International Congress Center outside of the Bavarian capital. He spent a month developing a plan and sent it to Al-Qaeda through the network of Sharia banks and money-lenders connecting the Islamic world. Approval was quickly given with minor modifications. The mandate was unequivocal: murder and mayhem on a massive scale. The world would be stunned by the massacre of hundreds of its brightest young men and women.

Security at the Youth Congress would make it virtually impenetrable by outsiders, so Sebastian decided to *become* the security for the event.

He knew that the Bavarian State Police would be responsible for protection at the Youth Congress including elite special response units called *Spezialeinsatzkommandos* (SEK). According to media reports, the police would work in conjunction with contractors from DSH, Europe's largest private security company founded by the powerful Hanno Kasper. Sebastian decided that an *ersatz* team of the SEK's secretive Alpine unit would carry out the attack. It was likely that the real members of the unit would be unfamiliar to Munich-based forces, as the Alpine contingent was stationed in Berchtesgaden. Besides, Sebastian liked the stylish uniforms, especially the edelweiss insignia and *Bergmütze* caps that were almost identical to those worn by the Third Reich's *Gebirgsjager* units during World War II.

He recruited 23 men from a secure database of over one thousand dormant operatives based in the European Union. All were young, light-complexioned and Muslim. A family of Turkish tailors in Karlsruhe made copies of SEK uniforms from photographs found by searching Google. Stolen identity documents were copied by an Algerian forger in Marseilles.

Military boots, belts, and other gear were readily available from street markets and military surplus merchants. Two dozen Heckler & Koch MP5 submachine guns, an equal number of H&K P7 semi-automatic pistols, and 5,000 9x19mm Parabellum cartridges were purchased from a Slovak arms merchant. The ammunition included 3,000 hollow point rounds designed to inflict maximum carnage.

To avoid having to buy the components for mass casualty explosive devices, Sebastian purchased ten 9-kilogram satchel charges filled with US M2 and M112 plastic explosive blocks. Sold by a prominent Bagdad businessman whose brother was Iraq's Minister of Defense, the explosives were in canvas backpacks stamped "US Army." The Iraqi also provided 30 MK2 concussion grenades but was unable to procure the lethal M67 fragmentation variety.

Sebastian needed a staging base in Bavaria that was close to Munich but safe from scrutiny by both the authorities and the public. His researchers discovered an abandoned camp in the *Bayerischer Wald*, built by the SS during World War, subsequently used by the German Federal

Board Guard, but abandoned since the fall of the Berlin Wall.

He bought a second-hand BMW 330tdi and used its GPS system to navigate to the old SS camp. The main entrance was an unused logging road, its ingress almost hidden in thick pines lining the Brennes-Lam highway. A rusted steel gate posted with a faded *Eintritt Verboten!* sign was set in a barbed wire fence attached to concrete posts that disappeared into new forest growth. Decaying wooden barracks loomed on either side of a gravel road that was steadily being swallowed by trees. Sebastian had found the place eerily quiet except for a bitter wind rustling the pine branches.

At the camp's center was a parade ground dominated by a headquarters building. The structure was two stories, solidly built of cinder blocks with a flat roof. The glass was gone from the building's windows, and the place was infested with rodents and littered with broken furniture and rubbish. A long, open vehicle shed near the headquarters building was in fair condition, and a track at the rear of the camp connected to the Neukirchen road – a perfect back-door escape route.

Sebastian always made sure there was a back door.

His men arrived in small groups, driving five used Mercedes G-Wagens. All cell phones and tablets were confiscated. Sebastian and two of his lieutenants – both ethnic Bosnians who had served in the German army - trained the men relentlessly for eight days. A team was detailed to paint the vehicles to be indistinguishable from those used by the Bavarian SEK. With the World Youth Congress scheduled to convene the following day, the terrorists were honed to killing perfection.

Now, unable to sleep on the upper story of the headquarters building, Sebastian went over the day's events in his mind, mentally checking off that all the last-minute preparations had been executed. The teams had been assigned to their vehicles. He was content that each man knew exactly what was expected of him.

When dusk settled on the camp the prior evening, Sebastian had ordered the men to form up on the parade ground for inspection. He wore the perfectly tailored uniform of an SEK *Polizeirat* – a captain. The terrorists stood at attention in two neat lines, wearing green Bavarian police attire, Aryan faces glowing with zealotry under the *Bergmütze* caps. They looked so much like resurrected Nazi soldiers that Sebastian thought they could have stepped from the set of a World War II movie.

Sebastian had gazed over their heads to the doorway of the old SS headquarters where a sculptured design had been crudely plastered over. Years of freeze and thaw had crumbled the plaster, exposing a swastika clutched in the talons of the Third Reich's eagle. A shift in the dying daylight made the eroded sculpture seem freshly chiseled. He remembered whispered stories from his childhood about his grandfather's service during World War II as a trooper in the German SS 13th Waffen Mountain Division.

Sebastian suddenly felt a powerful sense of *deja vu,* something he had read about but never experienced. He dismissed it and addressed the men in German, cynically using the Mujahideen rhetoric they expected.

"Brothers! We are Allah's warriors in the Jihad against the Great Satan. Tomorrow we will strike the greatest blow against the Crusaders and Zionists since our martyred brothers brought down the Twin Towers. All of you are heroes! Rest and gird yourself for the holy battle. May Allah be praised!"

Sebastian closed his eyes and tried to slow his pulse that surged in anticipation of tomorrow's historic operation. He was so sexually aroused that he considered spilling his seed, but the vestiges of his Muslim upbringing stilled his hands. *Plenty of time for that later*, he told himself, *but it will be with real bimbos instead of a thousand fat virgins in Paradise, like some of these poor fools who will die tomorrow believe!*

"There," whispered Holcombe. "Under that tree. Just seen him move."

Fox team hunkered in the forest across from the steel gate with its *Eintritt Verboten* sign. They had been there for ten minutes, catching their breath after rapidly trekking from the drop zone and reconnoitering the entrance to the Werewolf camp. Sutton squinted into the darkness, grateful for the private's keen eyesight. A moment later his vigil was rewarded when a lighter flared, illuminating the sentry's face beneath the bill of his *Bergmütze* cap as he lit a cigarette.

"He's mine," Roth hissed. He handed his Thompson to the nearest man, divested his other equipment and melded with the night.

Roth found a place thirty yards from the gate where a fallen tree had smashed a gap in the rusted barbed wire fence. Slipping through it, he circled back to the small red glow of a cigarette beneath a tall pine. *Another fool smoking on duty,* he thought. The carelessness of the Nazi sentries was surprising, though hardly unwelcome.

Water from an intermittent drizzle dripped from the pine boughs, masking his footsteps. Roth crept within five feet, waited until the sentry flicked away the butt, then launched himself onto the man's back, knocking the wind from his lungs as he rode him to the ground. He jerked the sentry's right arm into his upper back, nearly dislocating the shoulder. The man gasped, babbling, until the point of Roth's British commando knife pricked his throat.

"Ruhe." Roth rasped. *"Bewegen Sie sich nicht!"*

The German froze. Roth asked four questions that were answered in a Hamburg accent. *"Gut,"* whispered Roth as he plunged the stiletto into the soft skin beneath the sentry's right ear, penetrating the brain. For good measure he slit the spasming man's throat. He wiped his bloody hands and knife blade on the German's tunic, dragged the corpse into a ruined sentry box, then returned to his teammates.

"I interrogated the sentry," he reported. "Edelweiss insignia – must be from one of the SS mountain units. He said there are only twenty-four troops here. Couple of sentries on the roof. Submachine guns, no heavy weapons."

Sutton thought for a minute, weighing the risks for his team against the need to strike a blow against the elite killers of the German army.

"Okay," he said. "We'll take them out."

After Roth led them through the fence, Sutton took the point. The place looked like it had been abandoned for a long time, judging by the rows of ghostly, tumble-down barracks they passed. *Another intelligence failure; typical SNAFU,* he mused.

When the headquarters building loomed, Sutton halted the team and went ahead on his own to reconnoiter the structure. Keeping in the deeper shadows of trees and surrounding structures, he strained his eyes and ears. He came to an open shed with six vehicles inside, five green trucks and a strange, futuristic automobile painted in green and silver. All the vehicles had *"Polizie"* on their sides with a badge of some kind. He shook his head in bewilderment. *Something else to tell the intelligence debriefers when I get back ... If I get back.*

The clouds thinned to emit tepid moonlight and he saw a pair of silhouetted figures on the roof. Sutton also noticed that there was no reflection in the windows, as if they were devoid of glass. When the clouds congealed again, he sprinted to the building for a closer look.

His eyes had not deceived him – all the windows had only glass shards in their frames. Crouching, he circled the building again, hearing snores from the black interior beyond the windows on the ground and upper floors. He pressed against the front door, sheltered by a frieze of the Third Reich's eagle, and formulated an attack plan. Then he sidled to the end of the building, took a deep breath, and ran across the parade ground.

Sutton briefed his men on the building's layout and deployed them. Sarnoff would guard the vehicles to prevent the enemy from escaping. The garage would be their rally point. Roth and Private Loomis would take the building's rear, while Sutton and the other two privates assaulted the front.

43

The Rangers waited until a cloudbank hid the moon, then flitted across the open space. Each man slung his submachine gun and unclipped a pair of fragmentation grenades from his chest harness. At Sutton's signal, Holcombe and Kemp pulled the safety pins with their teeth and squatted beneath the chest-high windows.

Sutton gripped his grenades around the spoon handles and stepped a few paces away from the building. He lobbed one grenade onto the roof and quickly followed it with the second. A voice called *"Was zum Teufel ist das?"*

A pair of explosions shattered the night. After a shocked pause, a scream sounded from the rooftop.

Holcombe and Kemp hurled grenades through four of the ground floor windows, ducked beneath the sills and waited for the blasts. The building shook and debris flew out the windows. A dismembered hand landed at Sutton's feet as he unclipped two more grenades and tossed them into upstairs windows. He heard detonations at the back of the building from Roth's and Loomis' attack.

Amid a cacophony of cries, the Rangers unslung their Thompsons and sprayed the interior with bursts. 45 caliber bullets ricocheted off the inside walls, silencing the maimed men on the ground floor who had survived the grenades. Cordite from the explosions mingled with the stench of ripped entrails. The Rangers discarded empty submachine gun clips and snapped in fresh ones.

"Let's go!" Sutton shouted. He backed away from the building, covering the second story as the two privates moved away.

A figure appeared at an upper window and threw out a small object. Sutton fired and the man disappeared. Sutton pivoted, frantically looking for the thing thrown by the German. It lay in the path taken by Holcombe and Kemp, who failed to see it in the dim light.

"Grenade!" Sutton yelled. The privates stopped and looked around.

Sutton had been a star running back at Lee's Summit High School, renowned for his speed on the gridiron. He was stronger and faster now than he had been as a teenager and he charged like a runaway freight train, hollering "Get Baaack!" to the bemused privates. He covered the distance to the grenade in under four seconds, diving the last few feet to form a bulwark for his men.

Sutton was less than a yard from the grenade when it exploded, somersaulting him backwards like a rag doll flung by a careless child. The back of his helmeted head slammed into the ground first, followed by the rest of his limp body.

6

As the first detonations rocked the building, Sebastian gripped his mattress and rolled onto the floor with it protecting his back. An instant later a grenade went off in the corridor outside his room. Shrapnel sprayed through the open doorway, lancing his mattress and sleeping bag. The mattress collapsed, hissing like a basket of cobras, but he was unscathed. He wriggled out of the sleeping bag and reached for his hiking boots as concentrated machine gun fire raked the building's ground floor below him.

It's all over. The counter-terrorism forces have finally caught up with me. Not totally unexpected, but dreadfully inconvenient. Someone must have betrayed them. He'd find whoever it was and make them eat their own testicles before he flayed them alive. But first he had to escape from the trap.

He had slept in his civilian clothes for just such an eventuality. Zipping a leather jacket over his turtleneck, he grabbed the MP5 submachine gun beside him and crawled to the hallway as a burst of gunfire drilled through a window a couple of meters away. A man standing there gasped, spun, collapsed beside him. Sebastian recognized one of his Bosnian lieutenants. Blood pooled around the man's head.

A grenade boomed outside. He heard the rip of 9 mm automatic weapons firing from his floor on the opposite side of the building. He was glad to know that some of his men were still alive and fighting back. That would buy him a little time.

He scrambled down the corridor toward the gunfire, passing two corpses rent and disemboweled by grenades. He rounded up four men who were still alive and returning fire.

"I'll go out and get one of vehicles," he told them. "I'll drive it to the rear door and collect you. We'll fight our way out of here. Hold your fire for sixty seconds to allow me time to go downstairs, then open up with everything you've got to give me covering fire."

The terrorists grunted their assent. Sebastian smiled and scuttled towards the staircase.

Of course, he had no intention of coming back for them. They would die here or be captured, but *he* would live to enjoy his wealth and liquidate his betrayer. He would take one of the vehicles, smash through the ring of anti-terrorist troops, and flee through the hidden escape route.

He reached the lower level and moved towards the rear door. The floor was slippery with blood and stinking excrement from ripped entrails.

Sebastian stood at the door and looked through a bullet hole. There was no sign of the attackers. He cocked his sub-machine gun, gripped the doorknob, turned it. A barrage of machine gun fire roared overhead. He pushed the door open and dashed for the garage.

Roth and Loomis took cover when the building's survivors first began shooting, holding their own fire so they wouldn't give their positions away from muzzle flashes. After the enemy guns fell silent, Roth tapped Loomis on the shoulder and motioned to follow him to the rally point. They were fifty yards from the garage when the Germans unleashed their volley from the building's upper floor. Both men flattened themselves on the ground as bullets flailed the pine trees around them.

Roth's peripheral vision caught movement – a dark shape outlined against the stucco headquarters building, running in the direction of the enemy vehicles. He aimed his Thompson towards the figure, forefinger curling on the trigger, but stopped when he realized it could be another Fox team member heading for the rally point.

"Let's go," he snapped, rising to his feet.

"Lieutenant's dead." Private Kemp cowered as enemy machine guns churned the ground a dozen feet to his left. "Took the full blast of that grenade. I saw it."

"Gotta check," Holcombe answered, running his hands over Sutton's body. "Ain't no blood."

"C'mon, Dan! We gotta get out of here!"

"Hold on ... Here's his neck ... Gotta pulse! Glory be, he's alive!"

Holcombe took Kemp's submachine gun and pack, then helped lift the unconscious officer onto the bigger man's back. As Kemp lugged Sutton in a fireman's carry, he shook his head, amazed that the lieutenant had lived after throwing himself on a grenade.

"Praise the Lord," whispered Holcombe as he brought up the rear. "It's a miracle."

Sarnoff watched the attack from the garage. He was in a foul temper, believing that Lieutenant Sutton had assigned him to guard the enemy vehicles as punishment for sassing the Jew sergeant. Sarnoff didn't like Jews because his dad once told him they had started the revolution back in Russia that murdered his family and forced him and Sarnoff's mom into exile. Truth be told, Roth scared the shit out of him with his cold blue eyes and Kraut accent. Guy just didn't belong.

He glimpsed a shadowy figure approaching and clicked the tin cricket on the Thompson's stock to give the recognition signal. The form disappeared. Wary now, Sarnoff stepped outside the garage with his weapon raised. More movement from a different direction. Tin cricket clicks. Kemp's voice called, "Sarnoff, give us a hand."

"Okay," Sarnoff replied, "I'm com—"

Sarnoff's last conscious image was of red flowers blooming in the darkness. His final sensations were the overwhelming agony of hammer blows on his torso as the bullets hit him. He was dead before his body toppled to the ground.

Sebastian rose from the kneeling position with the MP5 pointing towards the man he had shot. As he continued towards the garage, he wondered at the American voices he had heard. *What were they doing here? US Special Forces working with the Germans?*

He had taken only three steps when he heard the thud of running boots behind him. Sebastian wheeled, submachine gun swinging toward the noise.

Roth opened fire from ten yards, expending half of his Thompson's thirty-round magazine. Nine of the .45 caliber soft-nosed projectiles found their target, exiting from Sebastian's back in fist-sized holes, blowing off his left arm and disintegrating his neck so that his head flopped onto a shoulder, held only by a skin flap. The terrorist puppet master's cadaver was hurled backwards, coming to rest a few yards from his last victim.

Roth ran forward, kicked the MP5 away from Sebastian's remaining hand, and made sure that the threat had been eliminated. Loomis followed and knelt by Sarnoff's body. A moment later the other two Rangers trotted up.

"Report," Roth growled.

"The lieutenant's out," Kemp gasped. "Don't know how bad."

"What about Sarnoff?" Roth asked as Loomis joined them.

"Dead."

"Okay. Leave Sutton. Holcombe and Loomis disable those vehicles. We're pulling out in five minutes."

"Fuck no," Holcombe said. "We ain't leaving the lieutenant. He saved our lives!"

"You can't carry him!" Roth snapped. "He needs medical attention. The Germans will take care of him."

"They'll take care of him all right," Kemp said. "Just like the SS took care of all our boys they butchered at Malmedy last Christmas!"

"I'm with 'em, Sarge," said Loomis. "Sutton's going with us."

Roth ground his teeth, looking back at the headquarters building. The surviving SS soldiers there would have radioed for reinforcements. There was no time for argument or coercion.

"All right. We'll take one of the Nazi vehicles."

Roth went through Sutton's pockets, taking his maps and target list. Ignoring the strange green and silver police car, he managed to start one of the large, jeep-like Mercedes and drive it out of the garage. The other men threw grenades into the remaining vehicles, setting them ablaze. The privates then climbed aboard the G-Wagen, gingerly easing the unconscious Sutton into the rear seat.

Roth sped up the road towards the camp's main gate, switching on the headlights after they were out of sight from the headquarters building. When they reached the locked steel gate, he turned into the forest, maneuvering around trees until he found the gap in the fence caused by the fallen pine. Kemp and Holcombe quickly cleared enough boughs and wire to allow passage. Roth steered the truck onto the logging road and headed east.

The grenade detonations and machine gun fire were audible five kilometers from the old SS camp. All local police units were on full alert after the attacks on Höhenbogen Kaserne and Mühldorf airfield, and they were soon aware that a battle had occurred somewhere in the *Bäyerischer Wald*.

Nonetheless, nearly an hour passed before the combat site could be determined. Telephone calls to police stations from residents in the vicinity provided a general location. Due to bad weather conditions, police helicopter patrols had been grounded, but the crew of a Eurocopter EC135 based at Passau volunteered for a reconnaissance mission.

From a distance of five kilometers, they could see the low clouds glowing from a substantial fire. The pilot flew straight towards it. At 05:12 the EC135 arrived at the SS camp and hovered over the headquarters building. Its powerful searchlight illuminated mangled bodies sprawled on the flat roof, then tracked to a wooden building nearby that was burning along with a row of vehicles inside it. The probing light found another pair of corpses lying on the ground.

The helicopter crew failed to see four men hiding in the forest half a kilometer west of the headquarters building. The surviving terrorists – now wearing civilian clothing - waited until the EC135 flew away, then jogged the remaining distance to the hidden rear entrance. Two kilometers away they found a VW Passat parked outside a *gasthaus*. Breaking into the car, they hotwired it. Half an hour later they were on the E56/3 autobahn speeding at 150 kilometers per hour to the Austrian border, en route to a safe house in Linz.

7

Washington, D.C.

"Want me to call you a cab, Eddie?"

Edward Cassera looked up and tried to focus on the face of the bartender. He shook his head and raised a glass to his lips, blinking as he found it empty.

"Gimme another Bud, Vince," he said.

"It's almost nine, Eddie. You been here since five-thirty and killed half a dozen Buds. Why don't you go home or get yourself some dinner?"

Cassera dropped a pair of twenties on the bar and slid off the stool, favoring his gimpy leg. The bartender shook his head, more in sympathy than in criticism, and used his prosthetic right arm to remove Cassera's glass.

Cassera swayed on the sidewalk outside, hoping the cool early spring air would clear his head. The bar was in an as yet ungentrified section of Arlington, Virginia, near Fort

Myer. Cassera went there when he needed the company of other veterans, men who spoke about mundane things but understood one another, who shared similar memories and pain of a type that no VA doctor could ease.

It was his own damned fault. He had been doing fine, sleeping okay, no bad dreams for weeks. Then he had to go and blow it all by visiting the Vietnam Memorial on his lunch break. He didn't know what compelled him to do it — he just wanted to get out of the office, walk on the Mall, forget about all the paperwork and bureaucratic bullshit. But something drew him and before he knew it he was moving down the ramp, past the tens of thousands of names etched into the black wall. An elderly couple laid a wreath with the words "We'll Always Love You Sonny." Beside them a legless black man in a wheelchair, layered in faded fatigues with the Purple Heart and Bronze Star pinned to his breast, wept as he traced the outline of a name. Cassera passed candles, photos, flowers, men his age hugging each other.

And there it was. The Name. For a moment, Cassera was back in a stinking rice paddy, watching his blood tinge the green water. And there was that skinny black teenager in a sleeveless combat jacket, the youngest, rawest grunt in his platoon, helmet like a stew pot on his head, saying, "Don' worry, 'Tenant, I git ya outta here."

Tears blurred Cassera's eyes and he hurried up the opposite ramp as fast as his damaged body allowed. He was late getting back to work, but couldn't give a flying fuck.

Now he limped down Wilson Boulevard, past cheap restaurants and a tailor shop run by two generations of Vietnamese hookers who offered comfort to veterans upstairs. Cassera needed comfort, but he didn't want any more reminders of his youth. He flagged down a cruising cab and gave his address in Foggy Bottom, dreading the sleepless night ahead.

Three thousand eight hundred miles away, a Mercedes G-Wagen painted with *Bayerische Polizei* markings raced along a forest road. A mile from the Werewolf camp, Roth pulled over, opened one of Sutton's maps and studied it with his flashlight.

Private Kemp, in the front passenger seat, nervously fingered his submachine gun and glanced at the dark evergreens around them. "What's up, Sarge?"

"We have time for one more target."

"Goddamit! It's getting light already. The Krauts must be looking for us!"

"Major von Scheller's house is nearby. It will take only minutes to execute him and be on our way."

"Hey," Holcombe called from the rear seat, where he cradled Sutton's head in his lap. "The lieutenant said no assassinations!"

"Yeah, that's right, Sarge," Kemp said. "Let's just leave that pilot guy and get our ... *ow!*"

Roth's flashlight blinded him. Kemp heard the snick of a pistol being cocked to chamber a round. The light beam shifted to illuminate the Walther in Roth's hand.

"Sutton is incapacitated. *I* am in command now. If you disobey my orders I have the legal right to shoot you. I will not hesitate to do so. Is that understood?"

"Take it easy, Sarge!" Kemp recoiled, hands raised defensively.

"Understood?" Roth shouted, glancing over his shoulder at the men in the back seat.

"Yeah, Sarge," the privates muttered in unison.

Roth grunted and lowered the pistol's hammer. He would not have shot Kemp, but had no patience for American squeamishness or the way in which even lowly privates questioned orders. He was engrained with the belief that authority was imposed by fear. Roth was puzzled by, and envious of, Sutton's ability to lead by example. The lieutenant was tough and decisive, but never physically threatening, and the men respected him for it.

Roth returned his attention to the map. He fixed the landmarks in his mind and scanned the target list. A photograph was clipped to one of the pages. He tucked it into a pocket and put the idling Mercedes back into first gear.

After another mile the road connected with a highway. Roth turned east onto it. He gnawed his lower lip as the horizon lightened with approaching dawn. They had been lucky not to run into a German patrol. The team could abandon Sutton and shoot their way past a *Völkstürm* unit of old men and boys, but they wouldn't stand a chance against *Wehrmacht* or Waffen SS troops. He didn't mind dying if he took some Nazis with him, but he had volunteered for the Bandstand mission to wreak as much havoc as possible, and Bavaria was ripe with opportunities for vengeance.

His sharp eyes caught the landmark described in the target list – a gate flanked by stone columns chiseled with heraldic plaques. The baroque iron gates gaped, rusted and overgrown. Roth drove through them onto a gravel driveway. Beyond was a derelict cottage. Roth pulled the Mercedes behind it so it was hidden from the drive. He ordered the Rangers to touch up their black camouflage face paint and check their weapons.

"Let's go," he snapped.

Kemp and the other two Rangers whispered to each other. Roth hefted his submachine gun in a peremptory way, and the men obeyed.

"What about the lieutenant?" asked Kemp.

"Leave him. We'll be back soon."

Scattered raindrops increased to cold drizzle, dripping from the men's helmets as they slipped waterproof ponchos over their heads and unslung weapons.

"What's the plan, Sarge?" asked Loomis.

"Follow me and do as I say." The expectation of Nazi bloodletting thickened Roth's German accent. "Keep quiet. We are close to the main house."

They tramped to the driveway, hunched against the rain as they splashed through puddles. Their eyes flicked warily at the great oaks and firs hemming the lane.

"*Ach, ja,*" Roth whispered, like a hungry man about to feast.

The gravel drive widened to an ellipse enclosing a fountain overgrown with weeds. Beyond loomed a large house with stucco walls crowned by a mossy tiled roof. A *porte cochère* at the front door sheltered a grey Volkswagen. *The Nazi pilot must indeed be one of Hitler's favorites,* thought Roth. Very few of the new "people's automobiles" had been made, and they only went to the elite.

The Rangers reconnoitered the house. In the rear they found a servants' wing and a stable block. Roth squatted beside barren rose bushes bordering a stone terrace and motioned for the others to join him.

"This will be a piece of cake," he whispered. "Von Scheller was badly wounded on the Eastern Front in January and is recuperating here now. His Luftwaffe orderly is with him and will be armed. The intelligence report says the only other people in the house are von Scheller's mother and one or two servants. They will offer no resistance."

Roth outlined his assassination plan, calmly screwing the long silencer tube onto the muzzle of his pistol while the other men numbly listened. Even though they were combat veterans, and had seen violent death in all its forms, they grieved over the loss of Sarnoff. And here they were, more than two hundred miles behind enemy lines in the heart of Nazi Germany, burdened by an unconscious officer and commanded by a fanatical sergeant. The adrenaline charge of battle had ebbed, replaced by fatigue and fear.

Roth crossed the terrace to a pair of French doors. He tried the doorknobs, then smashed a pane with his pistol. Thrusting his hand past the glass shards, he groped for a latch and stepped inside. He was in a parlor dominated by heavy Wilhelmine oak and velvet furniture from the previous century. Chintz curtains draped the windows, dark paintings crowded the whitewashed walls, and a blackened Gothic crucifix dangled in a comer.

The others followed, their tension as palpable as the room's mustiness. Roth eased open a door and crept into a landing beneath a wide staircase. A chandelier sprouted from a floral-painted ceiling over the floor's checkerboard marble tiles. Roth's boots tapped as he started across it. He froze as something scratched behind a door on the opposite side of the landing. The scratching was joined by a dog's whine, then barks rising to a frenzy that were hushed by a man's voice.

Roth ran across the floor, tore open the door, and moved into the darkened room in a fighter's crouch. A small dog leapt at his ankle, snarling and worrying his boot. He ignored it and shone his flashlight on a figure sitting up in a four-poster bed – a man obviously in his 80s wearing striped pajamas. Roth strode across the room and gripped the old German's throat. The man gasped and fell back onto the pillow. Roth released the man's windpipe and pressed the silenced pistol into his cheek.

"Where is Major von Scheller?" Roth asked in German. "Hans-Ulrich von Scheller?"

The elderly German seemed confused. *"Ich,"* he whispered. *"Ich."*

"Von Scheller!" Roth snarled. *"Wo ist Major von Scheller?"*

Roth snapped on a bedside lamp and thrust his free hand inside his pocket. He pulled out the photograph from the Bandstand target list and shoved it in the man's face. "This man is Major von Scheller. Tell me where he is!"

The aged man gazed at the photo of a smiling young officer wearing the Third Reich decoration of the Knight's Cross at the throat of his World War II Luftwaffe uniform. A strip of paper pasted to the photo's base read, "Major Hans-Ulrich von Scheller. Taken October 1944."

"Now. Where is this man?"

The German's faded blue eyes blazed at Roth. *"I* am Major Hans-Ulrich von Scheller," he said coldly.

A *Mobile Einsatzkommando* of the Bavarian state police arrived at the old SS camp's main entrance at 0552 hours and found it barred by a locked steel gate. They failed to notice the opening in the fence thirty meters away. The police vehicles were forced to wait for bolt cutters and oxy-acetylene torches to open the gate, but a young *hauptmeister* eager for promotion climbed the gate and went in with a heavily armed squad in body army and helmets. They discovered a corpse with a slit throat in a guardhouse wearing a *Bayerische Polizei* SEK uniform.

The *hauptmeister's* squad performed a reconnaissance of the headquarters building exterior and waited for the main force. By that time, it was growing light enough to discern the two bodies lying outside the building that the helicopter's crew had seen from the air.

When he arrived, the commanding *Polizeioberrat* deployed a double ring of men and vehicles around the structure. He surveyed it carefully before ordering an assault.

Two teams of genuine SEK officers stormed the building at 06:16. At 06:23, the assault team's leader radioed that the structure was secure. He didn't mention that two of his supposedly hardened men were vomiting their guts out after slogging through the abattoir inside. When the white-faced Bavarian policemen were able to control their bile long enough to inspect the ravaged corpses, they were baffled by the fact that all were clad in uniforms similar to their own.

An unconscious man with a head wound was discovered on the upper floor at 06:29. After a swift examination by a medic, he was photographed, fingerprinted and carried to a helicopter that had landed on the old parade ground. He was the only living person found in the building.

At 06:42, while technicians from one of the *Unterstützungskommandos* –Special Support Groups - based at Dachau snapped photos and detectives squinted at tire prints, the *Polizeioberrat* stepped outside the old SS building and speed dialed the chief of the BfV, Germany's domestic intelligence agency, on his secure SIP edition Blackberry. He frowned at the false police identification documents in his hand as he waited for the connection to be made.

He got directly to the point.

"Mein Herr, we have discovered what appears to be a direct threat to our national security. Please ask the Interior Minister to mobilize all forces."

Paula von Scheller had looked forward to a three-day weekend in the countryside, hoping to cleanse her heart of hurt and betrayal, be pampered by people who truly loved her, and seek her grandfather's wisdom. They had talked late into the previous night, sharing a decanter of sherry and listening to Vivaldi's Four Seasons.

"The music is a metaphor," her grandfather said gently, as the log in the fireplace collapsed in embers. "I have reached my Winter, but you are in the Spring of your life and have so much ahead. You must release the past and start anew."

"But I loved him so much!" she sobbed.

"That swine is not worth a single one of your tears!"

The previous week, Paula had discovered her fiancé in bed with another woman. Her last class of the day at Universität Regensburg had been canceled, so she planned to surprise Helmut with his favorite supper before he got home from his job at the Sparda-Bank Ostbayern. She stopped at Kaufland en route to his flat, picking up the ingredients for Spätzle, Schweinebraten and Knödel, with a nice Domina to wash it down.

She had let herself into the apartment with her key and headed for the kitchen, passing the bedroom. The door was open, and she was already past it when the image of a naked woman writhing astride a man registered. She took two steps back, stared in open-mouthed shock at the couple on the bed, dropped the grocery bags, and fled.

Helmut asked her to take him back – she told him it was over. *Fertig!* Yet in her subsequent turmoil, she kept wondering if she had made the right decision. Her grandfather's words comforted her. He was right. She had to start anew.

She put the old man to bed, stroked his pampered Cairn Terrior, Loki, and went to her own cold room. She turned on her iPad, read a few Neruda poems, listened to some *Florence and the Machine*, then cried herself into an uneasy sleep.

At her apartment in Regensburg, Paula usually awakened at 06:30 to allow time to prepare for her long days of classes and clinics. Sleeping late was an unaccustomed luxury, so she was annoyed when Loki's yapping awakened her. She glanced at her nightstand clock, groaning as she saw it was only nineteen minutes to seven. She rolled over and tried to get back to sleep, willing the usually placid little dog to shut up.

Paula sat up as heavy boots pounded up the stairs from the ground floor. Her heart raced as doors were flung open along the hallway outside.

Her bedroom door burst open, crashing against the wall. What she perceived as a helmeted black man stood in the doorway, a nightmare dressed in an American army uniform festooned with guns and grenades. The creature saw her and charged across the room holding a black stick that her shocked mind perceived as a giant penis. A scream formed in her throat and her mouth opened to vent it, but the black-faced man clamped a hand over her mouth.

"Don't scream!" the intruder pleaded. "I gotta kill you if you scream."

Paula's brain fashioned order out of her chaotic thoughts. She realized that the intruder had spoken in English with an American twang. The stick in his hand was a machine gun and the eyes in his blackened face were wide and blue. The dirty hand covering her mouth was shaking.

"You understand me?" the man asked. "You speak English?"

Her nod was lost in her trembling. She was gripped by a terrible fear that something had happened to her grandfather.

"You gotta come downstairs." The intruder gnawed at his lower lip. "Promise you won't scream if I take my hand away?"

She nodded again. Tears welled at the corners of her eyes.

"You, uh, gotta get out of the, uh, bed and come downstairs with me," the man said shyly. He took a few steps backwards. "Come on now."

Paula pushed aside the eiderdown and slid out of the bed, clutching the neck of her flannel nightgown. The man looked at her ankles, then stiffened as she started towards a chair.

"*Mein morgenrock,*" she gasped, pointing at the garment draped over the chair. "My dressing gown, please," she repeated in English, shocked by the unnatural sound of her voice.

"Okay. Just don't try nothing cause I'm gonna be right behind you."

Paula glided trancelike out of her room and across the landing, hoping she would wake up and discover that this was a bad dream. She went down the staircase past the large fresco of the von Scheller arms on the wall, hearing the intruder's heavy breathing behind her.

As she stepped onto the ground floor, the kitchen door opened. Another black-faced soldier herded out Sepp and Maria, the elderly couple who served her father as handyman and cook. Sepp squinted across the hallway at Paula, toothless mouth working. Maria clutched her shabby dressing gown with one hand and gripped her husband's arm with the other. Her red peasant face wore a look of terror as their captor prodded them forward.

"*Schatzilein.*" Maria cried as she spotted Paula.

"Shut up, old lady," their guard hissed.

"*Maria, sei still!*" Paula warned. A gun muzzle jabbed her back.

"Watch your mouth, lady!"

A third soldier clattered down the staircase. He eyed the frightened Germans.

"Top floor's clean," he announced. "No sign of anyone else in the house."

"Same here." Paula's guard pointed his submachine gun at the open door of her grandfather's bedroom. "In there. Move!"

Her grandfather lay on his bed, duvet pulled off to expose the thin body trembling in baggy pajamas. His right trouser leg was cut short over the stump of his leg, and his knotted hands lay at his sides as he spat answers to questions asked by a German-speaking trespasser with sergeant's stripes. Loki barked and snarled from a corner.

Relief suffused the old man's face as Paula entered the room. She threw herself into his arms and sobbed as she had not done since childhood.

Roth was tired of this old man, this house, the furious little dog in the corner. All he needed was a hysterical woman to deal with. He cursed and turned away from the scene on the bed, fixing his eyes on the dog. He aimed his pistol at it.

"Loki!" croaked von Scheller. *"Meine arme kleine Loki!* Don't shoot her!"

Roth hesitated, remembering his grandmother's Pomeranian that he romped with when he was a child in Berlin. The old lady mourned for weeks when the dog had to be put down. The thought led to another, an image of the way *she* had died. *Be strong, Hugo,* he imagined her saying, *you are in command.* Lowering the pistol, he turned to Holcombe, who had escorted the younger German woman into the room. "What did you find?"

"The girl was upstairs and Loomis found the old Kraut couple out back. That's it. Ain't nobody else here unless they're hiding."

"That's what the old man told me. Was there any sign that someone else was here recently? Uniforms or equipment?

"Didn't have time for a good look but it seemed like most of the furniture upstairs was covered with dustcovers like it ain't being used." Holcombe frowned. "Hey, we got the right house, Sarge?"

Roth eyed the weeping German woman, smacking the barrel of his pistol against his other hand. His eyes returned to Holcombe.

"This is the von Scheller house, but it appears the Nazi hero has been moved. Once again our intelligence reports were wrong."

Holcombe gestured towards the bed. "So what'd the old guy say?"

Roth laughed with contempt. "The old man is senile. He says *he* is Major Hans Ulrich von Scheller. That may well be his name and former rank, but he can only be the grandfather of the Luftwaffe officer we are seeking. *That* Nazi is twenty years old!"

Private Kemp spoke from the doorway.

"So what do we do now, Sergeant? It's broad daylight and you can bet your life the Krauts are looking for us."

Roth ignored him, turning to fire more questions in German at the old man. Von Scheller hugged his weeping granddaughter and growled responses. Roth said something in a menacing tone before turning to Holcombe and Kemp.

"They expect no visitors and people rarely come here because it is so isolated. This is a good place for us to spend the day. Tonight we will continue east on foot. Perhaps

Sutton will recover by then. It seems fitting that the US Army should shelter in the home of the Nazi hero von Scheller."

The privates looked at one another, obviously relieved.

"We gotta get the lieutenant," said Holcombe.

"Yes, but you will have to carry him here. Leave the car where it is and camouflage it with bushes."

An ormolu clock on the mantelpiece chimed seven o'clock.

8

At 07:16 a Fujitsu-Siemens Stylistic ST6012 tablet began ringing in a 19th century villa on the shore of the Heiliger See in the city of Potsdam, west of Berlin. The spacious home belonged to retired General Hanno Kasper, chairman of Deutscher Sicherheits und Hilfdienst GmbH Berlin (DSH), Europe's largest private security company.

Kasper was in a room outfitted as a gym, laying on a padded bench and pressing a fifty-kilo barbell. At the age of 78 he was in extraordinary physical condition, still as lean and toned as he had been three decades earlier when he had led the world famous hostage rescue mission code-named *Feuerzauber* at Mogadishu airport.

Normally, Kasper would have refused to answer the call: one of his rules was that he was not to be disturbed during holidays and weekends with his family unless there was a national emergency. But this tablet – equipped with a Secure Communications Interoperability Protocol or SCIP – was with him 24 hours a day. Only five people – the most senior members of the German government – had the

71

tablet's number. Each of the five had been assigned a ring tone so he would know in advance who was calling.

He racked the weights, rolled easily to his feet, and unhurriedly walked to a side table where the tablet was insistently playing the first movement from Beethoven's Fifth Symphony.

"Kasper," he barked. "Good morning Madame Chancellor."

After listening to the German leader's description of the night's events, he asked a few questions, grunted, "*Sie wird gestoppt*"("they will be stopped") and killed the connection. With the same sense of calm that always came over him before an operation, he stretched for five minutes to clear his mind. He met his wife Petra on the way upstairs to his bedroom.

"We have an alert," he told her. "Frau Nein thinks it's something big."

A familiar look of anxiety shadowed her face. "Overseas?"

"No, here in the *Bäyerischer Wald*. Terrorist attack on an Ami base and a number of bodies in false Bavarian SEK uniforms. The news hounds will be on it soon." He continued up the stairs.

"Have you time for breakfast?" Petra called after him.

"Coffee. The car will be here in ten minutes."

Kasper showered and shaved, then dressed in his trademark paramilitary uniform of double breasted black leather jacket over gray shirt and trousers. He belted the holster for his Glock 31 .357 SIG semi-automatic on his slim waist and covered his closely cropped white hair with a black beret embroidered with the DSH logo. As a final act, he reverently took the Iron Cross awarded to him by the Führer from its case and pinned its black, red and white hanging ribbon to his tunic.

In the kitchen, he accepted a cup of coffee from Petra, trying to soothe her by talking about their grandchildren while drinking it. He kissed her and went out to the armor-plated Mercedes CLS 550 Coupe waiting in the driveway.

The car was Kasper's personal command vehicle modified to his specifications. In addition to its 4.6L twin-turbo V-8 engine, the car had double bulletproof windows; one standard and a one-way type with adjustable opacity. The big Mercedes was also equipped with a secure communications terminal and Kasper used it while his driver wove through the light traffic. Although he no longer had official authority within the German forces, Hanno Kasper's role as security advisor to the Chancellor and *de facto* chief of the German Crisis Section gave him extraordinary powers that were not only tolerated but welcomed by the variety of often competing federal and state organizations charged with protecting *Deutschland*.

Kasper's first call went to the *Brigadegeneral* commanding KSK *Kommando Spezialkräfte*, the elite counter-terrorism and special operations unit based at Calw in Baden-Württemberg. In addition to operating internationally in Afghanistan and other foreign conflicts, the KSK had broad legal authority for the "Defense of Germany." Kasper knew that the Brigadier General, one of his former subordinates and loyal disciples, would be expecting his call, having received his orders from the Minister of Defense.

The KSK always had a Special Commando Company numbering one hundred men on standby alert. Kasper ordered the general to be ready to deploy the company to Bavaria.

His second call went to the Luftwaffe's liaison office in the Bendlerblock building in Berlin, directing that a pair of C130J transports be flown to the Black Forest Airport at Lahr, the airfield nearest to the KSK base.

The final call was to the Bavarian *Polizeioberrat* at the former SS camp. Kasper jotted notes from the officer's report, then hung up as the big Mercedes exited the A10 autobahn at the Schönefeld airport off-ramp.

The guards at the airport's restricted western gate checked their ID, then lowered the steel anti-terrorism barrier and saluted Kasper as the car sped through. It drove directly onto the runway, braking beside a *Bundeswehr* EC 635 helicopter with the Iron Cross painted on its sides. Its rotors spooled as Kasper climbed aboard and strapped himself in beside the pilot. The aircraft lifted into the overcast sky and climbed on a southeastern course for the Bavarian Forest.

"What is our flying time?" Kasper asked.

"Two hours at cruising speed, *Herr General.* Ninety minutes at maximum power."

"Give me maximum.'

"*Jawohl!*"

Kasper studied the youthful pilot from the corner of his eye. He looked not much more than twenty, though he was probably five years older than that. He had a good Aryan face, and seemed to know his business well.

Many of Kasper's generation of former military and police officers criticized Germany's young soldiers and policemen. Overly educated, said some. Coddled by the state, others whined. Kasper refused to share their views, and in return was held in an esteem bordering on hero-worship by tens of thousands of men in the increasingly hawkish German forces. He had been influential in ending conscription for the *Bundeswehr*, believing that a professional military best served the Fatherland's interests.

Hanno Kasper often spoke at schools and sporting events, reminding his youthful audiences that he had been fighting to defend Germany against her enemies since the age of twelve. He was pleased with the reactionary trend among German youth, even though he despised the skinheads and other radical right-wingers for their lack of discipline. Young Germans no longer felt that they had to apologize for what Hanno termed the "excesses" of the Nazi era. Germany had regained its rightful place as the most powerful nation in Europe, and the current generation was increasingly anti-immigrant and disgusted with having to pay for the sloth of third-rate countries such as Greece.

As much as he despised the German chancellor - who Kasper and his cronies privately called *"Frau Nein"* or *"Mutti"* ("Mrs. No" or "Mom") - he had heartily endorsed her public comments that Germany's attempts to create a multicultural society had "utterly failed," and that the idea of people from different cultural backgrounds living happily "side by side" did not work.

Kasper thoughtfully fingered his Iron Cross. He had often been criticized by the liberal media for wearing it publicly. Damn the liberal *Sitzpinklers* – yellow belly cowards! To him, the Iron Cross was a symbol of Germany's strength – still proudly emblazoned on everything from the *Bundeswehr* helicopter he rode to the Defense Ministry's Web site.

In the Siberian prison camp where he had been shipped as a twelve-year-old child after being captured by Russians in Berlin, he survived by eating rats, stealing food from weaker prisoners, and when there were no rats to eat or food to steal, drawing his will to live from the Iron Cross.

He lay awake at night gripping it, careful to conceal it from the other inmates. Somehow, he believed, the Führer's mystical strength flowed through it and into his heart. There was no other way to explain that after four years, he was one of the 600-odd survivors of a camp once occupied by twelve thousand men.

Hanno Kasper had been repatriated to Bavaria in 1949, a sixteen-year-old scarecrow who alighted at Trostberg station under the pitying gaze of well-fed American soldiers from the Occupation Forces. His mother had fainted when he appeared at her door. Still, it hadn't taken long for him to return to his former self.

He had finished school, joined the Federal Border Police, and then the West German Army after it was reactivated in 1955. He had risen steadily through the ranks due to a combination of zeal and ability, as well as the fact that most German officers in the 1950s and early 1960s had served in the Wehrmacht during World War II and favored the young man whom Hitler had personally awarded the Iron Cross.

Kasper trained with the British Special Air Service and the US Delta Force before forming the German Army's KSK *Kommando Spezialkräfte*. After leading the successful Mogadishu hostage rescue mission, he became an internationally known figure. Following his retirement, he formed DSH, acting as a counter-terrorism advisor to a dozen Western governments. DSH provided a variety of security-related services and currently had annual revenues of nearly a billion Euros.

As a military officer, Kasper had been forbidden to play an overt role in German politics. After retiring, he had become a key leader of the *Phönix* organization, which he had helped to expand to a membership of over sixty thousand men and women by providing funding from his enormous share of DSH profits. The *Phönix* political tactics were far subtler than the theatrical ranting and torchlight parades of neo-Nazi groups such as the banned HNG. The secret organization backed only viable conservative parties such as the Christian Democratic Union and the Christian Social Union.

Kasper and other leaders had not forgotten Hitler's tenet that the youth were "the guarantors of the future," and so *Phönix* recruited young men and women from the lower echelons of government, the military, and the business community. Their strategy had proven to be successful. *Phönix* members held influential positions in the Ministry of Defense, in all three branches of the armed forces, in eleven of the sixteen state police forces, in Germany's parliament, the Bundestag, and in the majority of state governments.

Their goals were the same as their forefathers: a proud Germany reasserting its dominant role in Europe and freely pursuing its natural evolution as a world power. Over the years, many of the *Phönix* objectives had been realized: the defeat of the Soviet Union, German reunification, withdrawal of foreign military forces from German soil, and dominance of the Eurozone economies. They had yet to achieve their dream of mass deportation of Turks and other subhuman immigrants.

Kasper returned his thoughts to the present, charging through the air towards another adventure. He looked down at the neat farms, forests and lakes – all the German order, cleanliness, and efficiency that were a paragon for the rest of the world.

Somewhere ahead of him in the cloud-sheathed *Bayerischer Wald* lurked terrorists, devoted to the destruction of his Fatherland. His face grew hard, rage building as he stared through the helicopter's windshield. *No more whining terrorist prisoners to be given light sentences by the liberal justice system,* he vowed. *None shall be taken alive!*

9

The *Bundeswehr* helicopter drifted at treetop height over the firs, circling the derelict wooden barracks and the stucco headquarters building. Kasper motioned to the pilot, and the aircraft alighted near three other helicopters, including a US Army UH-60 Blackhawk.

A Bavarian policeman ducked under the windmilling blades and held an umbrella over Kasper as he scooted out of the cockpit. Kasper brushed him aside and strode towards an officer in body armor and black commando battledress with drizzle running off his Kevlar "Fritz" helmet. The SEK team leader halfheartedly clicked his heels and introduced himself.

"Polizeioberrat Keitz, Herr General."

A helicopter from the RTL *aktuell* news program swooped out of the clouds to hover overhead. Kasper caught the lens of a TV camera aimed at him and turned his back on it.

"Get them away from here!"

"General Kasper, I believe they have permission fro–"

"Do it!" Kasper walked towards the headquarters building. Keitz barked an order at an aide and hurried after the
stiff-backed older man.

"So what have you discovered?" Kasper halted by a
growing pile of black plastic body bags.

"Twenty corpses. The eighteen dead men in SEK uniforms are imposters. Their ID papers are forgeries. We have
not identified the cadaver in civilian clothes or the one in
a US Army uniform. All have been fingerprinted and photographed and the material transmitted to the Criminal
Records and Identification Bureau. The single survivor
we found has regained consciousness and is in hospital in
Regensburg."

Kasper picked up a brass shell casing.

"Anything new on the tire prints?" He squinted at the
spent .45 shell's base.

"*Nein.* There appears to have been one vehicle that
left here, almost certainly a Mercedes G-Wagen with false
police livery like the ones we found destroyed by grenades.
We have alerted the public."

"So some people obviously escaped from here. Any links
with the sabotage at Höhenbogen and Mühldorf?"

"Probably. Too early to know for sure, *Herr General.*"

Kasper pocketed the .45 shell. "You said there was a
corpse in civilian clothing and another in an American uniform. Have they been bagged yet?"

Keitz shook his head. "Some officers from the American
Army CID are examining them."

"Why are Americans here?" Kasper growled. "This is
now officially a German federal case."

"They were investigating the Hőhenbogen Kaserne attack. I gave them permission to join us because of the probable connection and the body with US uniform and ID."

Keitz guided Kasper around the bullet-pocked building towards the smoldering garage. Three men - two in civilian clothing and another in a US Army black beret and trench coat - huddled under umbrellas around a cadaver. Twenty feet away, a pair of legs clad in jeans and hiking boots protruded from a plastic sheet.

The Americans straightened and shook hands, their manner deferential after Kasper was introduced. All three wore perplexed expressions.

Kasper peered at the corpse's face. "So what do we have here, a Negro?" he asked in fluent English.

"Nope," said one of the civilian-clothed men, who had introduced himself as Warrant Officer Oldham. "He's got on black camouflage greasepaint."

"Another imposter then," said Kasper. "But wearing an American uniform instead of SEK clothing." He turned to Keitz. "They were probably planning to infiltrate terrorists disguised as soldiers and policemen into installations. The Baader-Meinhof gang tried it at Munsterlager years ago."

"That's what puzzles us," Oldham said. "Those corpses with fake SEK uniforms and ID might have conned their way into a kaserne or a secure civilian facility, but this guy wouldn't have gotten past the front gate!"

"And why is that?"

"Well, number one, he's wearing a World War Two uniform and helmet that he must have got from a costume shop or eBay – can't even get real ones from Army surplus stores. Number two, he's got what appear to be real World War Two ID papers that match the dog tags he's wearing. And to top it off, this guy was carrying an antique Tommy gun!"

"We found another Thompson submachine gun outside the headquarters building," Keitz added. "Both had children's toys - tin clickers - taped to the stocks. Very strange."

Kasper's eyebrows knitted as he remembered the .45 shell he had picked up. At that moment there was a shout and all five men turned to see a young policeman running towards them from the mobile command post. He handed Keitz a document still warm from the command post's laser printer.

"This just came from Munich," he said, barely containing his excitement.

Keitz scanned the message, then handed it to Kasper. "The man we found alive is an ethnic Bosnian named Rijad Jasarevic! He has been on our watch list of suspected terrorists for six years."

Kasper stiffened, nostrils twitching like a bloodhound scenting its quarry.

Keitz turned to the American detectives. "He's spilling his guts to the *Bundesamt für Verfassungsschutz*. Jasarevic told them that he and his comrades were planning to attack the World Youth Congress meeting that starts today outside Munich."

"A hostage-taking operation?" asked one of the Americans.

"No," the Bavarian police commander spat. "They were planning a massacre to rival Mumbai."

Kasper's face mottled with fury.

"We had intelligence warnings of an attack in Bavaria. Filthy terrorist animals!" he shouted, chest heaving. "I will not rest until I have hunted down and exterminated those that escaped!"

The younger men waited in embarrassed silence until the former Hitler Youth regained his composure. Kasper gazed into the distance, shook his head, and turned back to Keitz.

"That explains the SEK uniforms," Kasper said calmly. "Did the survivor say what happened here?"

"He said he was awakened by detonating grenades and gunfire. He glimpsed the attackers before a bullet creased him. He swears they wore American army uniforms. Like this one." Keitz nudged the corpse with his foot. "A mystery, *nicht wahr?*"

Kasper frowned. "Yes, but Jasarevic's leaders would have told him only what he needed to know. There may have been separate terrorist units involved in a coordinated action – some disguised as our police and others like Americans. Some teams would attack military targets while others went after civilians. This was a major terrorist operation, and I don't think it's over yet."

"So what the hell happened here?" One of the Americans gestured around the old SS camp.

"Perhaps these scum had a falling out and turned on each other like the mad dogs they are." Kasper faced Keitz, his eyes gleaming. "Jasarevic said there were twenty-four men disguised as SEK troopers in his band. We have eighteen dead terrorists and one prisoner, plus these two corpses, whoever they are. That means that some of the swine escaped. They can't have got far. We must neutralize them!"

He spun on his heel and marched towards the mobile command post, trailed by the young policeman who had delivered the message. Keitz started to follow.

"Wait," said Warrant Officer Oldham. "I need your permission for us to take custody of this body." He pointed to the dead man in the outdated US Army uniform.

"Take custody? I am afraid this is not within your jurisdiction. Just because the corpse is wearing an American uniform does not mean he is one of your people."

"It's more complicated than that." Oldham crossed his arms. "This guy also has US Army ID papers, even if they're over sixty years old. Under the terms of our treaty, the US government is the ward of any remains found on German soil that carry US military identification. Over the years we've had dozens of desertions from our forces in Germany. We know that a few of those deserters joined terrorist organizations. It's possible that this guy is one of them. Maybe he doctored up some old ID papers to match his dog tags. I don't know why he'd want World War Two papers, but we need to at least find out if he's one of ours. We'll coordinate our investigation with yours, of course."

The harried Keitz nodded. "All right, but I would like to keep his boots. If he turns out to be one of yours you can have them back, but we need to see if they match the footprints at your *kaserne* and the airfield."

Paula von Scheller watched as the intruders carried the unconscious man into the hallway, leaving a trail of muddy boot prints.

"Where we gonna put him?" asked one of the men, whom Paula had figured out was named Holcombe. She now knew all their names – Holcombe, Kemp, Loomis, and the German-speaking sergeant called Roth.

"There are beds upstairs," Paula said, her voice hoarse from crying.

Roth, who had been guarding Paula and the two servants, shook his head. "No, we will put him in the old Nazi's bed down here."

He strode into the bedroom and ordered her grandfather out of his bed. Paula hurried to assist, positioning the elderly man's wheelchair and supporting him as he slumped into it. She tucked a blanket around him as the soldiers laid their comrade on the bed.

"What's wrong with him, concussion?" asked Holcombe.

"Could be." Kemp shook his head. "That grenade went off just a few feet from him. It's a miracle he ain't hamburger. Any of you guys know how to help him?"

Loomis shrugged. "I could bandage a cut or bullet wound, but concussion's something else."

Roth stuck his head around the doorway. "Are you finished? We'll take turns on sentry duty. Holcombe and I will take first watch – you two get some sleep. Smoke if you want to. Holcombe, you stay here and guard the prisoners while I go upstairs to watch the outside."

"Guess I could do with some shut-eye and a bite to eat," Kemp said. He offered a pack of *Lucky Strikes* to Loomis, took one for himself, then lit both cigarettes with his Zippo. The two Rangers went out the door, passing Sepp and Maria as they shuffled into the room. The servant couple sat on a sofa and held hands, fearfully eyeing Holcombe, who stood by the bed looking at the unconscious man.

"Wish I could do something for the poor guy," Holcombe said.

Paula had also been studying the man. She cleared her throat.

"I am a medical student. Perhaps I could help him."

"No!" Her grandfather wheeled his chair close to her. "I forbid you to help these terrorists!"

"I'd be real grateful if you could take a look at the lieutenant, ma'am," said Holcombe.

Paula left her grandfather's side.

"Paula!"

"*Opa, please.*" She unbuckled the chinstrap of Sutton's helmet. "Could you bring me a wet washcloth, a towel, and bar of soap?" she asked Holcombe.

She removed the heavy steel helmet and liner from Sutton's head. The hair underneath was light brown and close-cropped. Holcombe brought soap, towels and a first aid kit from her grandfather's bathroom. Paula swabbed away the black camouflage paint to reveal a youthful face with straight nose and long eyelashes. Stubble had grown on the square chin and thin cheeks.

"Help me with his clothing," she said to Holcombe, and together they divested the man of his airborne combat jacket and khaki woolen shirt. The left sleeves of both garments were singed. She tossed the uniform onto a chair beside her grandfather.

Paula didn't notice the decorated button that dropped from one of the jacket pockets. Von Scheller saw it and reached down to retrieve it. He hid it in the palm of his hand, watching as Paula dressed the light burns on the unconscious man's arm with salve and bound them in a gauze bandage.

She examined the rest of his body but found no other injuries. With Holcombe's help, she turned the man over, clucking her tongue when she saw the lump at the base of his skull. The man groaned as she touched it – a good sign that he'd wake up soon, Paula knew.

"I believe this is what made him unconscious," she said. "He must have struck his head very hard. I don't think his skull is fractured, so hopefully he won't have brain injury."

Holcombe nodded. "Glad to hear it. You got any idea how long he might be out?"

"It is hard to say. A few hours? Maybe the whole day? He should be in a hospital." She rolled Sutton onto his back and arranged a pillow to cushion his head. As she did so, Paula saw the man's aluminum dog tags hanging from a chain against his olive drab tee shirt. She picked one up.

"'Arthur J. Sutton'. That is his name?"

"Yep. First Lieutenant Arthur Sutton." Holcombe rubbed his hands together briskly.

"Hey, it's kinda cold in here. I'll build us a fire." He went to work with kindling and his black crackle Zippo, crouching at the fireplace.

"You are Americans then?" asked von Scheller.

"Sure am."

"What right have you to invade my home and hold us prisoners! Where are you from – Hőhenbogen Kaserne, Grafenwoehr? If this is one of your damned exercises you Americans have gone too far this time! I shall see to it that my government takes the strongest actions against all of you! Who is your commanding officer?"

"Lieutenant Sutton there is my commanding officer, mister. Now you just calm down and we'll all get along fine. You think we could rustle up some breakfast?"

Von Scheller pushed his wheelchair closer to the fireplace.

"Don't insult me young man! Are all you Americans so deranged by drugs that you can't think about breaking the law? Your President Obama will hear of this atrocity!"

Holcombe stared at him. "Who in blazes is President O'Bama? Jesus, talk about deranged! Are you Nazis so brainwashed over here you don't even know that the President of the USA is Harry S. Truman?"

Von Scheller wondered if he had misunderstood the American's drawl.

Remembering the object that had fallen from Sutton's jacket, he opened his hand and looked at the campaign button with the face of the long dead US president printed on it. He decided that the young *Amerikaner* soldier was baiting him.

"Please do not joke with my grandfather," said Paula. "He knows many people in the government and means every word he says!"

Holcombe fed a log into the fire and stood, frowning at them.

"Look, lady, I ain't joking and I got nothing personal against you people. All I'm trying to do is follow orders and stay alive until this goddam war is over so I can go back home where I belong. You and your granddaddy would sure make my job easier if you'd stop pestering me!"

"War?" said Paula. "What are you talking about?"

"I assume he is referring to war games," said von Scheller. "But these fools have carried the realism too far!"

"Sheeeit!" Holcombe shook his head in exasperation. He stomped across the room to the bathroom, removed his helmet, and splashed water on his face. Von Scheller watched him through the open door.

"Where is your home?" Paula called as Holcombe toweled his face.

"Loachapoka, Alabama, USA."

"Oh, yes, that is in the South, isn't it? And how long have you been in Germany?"

Holcombe discarded the towel, turning his freckled, boyish face to the German woman. It seemed like he was not going to answer, but then an obviously sly look appeared.

"Just parachuted in last night. 'Bout fifteen thousand of us. Should have the whole of Bavaria captured by today. War'll be over soon."

His bathing completed, Holcombe dragged a chair to the fireplace and sat down. He took a K ration package from his pocket and opened a can of breakfast egg yolk and pork with a key worn around his neck on the same chain as his dog tags.

"Have you been in the American army long?" Paula asked.

"Um hum," Holcombe mumbled through a full mouth. He swallowed. "Went into town and joined up the day after Pearl Harbor."

"Pearl Harbor?"

"Yep. Monday morning, December 8, 1941. Lied about my age but they took me anyhow."

Von Scheller was bewildered. He remembered the old photograph of himself the sergeant had shown him during his interrogation, and the intruders' mystifying conversations and actions. He peered closely at Holcombe's uniform. It seemed unlike the pictures of contemporary American soldiers in newspapers and magazines – more similar, in fact, to photos in World War II histories. This *had* to be a hoax. An elaborate and cruel practical joke.

Von Scheller cleared his throat. "We are the victims of a hoax, Paula. These are not real American soldiers. They are probably left-wing students trying to punish me in some sick way for my service in the Luftwaffe."

Holcombe paused with the spoon halfway to his mouth. "The hell you say we're not real American soldiers! I'm a member in good standing of the best goddam fighting unit in the world, the US Second Ranger Battalion!"

"If that is true," Paula said," how can you claim you joined the army in 1941? You look no older than twenty!"

Holcombe banged the spoon and can on the floor.

"What the hell's wrong with you crazy Krauts? You trying to get my goat or something?" He took out a US Army pay book with his ID card clipped to it and tossed it to Paula. "This'll prove I'm the real McCoy!"

Paula examined the dog-eared piece of cardboard headed "Enlisted Mans Identification Card, European Theater of Operations, U.S. Army."

"Opa, these say his name is Private First Class Daniel R. Holcombe, Company B, Second United States Ranger Battalion." She looked up, her expression mingling wonder and disbelief. "It gives his date of birth as October 8, 1924. That's impossible!"

"Let me see them!"

Von Scheller scrutinized the documents, then handed them back to Holcombe.

"These prove nothing! Do you and your comrades really think you could fool us with your absurd World War Two charade?"

Holcombe's innocent blue eyes showed his bafflement. "Mister, I don't get you. What do you mean by 'World War Two charade?'"

"You have obviously dressed up in old uniforms with stage props such as your papers and even this Roosevelt button. For some warped purpose you are pretending you are in 1941."

"It ain't 1941!" Holcombe cried.

"Ah, so you admit it?"

"You know damned well it's 1945!"

Paula sighed. Von Scheller threw up his hands in exasperation.

"You expect me to accept that you truly believe we are in 1945? What kind of a fool do you take me for!"

Holcombe rubbed his forehead as if in pain. "Well why the hell shouldn't I believe it when it *is* 1945! What's wrong with you people?"

The young American seemed determined to perpetuate his masquerade, von Scheller thought, and well prepared too. He decided to trick "Private Holcombe," make him slip up in his ridiculous story. Von Scheller paused to remember public figures and events of the 1930s and '40s. His mind returned to the summer of 1939, when he had visited the New York World's Fair as a student.

"Did you listen to the radio much before the 'war' started?" he asked.

"Sure. Why do you want to know?"

"Oh, I am just curious about your country. What were some of your favorite radio shows?

Holcombe scratched his jaw. "Well, I like *Spotlight Band* and *Grand Ole Opry*. Ma and Pa and me used to listen to *Information Please* and *Quiz Kids* 'cause it's educational. Of course, everybody likes Jack Benny. Edgar Bergen and Charlie McCarthy are a real hoot, and so's old Bob Bernie and Joe!"

Von Scheller was surprised to find the imposter so knowledgeable. He pursued his questioning. "Do you remember the names of any of the radio commentators you listened to?"

"Sure do. Let's see, there's Elmer Davis on CBS and, uh, Dorothy Thompson, Raymond Gram Swing, and Lowell Thomas. And of course, Orson Welles. Jesus, that *War of the Worlds* thing of his was scarier than hearing about Pearl Harbor!"

Von Scheller remembered newspaper accounts of Welles's notorious radio program.

"When was that broadcast?"

Holcombe rubbed his crew-cut hair. "Around Halloween about seven years ago. '38, I guess."

Von Scheller was impressed. The young American had done his homework well.

"Do you have a favorite sport?"

"Sport? Well I guess baseball's my favorite now, but when I was a kid I was crazy about boxing."

"Is that so?" Von Scheller had discovered a subject he was more than superficially acquainted with, having been a fan of American boxing in the 1930s. "Did you like Joe Louis?"

Holcombe grinned. "Yeah, he's swell! Got a *Big Little Book* about him for Christmas one year. Must have been about thirteen then. We was so poor my Daddy had to give up buying hisself a new hat so he could get me that book."

"Tell me about Joe Louis, please."

"Let me think, now. He knocked Max Baer out in the fourth round in the fall of '35. Baer beat Primo Carnera the year before. Then Joe Louis kay-ohed James J. Braddock the heavyweight champ in '37. My daddy and brothers and me went down to Clinton's store that night to listen to the fight on the radio with all the good ole boys. That was really something!"

Von Scheller swallowed. The American's knowledge of boxing lore from nearly 75 years ago was as accurate as his familiarity with radio programs and personalities of the time. A chill coursed up his spine as he began to sense an anomaly beyond comprehension.

He looked closely at the fresh-faced young man. There was something *different* about him ... guileless. He was either an incredibly good actor, or he had been hypnotized into believing he was a World War II soldier with an elaborate personal background to match. But *why?*

Then another thought occurred. Could it be ... ? No, it was *impossible!* The questioning must continue. Certainly the young man would make a glaring mistake that would dispel such disturbing thoughts!

"So, Private Holcombe, I would like to know what your favorite new songs are and who are your favorite film stars?"

"Film? Oh yeah, *movie* stars." Holcombe blushed behind his freckles. "Well, Hedy Lamarr and Carol Landis are about the best-looking babes in the world. Lupe Velez too. Songs? My favorites at the moment, aside from Country, are 'Don't Fence Me In' and 'Sunny Side of the Street.'"

"Could you sing them for me?"

Holcombe fidgeted. "Ain't too good at singing, but guess I could whistle 'em for you."

Von Scheller closed his eyes as Holcombe whistled "Don't Fence Me In." The layer of years peeled back to early December 1944, the Eastern Front. Evenings in a snow-bound hut used as the officer's mess by the survivors of his Stuka dive bomber *Gruppe*. One of the men had modified a radio to pick up the BBC's forbidden broadcasts. The weary Luftwaffe pilots enjoyed the American swing and boogie-woogie music. They had sung along with "Don't Fence Me In" and tapped the plank tables to "Sunny Side of the Street."

Some, drunk on *korn,* had wept as Anne Shelton sang "Lili Marlene" over the crackling airwaves. And there had been a BBC news reader, a calm, stately voice that inspired trust in contrast to the lies of Radio Berlin. The man's name surfaced from the past, an obscure morsel of World War II trivia that only a scholar or genuine veteran could know.

He interrupted Holcombe's off-key whistling. "Thank you. That was very nice. Tell me, did you serve in England before coming here?"

Holcombe nodded, concentrating on opening a can of K-ration peaches.

"Four months at a dump called Chilton Foliat in some-place called Wiltshire. Rained all the time. We was quar-tered with the 506th Airborne. Trained in Scotland, too."

"Did you ever hear of a man called Bruce Belfrage in England?"

Holcombe pursed his lips in thought. "Bruce Belfrage? Hmm, ain't he the Limey guy who reads the news on the BBC?"

Von Scheller gaped at the young American, his heart pounding.

The Luftwaffe C-130J Hercules, iron crosses blazoned on its skin, turned into the wind on runway two at the Black Forest Airport. Inside the transport's cabin, one hundred fit and highly trained young men of the German army's KSK unit listened to the revving of the turboprop engines. The brakes were released and the Hercules roared down the runway. As it rotated into the overcast sky, the hearts of its passengers lifted with it. First one voice, then another, then the entire company took up an old SS march-ing tune that their grandfathers had sung – a song known as the "Host Wessel Lied."

The body of Private Nicholas Sarnoff - photographed, fingerprinted, and tagged - was zipped into a thick plas-tic body bag and delivered by helicopter to the Landstuhl Regional Medical Center. Warrant Officer Oldham accom-panied the corpse to the hospital mortuary.

Sarnoff's corpse was stripped of all clothing and jew-elry. Its fingers were inked and rolled against an official fingerprint card for the second time that day. The head

95

was placed in a cradle and photographed from six different positions. A new tag was affixed to the big toe of the left foot, and the cadaver was stretched on a stainless steel table with a drain hole at the bottom. A bored orderly draped the corpse with a sherbet-green sheet and returned to his *Penthouse* magazine.

The US Army Medical Command colonel who served as chief pathologist at the Medical Center came as quickly as possible. His wife was on a shopping junket to Paris, and he hoped to get over to Koblenz before lunch to visit a certain little nurse. Normally, he would have told the mortuary to keep their cadaver on ice until Monday, but the urgent autopsy request had come from a buddy of his who commanded the Military Police Criminal Investigation Command unit at Kaiserslautern.

Surgical mask donned, eyes narrowed behind his glasses, the medical examiner told the orderly to turn on the video camera and remove the sheet from the corpse. The doctor checked the wall clock.

"Landstuhl Regional Medical Center Germany," he said. "11:36 hours, April 22nd. Colonel Meyer, Medical Examiner.

"This is the body of a well-nourished, well-developed white male weighing an estimated one hundred seventy pounds and measuring seventy-three inches in length. The head is of normal shape, the limbs are normal and of normal proportion to the body ...."

10

Edward Cassera stood in the lobby of his condo building, watching a parade of other residents depart for their jobs as he waited for the motor pool van. He grimaced, ill tempered from his hangover and a sleepless night. Cassera brightened as a pair of Asian nurses hurried past on their way to the Metro. *At least I can still get turned on by gook chicks,* he thought.

The Department of Defense van pulled to the curb outside and Cassera limped to it through the April drizzle. He wedged himself between a secretary from the Defense Audiovisual Agency and a rotund Pentagon Food Services manager with a streaming cold who wiped his nose on his sleeve. Eddie disinterestedly listened to some of the passengers discussing news reports about a terrorist attack in Germany.

Morning rush hour traffic was heavy for a Friday, and it was nearly 09:00 when the van stopped in front of the nondescript office building in Crystal City. None of the passengers - mid-level government bureaucrats like himself

97

- hurried to their jobs. Like the others, Cassera had learned early in his career that (A) once you had a GS position it was almost impossible to be fired from it and (B) nobody really gave a shit.

He rode the elevator to the eighth floor with a 40-something secretary from Public Affairs. The woman had a nice pair of boobs; she scowled when she saw Eddie ogling them. Cassera sighed as the woman hurriedly exited on the fifth floor. *Can't blame her,* he mused. *Who wants a balding guy with a bum leg and a beer gut who just had his 61st birthday?*

He left the elevator and went down a corridor to the offices of the Defense Prisoner of War/Missing Personnel Office. Milly, the secretary he shared with two other DPMO investigators, was absent from her desk. He helped himself to a cup of coffee and a donut from the lunch room before going into his windowless office.

Cassera hung up his overcoat, slumped into his chair, and looked at the donut, vaguely wondering how many calories it contained. He shrugged and took a bite. Eddie Cassera had long ago given up on his intent to do something about his unhealthy diet, drinking, settling down with a nice woman his own age, and a dozen other resolutions to fix his dead-end personal life. The willpower just wasn't there. Burned out, he no longer cared about much of anything.

Eddie eyed the stack of case files on his desk – service records, forensic reports, DNA tests, letters from family members and comrades of the Missing. He looked at the wall clock next to the framed DPMO motto "Keeping the Promise" – meaning that the US military was committed to bringing home the remains of America's warriors. *Well, we haven't kept our promise to find and repatriate a certain skinny black kid who went MIA over forty years ago*, he thought sorrowfully.

Cassera washed down a couple of Tylenol with the coffee, stretched and turned on his computer. As usual, he wondered how he was going to endure the day ahead, much less the remaining eleven months and seventeen days to retirement. But he still preferred the office routine to the bleak nights and lonely weekends in his one-bedroom condo.

There was a knock at his door. Milly entered with her overly bright lips and black-rimmed eyes behind spectacles that had gone out of fashion sometime in the '80s. She laid a large manila envelope on his desk stamped CONFIDENTIAL – IMMEDIATE ATTENTION.

"What's this?" Cassera asked.

"Just came in by secure email from Germany. The Director said to give it to you because everyone else seems to have taken today off."

"Germany?" Cassera opened the envelope. "Probably another case of bone fragments and dog tags found by some guy with a metal detector."

"Don't think so this time," Milly said over her shoulder. "It's from Army CID."

Cassera spilled the envelope's contents onto his desk. There was a PDF copy of a letter clipped to a sheaf of fingerprint cards, GSA forms, and photographs. He read the letter first:

```
From: 202nd MP Group (CID), Kleber Kaserne,
Kaiserslautern, Germany


IMMEDIATE ATTENTION. Request status PFC
Nicholas I Sarnoff serial number 35263776. ID
```

process report, fingerprints and photographs attached. Request fingerprint cross check FBI Integrated AFIS. No repeat No record Nicholas I Sarnoff 1965 to 2011 USA-EUR Records Center Heidelberg.

> **BG Lester Forbes**
> **Chief, 202nd MP Group**

Cassera shook his head in exasperation. "What the hell," he muttered. "Why can't the goddam CID use their own people over here to do their detective work? This guy can't be an MIA if they've got his fingerprints, for Pete's sake!"

Annoyed at the interdepartmental transgression, he rummaged through the documents. The photographs showing a dead young white male from various angles and ranges. Cassera laid these aside after a cursory inspection.

The next item was a long GSA form headed "Record of Identification Processes - Effects and Physical Data." The first subheading was "Items of Clothing and Equipment Found With Remains." Cassera scanned the list, brow wrinkling as he saw that every item of clothing, equipment, and personal effects seemed to date from the Second World War.

More than sixty articles were listed, including an M1A1 Thompson submachine gun, a khaki woolen 43 jacket with a blue *Rangers* badge on the sleeve, and three packets of K-rations packed in October 1944. Photographs accompanied the list. One showed an apparently blood-stained document headed "The Parachute School, Airborne Command,

United States Army," certifying that Nicholas I. Sarnoff had completed a course in "parachute packing, ground training and jumping from a plane in flight," and had been rated a "qualified parachutist" on January 14, 1943. Another picture showed an "Enlisted Man's Temporary Pass" authorizing PFC Sarnoff to visit Paris from December 2 to 5, 1944.

Among the personal effects were a cheap class ring embossed *Temple High School - Class of 1942* and three personal letters, copies of which were attached.

The second subheading said "Official Identification Found With Remains." These consisted of one US Army pay book issued October 11, 1942 to Nicholas I. Sarnoff, a US Army ID card, and a set of dog tags marked

```
NICHOLAS I SARNOFF
35263776 T42 43 O
MRS LOUISE SARNOFF
1623 WALNUT ST APT 4A
PHILADELPHIA PA P
```

Cassera knew that the pattern of these dog tags was used by the US Army from November 1941 to July 1943, which corresponded with the date of the pay book issued at a soldier's induction. He made a note of the next of kin's address in Philadelphia.

The remainder of the form provided a physical description of the cadaver. Under the subheading "Wounds or Injuries" was typed: "Massive gunshot wounds to thorax and abdomen (see autopsy report)."

Intrigued, Cassera read the autopsy report carefully. It stated that the subject of the post-mortem was a male

Caucasian in his early twenties who stood six feet, one inch in height, weighed 169 pounds, and had brown hair and blue eyes. The corpse had a three-inch scar on the external bicipital sulcus of the left arm and a tattoo on the right shoulder depicting a skull and crossbones with "Or Glory" on a scroll beneath. Cause of death was attributed to five gunshot wounds that had perforated the heart and other internal organs. A single bullet identified as a 9x19mm Parabellum had been found lodged against the ninth vertebra. At the time the autopsy was performed, the subject had been dead for less than 12 hours.

The final set of papers was a CID report stamped CONFIDENTIAL which related the circumstances under which the body was found. The transcript stated that the subject had been discovered in association with a number of other corpses and one living individual clad in false Bavarian Police Force special forces uniforms. The sole survivor had been identified as a suspected member of a terrorist organization. The report concluded by stating that the case had been given the highest priority by the German government, and that US Army CID was working closely with the German authorities.

Terrorists in Germany, Cassera mused, remembering the vaguely overheard conversation on the shuttle van. Clearing a space on his desk, he spread all the documents across it. He studied the dead man's photos, took a sip of cold coffee, and sat back in his chair, pondering the enigma in the papers on his desk.

Without the autopsy and CID reports, he might have thought there was a slim possibility that the fresh-looking corpse with its nearly 70-year-old personal effects was a genuine casualty of World War II. He knew of two precedents. The first involved an American B-17 bomber that had been covered by an avalanche after crashing in Greenland in 1943. In 1976, a US Navy weather plane had spotted the bomber's wing tip sticking out of a snow bank. Defense Department investigators excavated the crash site and recovered the bodies of eleven crewmen – mangled from the crash but otherwise preserved in their arctic deep freeze.

The second involved a German Heinkel He-111 bomber, which crashed on Norway's Dovrefjell Plateau in 1941, killing the pilot, gunners, and bombardier. Only the radio operator survived. With the help of Norwegian hunters who rescued him, the Luftwaffe crewman dug graves for his comrades deep into the permafrost.

In 1982, a Luftwaffe veteran's society decided to disinter the bodies and return them to Germany. Accompanied by reporters, TV stars, politicians, priests, public relations specialists, and an Austrian psychic, the lone survivor returned to the gravesite to witness the exhumation. The spectators gasped as the final layers of frozen soil were removed and the parachutes covering the corpses pulled aside to reveal four boyish faces unchanged since the moment of burial.

Cassera had been stationed with the military's Memorial Affairs unit in Frankfurt at the time. He vividly remembered coverage of the discovery on German television – close ups of the fat, bald, sixtyish survivor, sobbing as he looked upon the youthful forms of his comrades. Cassera could have sworn that among the emotions twisting the Luftwaffe veteran's face was jealousy that *they* were forever young and he was growing old. He sometimes felt like that himself when he remembered his lost youth and vanished friends in Vietnam.

Interesting as a frozen corpse case might be, it was impossible for the body in question to be a genuine World War II casualty. This was obvious from the reports that confirmed the cadaver had been found in the open in the middle of a forest, had been dead for only a few hours, and had apparently been killed by a modern weapon. The only plausible explanation was that the dead man had got his hands on an old American uniform, weapons, ID, and accessories.

Cassera found the whole thing pretty weird. The guy would have had to go to a ridiculous amount of trouble to equip himself with genuine World War II-era items. Christ, the guy even had old K-rations and personal letters dated 1945! But that part of the case didn't concern him. The CID report said the cops in Europe were working on the whys and wherefores.

Cassera's job as a DPMO investigator was to find out what had happened to the real Private Nicholas Sarnoff to help identify the corpse in Frankfurt that carried Sarnoff's ID. He thought that the request for a comparison of the cadaver's fingerprints with Sarnoff's was a waste of time as the real Nicholas I. Sarnoff must have been a World War II veteran – unless the ID papers were forgeries. But when you worked for the Department of Defense, even as a civilian, you'd better do what lard ass Generals wanted or the next pay grade promotion might get hung up. And anyway, the case was a welcome break from routine paper shuffling.

Cassera scanned the fingerprints into a computer program which had algorithms designed to detect and mark all minutia points, cores, and deltas on the print. He then logged on to the FBI's Integrated Automated Fingerprint Identification System (IAFIS) which had more than 60 million individual computerized fingerprint records. He uploaded the scanned prints, requesting a priority search. Usually, IAFIS search results were available in under two hours for criminal requests and 24 hours for civilian matters. Eddie knew that old paper fingerprint cards for the civil files were manually maintained in a rented shopping center space that served as a warehouse in Fairmont, West Virginia. If the dead man in Germany had ever served in the US armed forces his fingerprints should match ones in the IAFIS database. Because the DPMO did not have a secure IAFIS terminal, any positive search results would be sent to the FBI headquarters in downtown Washington D.C. and delivered by government courier.

Cassera doubted that the deceased was even an American – he suspected that the cadaver belonged to a German reenactor, a member of one of hundreds of European groups that dressed up in period military uniforms, from Romans to Second World War personnel.

Next, Cassera logged on to the National Archives' Access to Archival Databases (AAD) page and clicked on the World War II Army Enlistment Records link, which took him to "Electronic Army Serial Number Merged File, ca. 1938 - 1946 (Enlistment Records)." He entered Sarnoff's serial number. A record immediately appeared that matched the documents sent from Germany but had no additional information such as physical characteristics or particulars of military service.

Eddie refilled his coffee cup, snagged another donut, and returned to his computer. He accessed the Department of Veterans Affairs database, which contained no record that Nicholas I. Sarnoff had applied for post-war benefits or services.

Complete military service files were kept at the National Personnel Records Center (NPRC) in St. Louis and were not available online even for Defense Department investigators such as Cassera. He emailed Sarnoff's data to an NPRC archivist he had worked with over the years, flagging it High Importance and hoping the woman would be at work on this Friday instead of taking time off as so many federal employees seemed to do. She responded immediately, saying she would send the information as soon as it could be found.

For the next hour Cassera drafted a report on the identification of remains of GIs who had died at the Suan Prisoner of War Camp in North Korea in 1951. "Reported cause of death from eyewitness accounts," he wrote. "Starvation and beatings by North Korean guards." *No wonder I'm burned out*, he said to himself, imagining the horrors experienced by teenage boys who had been drafted to "defend America against international communism." Like all those dead and maimed boys he had known in 'Nam. And now half the fucking crap for sale at Walmart was from Vietnam and the other half was from "communist" China. Shaking his head, he left the office and walked down the street to a Frank & Stein.

He was finishing lunch when his Blackberry rang.

"Got your boy," the NPRC archivist said cheerfully. "Just emailed the complete file to you."

"Much appreciated." Cassera stood up from his plastic restaurant chair. "The VA had nothing on him."

"No wonder. He's an old-time MIA. Missing since April 1945."

"MIA?" Eddie's heart pounded. He sat back down heavily.

"Yeah. Sent you his 293 file . . . hey, you okay?"

"Sure," he replied hoarsely. "Gotta go."

11

Back in his office Cassera clicked on the archivist's email. He opened its PDF attachment to see the cover of a black folder bearing a yellowed label with the defunct War Department's seal. On it was typed: 293 File – Dead. Bodies Not Recovered – January to December 1945. Sarnoff, Nicholas I., 35263776.

The folder contained the missing soldier's service record, dental chart, medical record, line of duty, and addresses of next-of-kin. The last two pages were findings of the US Army Judge Advocate General (JAG) board convened to declare the man dead. There were no photographs.

Sarnoff had enlisted in the US Army in October 1942. During basic training at Camp Kilmer, New Jersey, he had spent three days in the stockade for "disorderly conduct - fighting." Sarnoff had volunteered for the 506th Parachute Infantry Regiment and sailed to England in September 1943 on the Cunard liner SS Samaria. Cassera grinned as he read that Sarnoff had been confined to the ship's brig for the last twenty-four hours of the voyage for throwing a plate of food at a mess steward.

Although considered a "bad egg" by his officers, Sarnoff's request for transfer to the US Rangers had been approved in early 1944. He had gone ashore with the 2nd Battalion on D-Day, fought through the Normandy campaign and been wounded. In February 1945 Sarnoff had been selected for a special mission code-named Bandstand – an operation still classified when his file was closed in 1946. He had disappeared during Bandstand.

Cassera skipped the dental chart and was about to do the same for the medical record when something caught his eye. He read it quickly, then scrabbled through the material sent from Germany until he found the official identification process form and the autopsy report. He scrutinized all three, comparing the anatomical details. When he finished, he felt just like he had on a day many years before as a high school football player when he was knocked down and left stunned by a 230-pound linebacker.

The physical descriptions matched on all three reports, with the exception of the Death or Glory tattoo and minor weight discrepancies. The height was identical, as was the age, musculature, and eye and hair color. What really shook Cassera was the dry World War II report on a shrapnel wound the original Sarnoff had received in Normandy – an injury that left a three-inch scar on his left arm exactly like the one on the body in the Landstuhl mortuary.

Cassera felt beads of sweat break out on his forehead. *Hold on*, he told himself, *it's all just a coincidence, a weird fucking coincidence!*

He took a deep breath, closed his eyes and tried to still his pounding heart. When he reopened them he was looking at the JAG board report in the 293 File. Sarnoff went

MIA on April 21, 1945, and had been officially declared Killed in Action on April 22, 1946. Eddie clicked on the date and time icon on the bottom right of his computer's monitor: Friday, April 22.

Holy shit, he breathed. Sixty-six years ago today. He jerked out of his reverie as Milly's nasal voice blared over the intercom.

"Courier just brought an envelope for you. Want me to bring it in now or are you busy?"

"Oh, uh, yeah, bring it in." He looked up expectantly as she entered.

"Hey, Eddie, you look kinda pale," she said. "You coming down with the flu or just hitting the sauce too much?"

Cassera ignored her as he reached for the envelope printed with the return address of the FBI's J. Edgar Hoover building. He ripped open the envelope and pulled out the Landstuhl mortuary fingerprints and a photocopy of another set on official FBI cards. A memo was clipped to the latter set. His breath caught in his throat as he read it.

The prints from the fresh corpse in Germany matched ones belonging to Nicholas Ivan Sarnoff taken on October 18, 1942.

"No," Cassera whispered.

"Yes," said von Scheller. "It is the same with all of them. Incredible!"

The gray afternoon was shading to early dusk from the persistent drizzle. During the remainder of the morning, Holcombe's wariness had lessened. He spoke with the von Schellers for hours, a homesick youth reminiscing about life on a hardscrabble Alabama farm during the Great

Depression and wartime experiences after being drafted. He had aired more knowledge of popular culture of the 1930s and early '40s, but was vague about world events and the strategy and politics of World War II, reflecting the perspective of an ordinary soldier.

Holcombe had allowed the Germans to bathe, dress, and eat. Old Maria brought Paula's clothes from her room and fetched bread, cheese, sausage, and coffee from the kitchen. Shortly after noon, Loomis and Kemp had joined them. They checked on the unconscious Sutton and smoked with Holcombe. Roth intruded half an hour later and ordered Holcombe to rest and Loomis to stand watch upstairs. The three men departed, leaving Kemp to guard the Germans.

Von Scheller had spent the next three and half hours conversing with Kemp as he had with Holcombe, his interrogative technique more refined to avoid alienating the young American. Kemp - a New Yorker - was more sophisticated than Holcombe. His combat hardened face lost its wariness when he talked of familiar personalities like Jack Armstrong, "The All-American Boy," who promoted his favorite breakfast cereal, *Wheaties*. He grinned as he reminisced about Saturday afternoon matinees at his neighborhood movie theater in Brooklyn - "they even got air conditioning" - when Buster Crabbe played Flash Gordon or Johnny Weissmuller starred as Tarzan.

Kemp had an encyclopedic knowledge of the 1939 World's Fair, where he claimed to have worked as an attendant at the "World of Tomorrow" in an exhibit called "Futurama," which portrayed a concept of the United States in 1960.

"My favorite was the sky dive," he said. "You know, the big tower with giant Life Savers candy on it? Must've done those parachute jumps a hundred times. Got me so hooked I volunteered for Airborne after basic, before I joined the Rangers."

When Kemp excused himself to use the toilet, von Scheller wheeled to Paula. He spoke softly and urgently in German to his granddaughter. "They seem genuine! Everything about them!"

Paula's eyes were troubled. "Opa, certainly *you* don't believe them! It must be a hoax like you said. It has to be!"

Kemp returned, squinted at them, then hunkered by the fire and jabbed it with a poker.

"I have tried every trick I could think of to trip them up!" von Scheller whispered. "I've asked them questions about the war and American culture of the '30s and '40s which they answered better than *I* could, as if their memories were fresher. I took that Life Savers parachute jump at the World's Fair, and I remember that 'Futurama' exhibition. In retrospect it was so naively utopian." He shook his head sadly.

"These men seem to know nothing beyond April of 1945. What strikes me about them - with the exception of their Berliner sergeant, who is a mystery - is that they appear to be very ordinary young Americans. Not overly bright, quite ingenuous, and basically friendly. If they are indeed pranksters, they are extraordinarily fine actors who have spent years studying American life in the '30s and '40s!"

Paula glanced at Kemp, then down at the unconscious Sutton.

"This one," she said, "the one they call Lieutenant Sutton, is not playacting. He has definitely been knocked out and his uniform appears to have been singed by an explosion. Holcombe said it happened during a battle with SS troops!"

Von Scheller nodded, pale fingers twisting a signet ring on his left hand. "You see? Why would they knock out one of their own and drag him around with them? There is no reason to do such a thing unless they are all insane, and the three Americans seem perfectly normal. No, my dear, I believe we are involved in something far more fantastic than a hoax."

Paula's face paled, her high cheekbones prominent under taut skin.

"Then who do you think they really are, Opa? What is this all about?"

Von Scheller shrank into his wheelchair, drained of energy by the day's emotional storm and his omnipresent pain. He massaged his forehead and sighed.

"I think these men genuinely believe they are American soldiers living in 1945."

"But, Opa, who are they *really?*"

Von Scheller gazed across the room at a seventeenth-century woodcut of Christ raising Lazarus from the dead. He chose his words carefully. "Either these men are victims of some brainwashing experiment - hypnotized and pro-grammed into assuming personalities of seven decades ago - or they are who they claim to be ... and we are witnessing a miracle."

Paula shivered. "It-it cannot be. Such a thing is impossible!"

114

Her grandfather's faded eyes blazed with an intensity she hadn't seen in years. *"You,* Paula, *you* have always been the one who believed in ghosts and ESP and parapsychology while I scoffed at such things because they were at odds with my Catholicism! Yet the Bible is full of miracles. If your supernatural beliefs are valid, then are they not miracles too? Can it be that when you are put to the test, you cannot accept things which you have told me for years are real?"

Paula was close to tears. She shook her head.

"These men are not ghosts, Opa. They are flesh and blood. What makes you think this is something other than a hoax or a brainwashing experiment?"

Von Scheller coughed, his entire body shaking with the effort. Paula held his hand until the paroxysm ended.

"A feeling up here." He tapped his bald head. "Some kind of awareness that seems to increase in proportion to the decay of this old body of mine. I lived during the time these men claim to be part of. I observed young Americans in those days. They had a unique manner, a naive idealism and belief in their own destiny that we cynical Europeans noticed. It's gone now – modern Americans are different. But I remember the quality well and these young men possess it ... a group consciousness which I doubt can be acquired through hypnosis or brainwashing."

Both von Schellers lapsed into silence, absorbing the magnitude of what the American soldiers represented. The only sounds in the room were the crackle of flames in the fireplace and Kemp's tuneless whistling of "Rum and Coca-Cola."

"What shall we do, Opa?"

Von Scheller fixed her with a steady gaze. "As long as these men believe they are still fighting World War Two, they are a menace to themselves as well as others. We must convince them that sixty-six years have passed and the war is long over!"

He nodded and began turning his wheelchair towards a pile of newspapers and magazines on a side table. Paula's fearful voice froze him: "What if *they* are the ones who are right? Perhaps *we* have been shifted to 1945!"

"*Mein Gott!*" He swiveled back to face her.

"If it could happen one way, I suppose it could also work in reverse." He looked nervously around the room, then peered through the window at the unkempt grounds and lowering sky.

"Everything looks unchanged. The grounds were much better kept in 1945."

He glanced at the nightstand beside his bed. "The radio! We can tell from the broadcasts if we are in our correct time. If so, perhaps the Americans can be swayed by it. For once I am sorry that I refuse to have a television!"

The radio was a box-like portable dating from the 1960s. One of the few diversions in the Luftwaffe veteran's spartan existence, the set was kept tuned to Bavarian State Radio – *Bayerischer Rundfunk*. Von Scheller listened mainly to classical music, although he also liked Bayern 1, which played songs from his youth as well as folk music, with breaks for news and commentary. Now, the warming old vacuum tubes pulled the opening aria of Handel's opera *Serse* from the airwaves. Kemp turned around at the noise, cheeks bulging with cheese and bread.

116

"You don't mind?" Paula said in English. "We thought it would be nice to listen to the radio."

Kemp shrugged. "Guess your radio stations don't play any Glenn Miller and Gene Krupa though."

Von Scheller moved the dial, hitting an Austrian station airing a panel discussion on the radioactive danger of a nuclear power plant in Japan that had been damaged by a devastating earthquake and tsunami the previous month.

"A least *we* know what time we are living in," he said.

"Yes," replied Paula, "but the radio is not much help unless we find an English language broadcast. Only the sergeant speaks German."

"True." Von Scheller frowned. "Sometimes I listen to the BBC World Service." He pushed his wheelchair back. "Come here and see if you can get it. I will try something else."

He wheeled to the side table and dragged the pile of newspapers onto his lap. The papers were all German, including *Welt am Sonntag,* the local *Kötztinger Umshau,* and the *Süddeutsche Zeitung.* He wished he had renewed his subscription to the English-language *International Herald Tribune.*

Von Scheller thumbed through the papers until he found a photograph in *Welt am Sontag* of Barack Obama at a White House press conference. The caption was in German, but von Scheller thought the words "USA-Präsident Obama" were near enough to the English version for Kemp to understand. What seemed equally important in the photo was the lectern in front of Obama decorated with the Presidential Seal and the words "The President of the United States."

"Mr. Kemp?"

"Hey," Kemp responded. "My name's Lou. You can call me that."

"All right ... Lou. I have some things here I wish to show you."

"Yeah?"

Von Scheller showed him the front page of *Welt am Sonntag.* "You can't read German, Lou?"

"'Fraid not."

Von Scheller's fingernail drew an imaginary line under the date at the top of the page. "You can read this, though, can't you? Tell me what it says?"

Kemp peered at the date. He blinked and read it again. "Well, uh, it says 17 April 2011."

"Yes, Lou, that was last Sunday's date: April the 17th, 2011. Today is the 22nd of April in the year 2011!"

Kemp frowned at the elderly German.

"'Fraid I don't understand you, mister. What do you mean by 2011?"

Von Scheller tapped the newspaper emphatically. "This is the *year* 2011. Right now. Today. It is not 1945!"

"I still don't understand. Have you Nazis ... er, people over here started your own calendar or something?"

Von Scheller extracted front pages from other newspapers and pointed to the dates.

"You see. They all say 2011. My young friend, impossible as it may sound, the War has been over for 66 years. We are now, truly, living in the year 2011. Something, a miracle of time perhaps, has happened to you and your comrades. Somehow you have jumped seven decades into the future!"

A slow grin spread over Kemp's face. "You're joshing me, mister."

"I swear in God's name that I am quite serious, Lou." Von Scheller showed the *Welt am Sontag* picture of Barack Obama.

"This man is now the American President. I will translate what it says here: 'USA President Obama at White House press conference replying to question on helping Japanese victims of the natural disaster.' You can't read German, but you can certainly see that this is the American presidential seal here."

Kemp picked up the paper and scrutinized it. He looked at Von Scheller with pity.

"You seem like a good Joe, mister, but I gotta tell you that this is either a bad joke or a trick the Nazis are using to fool you people. The real president of the USA is Harry Truman. The guy in this picture is a *negro!*" Kemp snorted derisively. "A black man could *never* be president of the USA, no-siree-bob! And why would we help the Japs when we're at war with 'em!"

Von Scheller placed a frail hand on the young man's arm and shook his head.

"My friend, no one is tricking you or us. The Nazis were totally defeated by the Allies in 1945."

"Opa," Paula called, "I can't pick up the BBC."

"Try some other stations," von Scheller snapped, his mind straining for another way to convince Kemp of the anomaly in time. "My library," he muttered. "My books on World War Two history and modern military aircraft."

Paula was twisting the radio's tuning knob, hunting for an English language broadcast. She turned the dial back to Bayern 1. At that moment it was 4:51 PM. Paula didn't know that at 4:30 every day, the station aired a program titled *Golden Oldies*. The broadcast this afternoon featured popular German, British, and American songs of the World War II era. The bouncy voices of the Andrews Sisters singing "Boogie-Woogie Bugle Boy" shrilled from the speaker.

"Hey!" Kemp was glad to be distracted from the disturbing conversation. "Guess you Germans have good taste in music after all. That's one of my favorite songs!"

Von Scheller groaned in frustration.

12

The old casement window rattled as if shaken by spectral hands. Rain thickened the early dusk, darkening the forest around the von Scheller house.

Roth stared at his reflection in the windowpane, watching raindrops trickle down the glass like tears he could no longer shed. He turned away, breath leaving a misty circle. The bedroom was cold and pervaded by mildew. The ceiling's bare light bulb was burned out, so he used his Zippo to ignite a candle.

With his usual efficiency, Roth had decreed a rest period for himself that afternoon. He had lain on a bed in the upstairs room, willing sleep yet feeling the lust of retribution like sexual desire. His mind leapt and churned with visions of pale Nazis drowning in oceans of blood.

Restless, searching for something indefinable, he moved to a chest of drawers and set the candle on it. The top drawer held half a dozen old cigar boxes. Roth opened one filled with black-and-white photographs. He picked up a handful, discarding shots of 1930s hunting parties, bathing-suited family groups at a lake, and a grinning adolescent boy waving from the passenger seat of a biplane.

Then came a picture of a young man in Luftwaffe officer's uniform posing with a girl in front of a restaurant. The man's face matched the photo of the Nazi hero von Scheller he had planned to assassinate. Roth recognized the building behind the young couple – Gruban-Souchay on the Kurfürstendamm, a *weinstube* and restaurant frequented by Berlin society. Roth's father, a prominent Berlin eye specialist, had regularly taken his family to Gruban-Souchay until the restaurant had stopped admitting Jews.

With hindsight, it was difficult for Roth to believe how blithely his family had ignored the diminishing number of restaurants and clubs they frequented in the years after the Nazis took control. His parents were invited to fewer and fewer parties, and the number of patients who patronized his father's formerly flourishing practice dwindled. Then came the Nuremberg Laws of September 1935 – decrees that effectively deprived Jews of all rights and legally reduced their status to that of *Untermenschen* or subhumans.

Roth and his two brothers were dismissed from their elite private school. After he was ruthlessly beaten by former classmates at a playing field, Roth noticed the new lines on his parents' faces.

The three Roth brothers were sent to live with their Uncle Nathan in Fair Lawn, New Jersey. Roth attended school by day, and at night he had joined his uncle at B'nai B'rith and World Zionist meetings in synagogue basements and Jewish Community Centers. But no amount of fundraising to aid the exodus of other Jewish refugees could quell the scorching rage that grew as letters from his family reached him by circuitous routes. These messages told of his father being barred from medical practice, and of his arrest and internment in Buchenwald for ten months before his release was secured through bribes. The final communication came from his mother, who reported the death of his grandfather. After refusing to wear a Star of David badge, the old man had been imprisoned, stripped, doused with buckets of cold water, and locked in an unheated cell, where eight days later he died of pneumonia.

Appended to that letter was a scrawled note from Roth's father. *"Vergessen Sie nie"* – "Never forget."

It wasn't until three years later, in November of 1944, that news of Roth's family reached him again. He had been a soldier in the US Army since December 10, 1941, the day after Germany declared war on the United States, and had killed Germans in North Africa, Sicily, and France. The account came from his cousin Max, in a letter that Uncle Nathan forwarded to Roth's unit in Italy.

In 1943, Max, along with the rest of Roth's family, had been packed at gunpoint into cattle cars for shipment to Mauthausen concentration camp. Roth's grandmother had suffocated aboard the cattle car, and his mother and club-footed sister had been marched to the gas chamber upon arrival at the camp. Roth's older sister was taken to an SS field brothel, where she had committed suicide with a razor. Roth's father was beaten to death by a camp guard for accidentally upsetting a wheelbarrow of sand. Max was alive only because he had been smuggled out of the camp by a priest who impersonated SS officers in his work for the anti-Nazi underground.

123

Now, as then, the images Max had relayed to Roth were as vivid and piercing as if Hugo had personally witnessed the extermination of his family.

Vergessen Sie nie. The words almost made him want to laugh. It was impossible to forget, as impossible as it was for Max to remove the numbers that the SS had tattooed across his forearm.

Roth looked again at the photograph of the missing Luftwaffe officer. He held it to the candle and watched it burn until the flame touched his fingers. He was about to slam the drawer shut when a blue presentation case caught his attention. It was embossed with a gold Luftwaffe eagle clutching a swastika in its talons. A parchment scroll secured by a red, white, and black ribbon lay beside it.

Roth opened the case. Nestled on sky-blue velvet was an elaborate Iron Cross. He unfurled the scroll and read the gothic German script of a citation dated November 10, 1945. It proclaimed that for bravery in the face of the enemy and devotion to the defense of the Reich, the Führer had awarded Major Hans-Ulrich von Scheller the Gold Oak Leaves with Swords and Diamonds to the Knight's Cross of the Iron Cross. It was signed Adolf Hitler.

Roth went downstairs. As he approached the old man's bedroom, he heard the younger German woman say. "My car. Let me show you my car! There was nothing like it in 1945."

"The one parked outside?" That came from Kemp. Roth was angry to hear him responding. He should have ordered him to keep his mouth shut.

"Seen one just like it in the German pavilion at the World's Fair," Kemp said. "Even had a picture of Hitler opening the new Volkswagen factory."

"Not that one! It's—"

Paula fell silent as Roth burst into the room. The dog whined and scurried under the bed. Roth looked at Sutton, then at Paula.

"He shows no improvement?" he snapped in German.

Paula shrank under his merciless gaze, and he felt a cold satisfaction.

"I believe he is coming out of it. The coma seems lighter."

Roth studied Sutton for a moment longer before moving to the hearth. The room was silent except for the ticking clock.

Kemp glanced at von Scheller, then cleared his throat. "Sarge, you wouldn't believe the weird stuff this old kraut's been telling me. He claims the war has been over for 66 years. Look, he showed me these newspapers and magazines. I can't read German but you can. Look at them dates on these – they're all 2011!"

The elderly man trundled his wheelchair to Roth. He proffered the stack of periodicals. "He is right, Sergeant," he said in German. "Please read these. The war *is* long over. America and the Allies won."

Roth glanced at the papers, then held von Scheller's eyes with his own, hands twitching.

"So, you are saying that we are now in the future, *nicht wahr?*"

"Yes! Through some miracle, nearly 70 years have passed for you in the blink of an eye!"

"Then your Thousand Year Reich must be Jew-free by now!" Roth hurled the newspapers and magazines into the fireplace. Von Scheller's face contorted in sadness as the papers were consumed.

Roth pulled the Nazi citation from his pocket, grabbed von Scheller's throat, and brandished the parchment in front of his terrified eyes.

"Liar! Adolf Hitler gave your filthy murdering grandson this!" He squeezed the old man's windpipe, heedless of Paula's cries and Kemp's shouts. "You're all the same. The earth must be cleansed of *your* race!"

"Let go of him, Sarge!" Kemp yelled.

Roth stepped back and pulled out his knife. He lunged for Paula, stopped only by Kemp catching his wrist.

"Roth! We're not killing any civilians, you fucking goddam loony!"

Roth spun and hurled Kemp back, pointing the knife at him. Kemp recoiled and drew his .45, aiming it double-handed at Roth. Paula wept as she held her coughing, gasping grandfather. Roth shook his head as if awakening from a nightmare, then returned the knife to its sheath.

"Okay, Kemp," he panted. "No need for that."

"Didn't mean no harm, Sarge." Kemp holstered his pistol. "Just trying to stop you from doing something that could get you locked up in Leavenworth."

"It's okay. You did the right thing. These Nazis were trying to trick you. Can't you see through their lies? It is always the same with them!"

Kemp looked at the von Schellers, then back again at Roth, seeming almost relieved. He nodded emphatically.

"You're right, Sarge, you're so damned right. Can't trust 'em. The old guy was really roping me in. Guess all that bad stuff you hear about the Nazis is true."

"They are much worse. Beyond your understanding, soldier."

Roth looked coldly at the bed where Sutton tossed and muttered as he emerged from his coma. *The lieutenant would be a major obstacle to his plans. An idealistic college boy with his typically lazy American way of leading a commando operation – strike the minimum number of targets, then scamper off with a self-congratulatory pat on the back into the arms of the Jew-baiting Russians.*

He glanced at the window. Night had almost fallen even though it was not yet six o'clock. Sutton would regain consciousness soon, and then he would lose his tiny command and the best opportunity he would ever have of carrying out his vendetta against the Germans.

"Kemp," he snapped, "be ready to move out in ten minutes. I'll get the others."

As the door closed behind Roth, Bavarian Radio 1 finished playing "White Cliffs of Dover" and began its 5:30 news report, leading with a story about terrorist attacks on an American base and a civilian airfield.

Von Scheller watched Kemp blacken his face with camouflage grease as the German-language news bounced off his uncomprehending ears.

"*Das Schicksal hat da mit uns gespielt,*" he said hoarsely.

"What'd you say?" Kemp scowled. "I don't want to hear you two speaking Kraut, understand?"

"I said, 'fate is playing games with us today.'"

"*You're* the one playing games today, bud! Pretty stinking low trick to act so friendly and try to con me the way you did with your crazy story about being in the future and all. I even saved your bacon from Roth. Shit!"

"It is no trick! You are making a terrible mistake. You *must* believe me. Please, please!"

"Leave it, Opa," Paula whispered, seeing Kemp's angry scowl.

Kemp turned to her, the blackface transforming him from an amiable young American back into an alien intruder. "And you can turn that radio off. I don't want to hear no more of that goddam Kraut gobbledygook!"

The door crashed open and Roth tramped in followed by Holcombe and Loomis – all blackened, helmeted, and wearing green ponchos. Kemp buckled the chinstrap of his helmet and slung his submachine gun as he joined them.

"So what about the lieutenant?" asked Holcombe. "We can't just leave him here!"

"Do you want to carry him on your back?" Roth replied. "I would not order any of you to carry him. He would slow us dangerously."

"I was thinking of the Kraut jeep."

"I told you that the entire countryside is on alert now. There will be roadblocks everywhere. Our only chance is to stay inside the forest and go on foot towards Czechoslovakia. I studied the map and worked out the best route for us."

"Can't we wait another hour or two?" Holcombe nodded towards the stirring Sutton. "Maybe he'll wake up and be well enough to go with us."

"We can't waste any more time here! The Nazis may be closing in on us already. Besides," he said, with a warning glance at Paula not to refute his lie, "the German cunt is a doctor and she told me that Sutton's head injury is very serious."

"What'll happen to him if we leave him?" Kemp said. "Think he'll be okay?"

"Of course," Roth replied. "The Germans seem to obey the rules of the Geneva Convention … for Gentile prisoners." He clenched his jaw, remembering how the Nazis had singled out Jewish POWs captured during the Battle of the Bulge and sent them to the Berga concentration camp.

"These people will hand him over to the authorities and he will be treated as a prisoner of war," he said, face a mask of bitterness as he looked at Sutton. *"He'll* be much safer than *we* will be until we reach the Red Army. Which is why we must hurry!"

Holcombe gestured towards the von Schellers. "We gonna tie them up? Loomis locked the two old geezers in the pantry."

"No, we don't have time. They are far from the nearest village and I have cut the telephone line. We will disable the car and the jeep on our way out. By the time they contact the Gestapo, we will be far away. Now, we go!"

The three privates filed out of the room. Roth paused at the door.

"I am sorry that I did not have the pleasure of killing your grandson and *your* brother," he said to the von Schellers. "But your monstrous regime is dying and my people will purge the world of your disease. When you see your Luftwaffe 'hero,' tell him that his days are numbered."

Paula and her grandfather heard the front door open and felt a bitter wind blow through the house and into the bedroom, making the fire roar.

They sat in unscholarly order in the auditorium of the Kőtzting gymnasium – one hundred earnest men in camouflaged German Army uniforms, load-bearing harness and Kevlar "Fritz" style helmets. They carried a variety of weapons, from high-tech HK G36 5.56mm assault rifles in both carbine and SAW versions with tactical lights and lasers, to HK 512 12-gauge shotguns.

Every man had completed grueling *Kommando Spezialkraefte* training, including a three week combat survival course at the International Long Range Recon Patrol School at Pfullendorf. They were youthful, fit and highly intelligent. KSK regulations mandated that no officer could be older than 30, and all NCOS were under age 32.

They waited expectantly, some whispering excitedly, others squinting at the topographical map mounted on the stage. Beside the map stood the short, muscular figure of *Brigadegeneral* Baldur Michalke, KSK's commanding officer.

A door opened to the right of the stage. General Michalke's head swiveled sideways, then swung back to the audience as he thundered '*Ach-TUNG!*" A hundred men rose in unison as the familiar tall figure of Hanno Kasper strode onto the podium.

Kasper had taken time to shower, shave, and change his shirt. He had learned the value of theatrical display during his childhood in Nazi Germany. Kasper knew that men wanted a leader who acted and looked the part, so he always groomed himself for the role. He joined General Michalke, topping him by a head despite his advanced age. Kasper threw back his shoulders in his black leather jacket, white hair accentuating his aquiline bronzed face and steady blue eyes. His jaw lifted as he surveyed the audience.

"Good evening, gentlemen." His voice was perfectly modulated, trained to carry commands. "You may be seated."

The men sank into their seats, spines stiffened in alertness.

"I have come from a meeting with the BfV chief detective and *Polizeioberrat* Keitz. The investigation into the attacks last night has just begun, but we have enough facts to allow us to plan our operation.

"The terrorist survivor, Jasarevic, has been interrogated all day in Regensburg. I spent some time with him myself this afternoon ... and he became very eager to talk."

A wolfish grin flitted across Kasper's face. The audience smirked with him, aware of his draconian way of dealing with subversives. Kasper drew himself up a fraction straighter.

"Jasarevic maintains that twenty-four *white* Muslim terrorists were involved in the plan to murder hundreds at the World Youth Congress. While he claimed that he did not know the terrorist leader - the only corpse found dressed in civilian clothing - our forensic specialists have identified him ...."

Kasper paused dramatically, bringing the young soldiers to the edge of their seats.

"He was a German national of Bosnian blood, the terrorist mastermind that we and the civilized world have sought for years. The one that Interpol called *Geppetto*."

The men turned to their companions to shake hands and slap shoulders. Kasper watched the display with fatherly approval, then nodded to General Michalke.

"*Ruhig sein!*" Michalke barked. "Be quiet!"

Kasper continued: "The terrorists had six false police vehicles for their operation. One of these, a Mercedes G-Wagen, is missing. Four of the terrorists escaped from the camp, presumably in this vehicle, and the public has been alerted to look for it."

Kasper knitted his hands behind his back and frowned.

"Now we come to a more puzzling part of the case. You are all aware of the terrorist attacks last night on the American Army's Hőhenbogen Kaserne and the civilian airfield at Mühldorf. Both attacks were made by the same team of six men who appear to have had Special Forces training because of their easy infiltration of the kaserne. *Kameraden*, we have established that these persons were also the ones who assaulted and almost wiped out the Muslim terrorists' force at the old SS camp."

A puzzled murmur arose, silenced by Kasper's imperious hand.

"Baffling, yes. I believe that the action was the result of a falling-out between two terrorist units. The unidentified corpse in surplus US Army gear was undoubtedly a member of the six-man team who struck the Amis and the airfield. Although the Americans claimed his body, we were able to retain the dead man's boots. These have been matched with prints found at Hőhenbogen, Mühldorf and the SS camp."

Kasper picked up a wooden stick and tapped the map with it.

"Here we are in Kőtzting ... " He moved the rod southeast into the Bavarian Forest. "Hőhenbogen Kaserne ... " The pointer scraped north a few centimeters. "Mühldorf ..." The stick cut due east, rapping a collection of rectangles.

"And this is the SS camp. The Czech border is only some twenty kilometers away. So, we are hunting for two separate terrorist units, probably still in this area. The Czech authorities have been alerted and have given permission for us to pursue the terrorists into their territory if necessary. As you know, the KSK can legally operate in any NATO country."

Kasper rapped the heavy pointer into the palm of his left hand as if it were a swagger stick. He eyed the determined young faces, gauging their frame of mind. The time was right: they were primed and ready. His face grew stern.

"Are the doors secured, Baldur?"

"*Jawohl*, trusted police sentries at each, *Herr General*. And we have searched the building. All reporters are outside."

"*Gut.*" Kasper stepped forward. "We are entering a new era! A rebirth we have struggled for over the past sixty-six years. Now the sordid permissiveness of the liberal era is dying. Discipline and strength will prevail. No longer will subversive leftist swine and terrorist murderers get light sentences from the courts. It is time to inaugurate this brave new age, and God has given us the opportunity to do so."

He breathed heavily, gripped with emotion as fervid as that experienced during the Hitler Youth rallies so long ago.

"We will find these terrorist monsters and we shall give them no quarter. Justice will be meted out instantly! Any reporters or photographers who venture too close will be arrested. No liberal witnesses to prevent our punishment of these beasts. You men are the vanguard of the new Germany

133

and to *you* is given the honor of protecting the Fatherland's rebirth!"

A hundred young cheeks grew taut, youthful hearts swelled with pride. Kasper felt the old sense of mission and destiny churning, expanding in his chest and screaming for release until he could restrain himself no longer. As memories of swastika banners and golden eagles crowded his mind, he stamped his feet and thrust his right arm out.

"Sieg heil!" he roared, "Hail victory!"

Stunned silence greeted his display. Then the elite young German soldiers were on their feet, many with tears of joy glistening in their eyes.

"Sieg heil!" they chorused. *"Sieg heil!"*

Kasper had a sudden image of the Führer smiling down from Valhalla.

13

Sutton was home. The old frame house on Maple Street in Lee's Summit. Upstairs in his bedroom. *Godawful sick headache. Must have been that moonshine Mitch Twiford's uncle got in the Ozarks. Brain feels ready to burst through my skull.* The room spun beyond his closed eyes. "Never gonna drink again," he moaned. "Goddam that Mitch!"

"He's awakening," a throaty woman's voice said, her German words filtering through Sutton's cotton-wool consciousness to be slowly translated. He heard the squeak and rattle of a trundling wheelchair. His eyes opened a crack, then squeezed shut as light stung them.

"Thank God," an asthmatic old man's voice said in German.

Sutton's head still hurt, but the throbbing had withdrawn to a place on the back of his skull that felt as tender as an overripe tomato in his grandma's Victory Garden. He opened his eyes for a second attempt, blinking away film. He saw the hazy face of an elderly man and in his dazed state took him for his grandfather.

"Golly, Pops. I'm never gonna drink that stuff again. I promise, Scout's Honor."

Another spasm of pain closed his eyes. A soft hand stroked his brow. The touch roused his senses: his mouth felt dry as old leather and his tongue as thick as a tom catfish.

"Thirsty," he mumbled. "Water. Gimme drinka water, Pops."

An arm slid around his shoulders, helped him sit up. A glass touched his cracked lips, spilled cold water into his mouth. He sucked it greedily, dribbling it onto his chin and throat. The liquid on his skin revived him further. He opened his eyes again, and looked across the foot of the bed to a funny old print on the white wall. Roebuck antlers hung above it. A presence caught his peripheral vision. He turned gingerly towards it, testing the pain. His gaze met a pair of wide green eyes studying him from an oval face. *Hmm, good-looking babe.* They scrutinized each other until the woman's face flushed. Sutton snapped into full awareness as memory scalded his brain.

"Holy shit!" He sat fully upright, reverting to the state of combat tension he had been in at the moment the grenade had knocked him unconscious. Muscles tightened near the massive bruise on his scalp, flooding his head with agony.

"You must be still," the woman cautioned in English. "You have a nasty bump on your head."

Sutton tested the swelling on the back of his skull with a shaky hand. He grimaced.

"Jesus! What a crack I must have got."

He turned back to the woman, taking in her dirndl skirt and matching bodice worn over a white blouse buttoned at the throat. The woman regarded him with a fascinated look usually reserved for exotic and possibly dangerous animals kept behind bars at zoos.

"So, I guess this must be a prison camp hospital or something." He sighed with resignation. "Oh well, guess I'm lucky to be alive and out of it now."

"You are not in a prison camp hospital," said the voice he had mistaken for Grandpa's in thickly accented English.

Sutton turned to a scrawny old man in a wheelchair on the opposite side of the bed. The man quivered with an excitement at odds with his frailty. His sunken eyes blazed at Sutton with the zeal of a Baptist preacher at a revival meeting. The old man and the young woman seemed to be Germans. He wondered if they were members of the Bavarian or Czech resistance "So where am I?" he asked in fluent German. "Who are you people?"

"Ah-ha!" the old man cried delightedly. "You speak German. How fortunate for us all!"

"You're German?"

"Of course."

"Are you members of Freedom Action Bavaria?"

"Freedom Action Bavaria?" The elderly German's forehead creased in puzzlement, then cleared as if he remembered something. "You mean the anti-Nazi movement? *Nein*, Lieutenant Sutton. We are not members of any resistance movement. But I can assure you that we are your friends and you are completely safe with us."

"How do you know my name?" Sutton asked, suspicion in his voice.

"Your four comrades spent the entire day with us. I had long conversations with the privates named Holcombe and Kemp. They told us who you are."

Sutton frowned. "I had five guys in my team."

The old man nodded solemnly. "Private Holcombe said that one of your men was killed during what he described as an attack on an SS camp. The same place where you were wounded. I believe the one killed was named Sarnoff."

"Sarnoff? Poor kid." Sutton shook his head, sighed, then looked around the room.

"So where are the others?"

"They left an hour ago. The sergeant, Roth, said they were going on foot to cross the Czech border and meet the Red Army. They will not get very far," he added sadly.

Sutton's mental gears were starting to mesh smoothly again. His suspicion grew. He glanced at the windows and the rainy night outside.

"An hour ago?" His gaze dropped to his left wrist, seeking his wristwatch. It was gone, and he looked at the old German with accusing eyes. "Hey, where—"

"It's in the drawer there," the woman said. "With your other things."

She opened the drawer, exposing Sutton's watch, military ID, and the Roosevelt button.

Sutton touched the button, then strapped on the watch and looked at the dial: 7:09. "So I've been out all day?"

"Yes," replied the old man. "Your men brought you here just after dawn this morning."

Sutton glanced at the closed bedroom door. "Yes? So tell me where 'here' is and who you are?"

He warily watched the old man's eyes shift to the woman, saw her nod.

The man in the wheelchair drew a deep, shaky breath.

"I am Major Hans-Ülrich von Scheller, former pilot in Number Twelve *Kampfgeschwader, Reichsluftwaffe*. This is my granddaughter, Paula. You are in my house, which is in the *Bäyerischer Wald* five kilometers west of the Czech border and twenty kilometers east of the village of Kőtzting."

It took Sutton a moment for von Scheller's words to sink in. The old guy's name was familiar but ... then he remembered his argument with Roth the previous night before their assault on the Werewolf camp.

"Von Scheller. Luftwaffe hero on the assassination list. Did Roth ... ?"

"No," said von Scheller. "Fortunately for me, your Sergeant Roth refused to believe that the 86-year-old man you see in front of you was the same person in this photo." He pulled a photograph from the frayed pocket of his velvet smoking jacket and handed it to Sutton. "Roth left this behind. Not a very good likeness really. Those sycophants at the old Propaganda Ministry used a bucket of make-up in the hope of making me look like some damned Hollywood film star!"

Sutton remembered the picture from the Bandstand target list. He read the typed inscription, then compared the photo with the tense face of the old man in the wheelchair. *A resemblance between the eyes and brows ... maybe the nose, too, but ....*

"You claim you're 86 but this is a picture of you? Says here this was taken last year." He couldn't keep the sarcasm from his voice. "So how'd you manage to change so much?"

Von Scheller shook his head, wrinkled face deeply solemn.

"Lieutenant Sutton, I must be perfectly frank with you even though what I say sounds impossible. That photo was taken nearly 67 years ago. I have, of course, aged considerably during that time."

"Sixty ... seven ... years ago?" Sutton wondered what crazy game was being played here. *Was he in a German insane asylum?*

"Uh, let's see, if that picture was taken in 1944, that means it must be 2011 now. That right?"

"*Ja!* The year *is* 2011!" Paula said. "You must accept that!"

Sutton looked from Paula to von Scheller. He vented a snort of disbelief.

"Wish I knew what this nonsense is about, but I don't have time to fool around. Uh, you got a bathroom handy?"

He flipped back the eiderdown and swung his legs over the side of the bed, suddenly aware that he was wearing only an olive drab T-shirt and boxer shorts. He glanced at Paula in mild embarrassment.

"Here." She handed him her father's dressing gown, watching as he stiffly put it on. Sutton tentatively stood upright, feeling the room pitch like the troopship in which he had crossed the Atlantic. He grimaced as steel pain claws dug into his skull.

Paula put an arm around his waist to steady him. He was taller than she had thought and the muscles of his torso were flat and hard under the robe. "I will show you," she said softly. "Take your time. Lean on me until the dizziness passes."

"Feel drunk as a skunk," Sutton mumbled in English.

"It's the concussion. You'll feel better soon."

Paula helped Sutton to a half-bath in the foyer outside the bedroom. Sutton locked the door and relieved himself, then looked into the mirror above the basin. Dark shadows underscored bloodshot eyes that peered from a face stubbled with two days' growth of beard. *Look like a hobo*, he thought, comparing his appearance to the neatly dressed Germans.

He opened the cabinet behind the mirror, locating a rusty razor amid a jumble of medicine bottles. An aerosol can beside it was marked shaving cream in German. Sutton had never seen such a container. He tried to unscrew the top, then turned it upside down and shook it. He gave up and covered his lower face with an ineffectual lather raised from a bar of soap. He shaved slowly, wincing from the dragging razor as well as the bandaged burn on his arm and the knot on his scalp.

He considered the von Schellers' words, their solemn, intense expressions. They seemed sincere, not what he imagined lunatics would be like. But what did he know?

His musing was displaced by an image of Roth's bitter face. Sutton was angered by Roth's disobedience in seeking to assassinate the Luftwaffe ace – not to mention abandoning him to the strange old German and his granddaughter. Remembering the sergeant's fanatical hatred of Germans, Sutton hoped he wouldn't lead his surviving team members on a suicidal confrontation with the enemy. *Roth must be glad to have me out of the way.*

Sutton rinsed his face, refastened the dressing gown, and stepped out into the chilly landing. He crossed the floor to a door he had noticed while en route to the bathroom. It opened onto an entrance hall lined with coat racks made from antlers and an umbrella stand that had once been an elephant's foot. Beyond was a double front door with stained glass set into its panels. He swung it open onto a cold, blustery night. Immediately outside was a grey Volkswagen sedan, one of the new automobiles designed by Ferdinand Porsche as a pet project of Adolf Hitler.

Frigid wind gusted under the hem of his borrowed dressing gown. Sutton shivered and returned to the interior foyer. He surprised an old woman on her hands and knees scrubbing the marble tiles. She gasped, crossing herself as fright crinkled her features. Paula appeared at the bedroom door.

"It's all right, Maria," she soothed in Bavarian dialect. "This one is our friend. He won't hurt you." She turned to Sutton. "Please come back inside."

"What's wrong with her? She acts like I'm Frankenstein's monster."

"Your men frightened her and her husband very badly when they invaded our house this morning. They suffered cruelly during the War when they were teenagers. They lost everything – both of their families - in the Allied bombing of Regensburg. Now they are like poor, timid mice."

Paula cleared her throat as they entered the bedroom, briskly changing the subject. "How is your head?'

"Feeling better. Guess it'll ache for a while, though." He spied his uniform neatly folded on a chair and started towards it. "Look, I'm going to have to move on. I'd, uh, hate to get the Gestapo on your backs for helping me and–"

"Wait," von Scheller called from the hearth. "Please come and sit by me."

"Well, I ... " He looked at Paula, who was watching him with that expression of odd intensity.

"Please," she whispered. "We only want to help you. You must trust us."

Sutton knew he shouldn't trust Germans. He had seen enough propaganda films and read too many stories about diabolical Nazi trickery. But, hell, these people seemed genuine. He knew how to keep his guard up.

"Okay."

The radio was on, classical music playing at low volume. Sutton took a chair next to von Scheller while Paula pulled up another and sat beside him.

"I have some books and papers that I would like you to look at very carefully," von Scheller began. "I assume you can read German as well as you speak it?"

"Sure can. I was a German and history major at college and did an immersion course at the Army language school in Chicago."

"Excellent. Please read these. We will not say anything or answer your questions until you have finished. Now, I understand that an intelligent and suspicious person will not easily accept photos and books that could be faked. But you will see that these photos and words would be impossible to fake. And believe me, Lieutenant Sutton, what you are about to discover is the most important event of your life."

"You don't say?" Sutton began to grin at von Scheller's melodrama, but the smile froze as he met the old man's impassioned eyes and compressed mouth. "Okay," he said. "I'll take a look."

Von Scheller reverently placed a German edition of *World War II: The Definitive Visual History* by Richard Holmes on Sutton's knees. Sutton examined the cover photograph of a pair of US Marines in the South Pacific before reluctantly opening the book.

14

Eddie Cassera checked his watch - 2:06 PM - then looked at his boss, Bill Miller, the DPMO Director. Reading glasses perched on the tip of his nose, Miller perused the sheaf of documents provided by Cassera. Miller said "Hmmm," without looking up. Eddie fidgeted, adjusted the knot of his tie.

Miller will think I'm nuts! Any second now and he'll kick me out of his office for wasting his time, after which I'll be the laughing stock of the whole Defense Prisoner of War/Missing Personnel Office.

Cassera and Miller were both military veterans and on a first name basis, if not friends. Nonetheless, Eddie was starting to regret his request for an appointment with the DPMO Director. He must have overlooked something that could explain the match between the fresh corpse in Frankfurt and the World War II MIA named Nicholas Sarnoff. But what? Eddie had spent the past hour verifying the data from the FBI, National Archives and the NPRC in case there had been a computer or human error, or the unlikely event of a prankster in one of the government offices. But everything on his side of the Atlantic checked out. If there was a falsification or error, it had to be in Germany.

Miller muttered something, drawing Cassera's attention back to him. Miller slowly shook his head while polishing his reading glasses with a handkerchief.

"This is something else, Eddie. Never seen the like."

Cassera tried to judge Miller's attitude about the case. "I've checked out everything from our end, Bill. It's got me stumped. So I thought I'd better get your view on it, seeing as it's a priority request."

Miller continued to shake his head. "Eddie, this is so far out that I'd swear you were shitting me if I didn't know you as well as I do. I'm just as goddam mystified as you are about it. The whole thing's like something out of that old *Twilight Zone* TV show."

Cassera was relieved. At least the boss agreed with him.

"Bill, give me your honest opinion on this case. Off the record. Do you think there's any chance that this kid's body in Frankfurt could be the Sarnoff guy who's been missing for 66 years? Jesus, Sarnoff would be 87 now!"

Miller's brown eyes seemed to gaze at something far away. When they refocused on Cassera his face was gentler, revealing the warm heart that Eddie knew was beating behind the official facade.

"Eddie, I'm a career civil servant like you and that means I've got to be an iron-clad pragmatist or I'll be out on my ass. But I've always tried to keep an open mind and I'll admit that I've come across some things that no one's been able to explain rationally." He sighed deeply

146

as if remembering something painful, then cleared his throat.

"Hell, I'm rambling. Eddie, as you well know, DPMO policy is to deal only with concrete facts when attempting to identify remains believed to be those of US Military personnel. We're basically historians, forensic scientists and archaeologists all rolled into one. Jumping to hasty conclusions can make us all look like fools and cause extra grief to an MIA's family. You've got a good record as an investigator and I'm satisfied with your basic work on this Sarnoff case. But we've still got some avenues to explore here. And I'll tell you, nobody is going to stick his neck out with an official confirmation until we've exhausted all possibilities for a positive ID check. Now, let's see what else we can do with this material here."

Miller slipped his reading glasses back on and shuffled through the forms, jotting notes on a legal pad. He paused several times before tossing his pen down.

"Okay," he said, "there's no dental chart for the cadaver in Frankfurt, and that's one of our essentials along with a DNA sample, which we should have soon. Seems like they did such a rush job on the autopsy they couldn't get a dental technician in." He shot a glance at his wall clock, calculating the time difference. "Too late now in Germany to get a dental chart done today, but I'll call the ME at home and ask him to get it done first thing in the morning even if it's Saturday."

He consulted his notes. "Next we've got Sarnoff's next-of-kin. How come you didn't check that out?"

"Same reason you just mentioned – I don't like approaching an MIA's family without more evidence that

147

we've actually found their boy. Besides, this guy's next-of-kin is probably deceased and almost certainly not living at the same address listed in 1942. "

"It's worth a shot." Miller flipped through pages until he found Sarnoff's next-of-kin. He read aloud: "Mrs. Louise Sarnoff, 1623 Walnut Street, Philadelphia. Who was she?"

"Apparently, his wife," said Cassera. "There were two letters found on the body signed 'Louise" – romantic stuff, so that makes sense. Also the JAG letter in the 293 File declaring Sarnoff dead was addressed to her. But the VA had no record of widow's benefits."

"That's because widows were ineligible for benefits if they remarried, which happened in 90 percent of such cases. But she probably got his death benefit. Servicemen in World War II had $10,000 National Service Life Insurance policies issued at no cost. MIAs were in a special category so the old War Department paid some of those claims directly. Check with the National Archives again as well as Social Security."

Eddie nodded and started to rise from his chair.

"Hold on a minute," Miller said. He looked at his notes, circled a nine-letter word with his pen, then turned back to Cassera. "There's something unusual in Sarnoff's service record. *Bandstand.*"

Eddie nodded. "I caught it. Sarnoff was a Ranger. He was on a top secret operation when he went MIA. Since the Bandstand mission was still classified in 1946, the War Department couldn't provide details about locale or circumstances relating to Sarnoff's disappearance. It'd be real helpful to know where the poor guy was lost."

"You'd better check out those operation records, too. Should have been declassified back in the 90s. The Army Military History Center's database will have them."

Miller reached for his telephone and punched in a number at Fort McNair on the opposite bank of the Potomac. He spoke for a few minutes and hung up.

"The Bandstand ops records will be sent over." Miller checked his watch. "Let's meet again in an hour. Good luck with finding the widow."

Cassera hurried back to his office with the sheaf of documents and began searching the National Archives database, cross-referencing the names of Nicholas I. and Louise Sarnoff with the terms "National Service Life Insurance" and "beneficiaries." He scored a hit within minutes.

A Louise P. Jablonski, widow of Private Nicholas I. Sarnoff USA, received a lump sum NSLI payment of $10,000 on February 4, 1947. Her residential address was in Cherry Hill, New Jersey. Eddie next logged onto the secure Social Security Administration database, entering Mrs. Jablonski's name and last known address. The woman had been widowed again in 1986 and was receiving Medicare and Supplemental Security Income benefits. She was currently living in Briny Breezes, Florida. The file listed her telephone number.

Cassera printed a copy of Louise Jablonski's Social Security data and rubbed his aching eyes. He wrote down her telephone number and pondered it. *What the hell*, he decided, *can't leave any stone unturned.*

The distant telephone rang eight times before it was picked up. "Hello?"

149

Cassera forced himself to speak slowly. "Is this Louise Jablonski?"

"Now I'm sick and tired of you telemarketers!" an elderly female voice said, "I told you to stop calling me!"

"*Wait!*" Cassera almost shouted, imagining that the telephone receiver was about to be slammed down on its cradle. "I'm calling from the US government."

"What do you want?" the old woman asked suspiciously.

Cassera took a deep breath, then quickly introduced himself and explained that he worked for the Defense Prisoner of War/Missing Personnel Office.

"We are trying to locate the relatives of a man who served in the US Army during the Second World War. The man's name was Nicholas Sarnoff. Are you a relation of his?"

The ensuing silence seemed interminable, broken by hisses on the line and the faint cawing of ghost voices. Cassera wondered if the woman was still there. He cleared his throat to get her attention. When she spoke, her voice was sad.

"Nicky was my husband, Mr. Casova."

"Thank you, Mrs. Jablonski. By the way, my name is Cassera." He spelled it for her. "Ma'am, I hate to revive painful memories for you, but as we both know, Nicholas Sarnoff disappeared in Europe in 1945. Just recently some remains were found which might be those of your former husband. We are trying to identify those remains so the man can be given a decent burial. We need more personal information to make sure he is correctly identified. I don't wish to trouble you, but would it be possible for me to visit you to ask some questions about your former husband?"

The ancient voice seemed on the verge of tears. "Nicky. My poor Nicky ... Yes, Mr. Casova, you are welcome to visit me."

Eddie heard a fumbling clatter, then the connection was broken. He sat thinking for a few minutes. No one would mind if he waited until Monday to continue the investigation. But the case had captivated him; he couldn't rest until the mystery of the cadaver in Germany was solved. Louise Jablonski was the living link to the real Nicholas Sarnoff. Besides, he told himself, she might be able to refer him to some of her former husband's blood relatives so that DNA testing could conclusively establish the corpse's identity.

Eddie called Miller and was readily given permission to go to Florida. He quickly opened Google and searched for Briny Breezes, Florida. The nearest airport was West Palm Beach. He logged onto Expedia and checked for flights from Washington National. US Airways had a non-stop departing at 4:30 PM. Unwilling to jump through the bureaucratic hoops of the Defense Department's travel office, he used his credit card to pay for a seat online.

Cassera made it through airport security with half an hour to spare. He bought a late edition of the *Washington Post* from an airport shop and opened it after his flight took off.

Terrorist Attacks in Germany US Base Hit Suspected Terrorists Found Dead

He read the stories under the headlines, wondering about the apparent connection with the corpse of Nicholas Sarnoff. Leafing through the paper, he noticed a story in the *Science* section: "Magnetic Convulsions Behind Sun Storms." The article said that solar storms causing massive convulsions of magnetic energy were exceptionally powerful that spring. Physicists were speculating that solar flares could influence weather patterns and even affect the space-time continuum. *Yeah, sure,* Eddie thought cynically before closing the paper.

He looked around the airliner's cabin. A trio of young soldiers - two white male privates and a black female sergeant - sat across the aisle. His eyes widened as he saw that they wore the "Electric Strawberry" insignia of the 25th Infantry Division – his old outfit - on the shoulders of their new UCP-Delta camouflage uniforms.

This really is a day for fucking coincidences!

Eddie overheard the sergeant proudly telling a flight attendant that they were "Warriors" – members of the 2nd Brigade's Stryker Combat Team – on leave prior to deploying to Afghanistan. *Sweet Jesus,* Cassera thought, suddenly feeling very old. How little things change. Back to square one after all that anti-war agitation. It could be the 1960s again and those kids heading to Vietnam to kill a commie for mommy. He felt his hip and thigh aching where the AK-47 slugs had shattered the bones. Cassera closed his eyes and remembered the hillbilly wail of a long-dead private as he cleaned his M-16 under a torrid Asian sky:

Oh mother dear
Won't you write our congressman
And get me out of here.

Compelled by his father's frustration at being no more than a cook during World War II ("My lousy pasta woulda made my Mama turn in her grave"), Cassera had joined the JROTC during his sophomore year in high school. He got his Second Lieutenant's commission in the summer of 1969. Three months later he was in 'Nam – assistant platoon leader in the 2nd Battalion, 27th Infantry Regiment, 25th Infantry Division. Man, was he proud!

The pride soon evaporated under creeping disillusionment. Eddie remembered miserable slogging patrols through booby-trapped swamps in an armpit of a place called the An Khe valley. Worried about pungi sticks and his men getting the clap from B-girls. Trying to catch up on sleep while mosquitoes hummed outside the netting and sweat saturated his thin GI mattress. Playing cards in the hooch during endless afternoons and evenings when they weren't on patrol. Swilling warm Swans Australian beer or the coveted Philippine San Miguel brand while listening to "Honky Tonk Woman" and "Bad Moon Rising" on the Sony tape player. Battery of 105 howitzers pounding in the distance. A Chinook thumping overhead from "the Golf Course" – the First Air Cavalry Division's base in the highlands. Somebody talking about a buddy getting wasted by a Chinese claymore. Answering grunts ... Good word for it, wasted ... Game goes on.

Sometimes he'd lie on his cot late at night with the earphone of his transistor radio in his ear. He'd listen to Hanoi Hannah and get angry. Then he'd switch to Armed Forces radio and soak up the sexy All American Girl voice of Chris Noel. He'd drift off to orgasmic dreams while tracks from the Beatle's new *Abbey Road* album helped to suppress his omnipresent fear.

Home by Christmas, they said. But Lieutenant Cassera spent Christmas 1969 under heavy sedation at the evacuation hospital in Qui Nhon, victim of a Viet Cong ambush. He was one of the lucky ones. On Christmas Eve nine of his men were trucked out to Tan Son Nhut airfield packed in labeled aluminum boxes. They were loaded aboard a C-140 for the long trip across the Pacific to Travis Air Force base.

Nice Christmas present for the folks back home.

But the skinny black kid who saved his life when Eddie was bleeding to death in a stinking rice paddy was never found, one of over 1,600 American servicemen still missing in Viet Nam.

Cassera spent a year at the VA Hospital in Los Angeles before being discharged. The Army looked after him well; he couldn't complain about it like so many other Vets did. He went to college on the government's dime, and after graduation the Army found him a job at the Memorial Affairs unit, forerunner to the DPMO after the Defense Department formed a single office in 1993 to oversee and manage POW/MIA issues.

Laughter fueled by complimentary booze drew his attention back to the young soldiers. *Better take care in Afghanistan or it may be your grieving next-of-kin I have to visit.*

Sutton closed the heavy copy of *World War II: The Definitive Visual History* with shaking fingers. He swallowed convulsively and turned to stare at the glowing logs in the fireplace, wanting to escape the old man's probing gaze.

It's not real, he thought fiercely. *This is a goddam nightmare. Must be an explanation!* He swung his head back, hoping to catch the Germans off guard with a hint of trickery exposed. But their faces showed only sympathy and kindness. He turned back to the fire.

He had carefully read the illustrated history of the war. The photographs dating from the late 1930s to early 1945 were genuine; he had seen a number of them in *Life* magazine. It wasn't until he came to a picture of Eisenhower accepting the surrender of the German forces on May 7, 1945 that he froze, frowning as he read the date and caption. He turned to the following pages in mounting disbelief, scrutinizing the shattered Reich Chancellery in Berlin near where Hitler had died. After gazing at the picture for several minutes, he had raised a stunned face to von Scheller.

The elderly man nodded with compassion. "You must continue reading."

The final days of the war passed before Sutton's disbelieving eyes – liberation of the Nazi death camps, Hiroshima, the Japanese surrender aboard the Missouri, VJ celebrations in Times Square, and a closing photograph of a young GI being welcomed home by his wife and child.

Sutton's mind was a maelstrom, mental defenses rejecting the pictorial and literary evidence. He tried to convince himself that he was the victim of a Nazi thought control experiment using cleverly fabricated photos. The Germans were skilled in that new science he had read about in college - psychology. The pictures *must* be fakes. But what about the photographs of the jubilant crowds in the familiar expanse of Times Square and a Russian soldier planting a Soviet flag on the shattered Reichs Chancellery in Berlin? Why would the Nazis go to such an immense amount of effort to fool one unimportant Ranger lieutenant?

He sat in shocked silence until von Scheller took the book from his nerveless hands. Then Paula moved her chair next to his and gently drew his attention to a small flat object, like a glowing picture frame, that she held.

"What's that?" he whispered.

"It's called an iPad. A miracle of modern technology."

Paula touched an icon on the tablet's screen, opening to CNN's "Newsroom" streaming live. Paula pointed to the date April 22, 2011. The video feed was labeled "Terrorists Strike in Germany." A reporter stood outside the main gate of Hőhenbogen Kaserne, telling her worldwide audience that US and German authorities believed the attacks to be the work of Al-Qaeda. Her commentary was interspersed with smartphone footage shot the previous night showing the base in flames. The report cut to the German chancellor stating. "We will not tolerate terror attacks on our soil," followed by President Obama on a sunny golf course saying, "The United States and Germany stand together in the global war against terrorism."

Sutton squeezed his eyes shut and shook his head vigorously. He opened them again to view a 30-second commercial advertising vacations to a country called Israel. His mind opened. At that moment he knew with crystalline awareness that he was caught up in something so profound that that it was beyond comprehension.

"Damn right it's a miracle," he breathed.

15

Roth halted on a stream bank and shielded a flashlight, compass, and map under his poncho. The other three men propped themselves against the trunks of alders lining the stream, too stiff in their sodden clothes to squat with the sergeant. They shivered miserably, quietly cursing the weather.

"We should've stayed in that nice warm house 'til this fucking rain and sleet stopped," said Holcombe. "I couldn't be wetter if I'd fallen in a creek."

"Guess the next thing he's gonna tell us is we're lost," said Kemp through chattering teeth.

"Shut up," Roth snapped, intent on his navigation.

"We inside Czechoslovakia yet?" asked Loomis. "Been walking for hours."

"Been walking in goddam circles," Holcombe said. "Betcha he don't know where we are any more than the man in the moon does!"

"I know exactly where we are," Roth said. He stowed the map and equipment in a pocket. "Keep your fucking mouths shut. This area is crawling with enemy patrols."

Holcombe hurled himself off the tree trunk and confronted Roth. Cold, fear, and frustration snapped his self-control. His helmet shook, flinging water like a dog after a swim in a pond. All the ingrained prejudices of a hard-scrabble Alabama upbringing surfaced.

"I'm sick and tired of being treated like a nigger, you stinking kike! Them stripes on your arm don't give you no right to treat us like shit! We got a right to know where we are and what the hell's goin' on!"

Roth stiffened as the other two Rangers joined Holcombe. "Private Holcombe," he said evenly, "do you remember what I told you about Army regulations?" He stepped back, hands closing on the submachine gun under his poncho.

Holcombe's resolve was bolstered by the presence of his two comrades, whom he knew shared his feelings. "Screw the regulations! You're jerking us around you mother-fucker, and we want to know what's goin' on!"

"Do you?"

Roth turned slightly and lashed the toe of his paratroop boot upwards. The kick caught Holcombe below his breastbone, driving the air from his diaphragm. Holcombe doubled up and crumpled to his knees as Kemp and Loomis grabbed his arms. They glanced up as Roth cocked his weapon with a metallic snap.

"This is getting tiresome." Roth spoke in an almost conversational tone, the poncho flap thrown over his right shoulder to expose the Thompson. "It would be so much easier for me to shoot you all and go on alone. No one would ever know what happened to you cowards."

Holcombe retched. "Oh shit," Loomis said.

"However," Roth continued, "unlike Lieutenant Sutton, I believe in doing my duty. That is the only way to defeat the Nazis. Now that I am in command, I have decided that we have many opportunities in this area to attack the Germans. You all volunteered for this mission to do exactly that, not to play games with Czech partisans or drink vodka with Russians. So, you can make the choice: follow me and do the job you were trained for - after which I will lead you to safe haven - or die on this spot."

Roth stepped further back to allow a wider field of fire. Kemp and Loomis scowled at him, wincing as sleet stung their faces.

"He wouldn't," Loomis muttered.

"He goddam would!" Kemp hissed. "Guy's a fucking Nazi himself!"

"Ten seconds," Roth called.

"Okay, Sarge, you win," said Kemp. "We're with you. Goes for Holcombe, too, I'm sure."

"A wise decision, but if any of you think you can shoot your kike sergeant in the back, may I remind you that you will be lost without the list of contacts in the Resistance. And that list is here"- Roth tapped his helmet -"in my head."

He strode forward and nudged Holcombe with his boot. "Now get that hillbilly pig on his feet or he'll never walk again!"

Holcombe revived enough to stand, and they set off again – away from the Czech border towards the village of Bodenmais.

Sutton hunched his shoulders, gazing at the lighted dial of the radio as he had done nearly every night while growing up in the 1920s and '30s. He listened intently to the words of the B5 *aktuell* newsreader.

"... terrorist bombings at Mühldorf airfield and the American base at Hőhenbogen Kaserne. Residents of the *Bäyerischer Wald* within a one hundred kilometer radius of Kőtzting are asked to be on the alert for suspicious activity. General Hanno Kasper, national security advisor to the Chancellor, has vowed that the attackers will be hunted down and brought to justice.

"In other news, revelations that a neo-Nazi gang committed racist murders have shaken the country's minority communities ...."

"'Mühldorf airfield and the American base at Hőhenbogen Kaserne,'" Sutton repeated wonderingly, again visualizing the footage on Paula's iPad. He remembered the anomalies during the previous night's attacks: no blackout at Hőhenbogen Kaserne, the smoking sentry with his strange song, the unguarded airfield with its brightly painted light aircraft, abandoned barracks at the SS camp. The puzzle pieces fell together. He buried his aching head in his hands as despair gripped him.

Paula turned off the radio when the 9:30 news ended. Her grandfather leaned forward, revelation brightening his features.

"Now I see!" he exclaimed. "These so-called terrorist activities at the American camp and the airfield. During the war, Hőhenbogen Kaserne was a panzer depot and Mühldorf was a Luftwaffe base! A World War Two attack on modern installations occupying old military sites. You must believe now, Paula!"

"I believe, Opa."

"And the dead terrorists at the former SS Werewolf camp that the news reports mentioned," von Scheller continued, his voice rising in amazement. "The authorities speculate that there was a fight between two terrorist bands. Holcombe and Kemp claimed they were in a battle with SS troops. I can easily see how they could mistake terrorists in modern SEK uniforms for the old SS, especially when fighting in the darkness inside what they were convinced was an SS camp!"

Von Scheller paused for a moment, his excitement replaced by seriousness.

"Paula, our guests from the past stopped the terrorists before they attacked the World Youth Congress. The news reports said they planned to massacre hundreds of young people attending that meeting."

The old Luftwaffe hero's voice grew hoarser as tears stung his eyes. He made the sign of the cross and heaved a deep sigh.

"Sutton and his comrades had a special purpose in coming here," he said so softly that Paula and Sutton had to lean forward to hear him. "God intervened in mankind's affairs by bringing these young soldiers from one terrible war to prevent the extermination of innocents!"

Sutton listened to von Scheller's explanation in growing turmoil. One part of him was accepting the radical shift in time, but the other portion of his psyche - the conservative Midwestern American nurtured during the 1930s - howled in protest.

He kept thinking about Dorothy in the *Wizard of Oz*. The movie had a special significance for him because of the tornado that killed his parents and elder brother when he was a child. After jumping from the plane the previous night he had felt like he had been sucked into the vortex of such a twister. He wondered if he would awake like Dorothy with his friends and comrades around him and realize that the experience was only a dream – or a nightmare.

Other than the miraculous device that Paula called an "iPad" he had yet to see any artifacts – aside from the shaving cream and books - that were chronologically incompatible with the world he had known in 1945. On the rare occasions when he had speculated about the future, usually after watching Buck Rogers movies or reading one of the new science fiction comic books during his youth, he had imagined gleaming domed cities, rocket ships, robots and machines that could fulfill every human whim. But here he was in a seedy house that was actually more 19th than 21st century. Come to think of it, there was something else.

"Hey," he said, face set in Missouri stubbornness, "I saw a car outside. One of those Volkswagens I read about in *Life* magazine before the war. I can't imagine car designs wouldn't change in seventy years."

Von Scheller nodded patiently.

"The basic design of that Volkswagen model did not change for some 50 years. The car outside dates from 1969. My man Sepp picks up mail and groceries from Bodenmais in it. You saw pictures of new cars on Paula's iPad. Most cars today look like those."

The old German's frankness was disarming, but it wasn't enough to convince Sutton. He vaguely remembered such a sleek vehicle at the SS camp, but hadn't the time for a closer look. His suspicions gained on his willingness to believe.

"That's just it – those are nothing but pictures. So far all I've seen are pictures of things and events after April 1945. Listen, I'm from Missouri and its nickname is the Show Me state because we Missourians don't believe anything unless we can see and touch it!"

There was an uncomfortable silence while Sutton looked with challenging eyes at von Scheller.

"You like cars, don't you, Arthur?" Paula asked.

Sutton turned, surprised at Paula's use of his given name. He saw a speculative gleam in her green eyes.

"Yes, I've been a real car nut for years. I've got a '32 Ford coupe back home. When the war's over I'm going to buy a new Buick as soon as they start rolling off the assembly lines." His voice trailed off as he wondered if his dream was now impossible.

Paula stood, smiling at him. "I have a surprise for you. I'll be back in a minute."

After she left the room, Sutton looked at von Scheller. The elderly man seemed sunk in gloom, his earlier energy dissipated. Sutton picked up his uniform, put it on, and sat to lace his high paratroop boots. He eyed his equipment on the floor, checking off helmet, holstered .45, knife, and musette bag.

Paula reappeared. "Please come with me, Arthur." He knotted his boots and followed her. She led him through the entrance hall, opened a front door panel, and gestured. "There was nothing like this in 1945!"

Sutton stepped into the doorway, seeing nothing at first but the Volkswagen and an indistinct shape in the sleet-misted darkness beyond it. Paula switched on floodlights over the *port-cochere*, dramatically illuminating the

163

shark-like silver body of a sports car. Sutton caught his breath, his expression rapt as a child on Christmas morning.

"What is it?" he whispered.

Paula thrust her face between his shoulder and the doorjamb, delighted by his reaction. "It's my car. A Porsche 911 Carrera. What do you think of it?'

Sutton licked his lips. *"Beautiful."*

She grabbed his hand and pulled him out the door, guiding him from the porch as if he were a victim of shell shock. Sutton felt neither cold nor sleet.

"It's like a ... like a fighter plane," he said as they slowly circled the car. "You know, a Mustang or a Spitfire."

"It's a 2009 model. 345 horsepower, zero to sixty in 4.5 seconds. Would you like to sit inside it?"

"Yeah." Sutton stroked the wet silver hood. "Please."

Paula opened the passenger door for him and scurried around to the driver's side. Sutton examined the instrument panel. "It's even like a fighter plane inside," he said. "This is just like being in a cockpit, only a lot more luxurious!"

Paula turned the ignition key. "The one big extravagance of my life. I bought it with an inheritance from a great aunt. Cost 70,000 Euros - that's about 90,000 American dollars - but it's worth it. Like driving a work of art."

Sutton looked at her, aghast. "$90,000! For a car? That's impossible. Before the war you could get a new Packard or Cadillac for less than three thousand!"

"Not these days." She grinned, put the Porsche in gear, and circled the forecourt. The 3.6 liter engine growled like a caged tiger. "I'll take you for a drive on the autobahn tomorrow," Paula said. "Then you'll really think you're in a fighter plane!"

Sutton admired her profile in the dim instrument glow. "Where was this earlier?" he asked. "I looked outside but only saw the Volkswagen."

"It was parked in the old stable block. Your men must not have seen it when they were looking around. I wanted to show it to them."

She cut the burbling motor and sighed. "Well?"

Sutton massaged his eyes. "Seems like a dream to me. If I'm really in the future, how did this happen? How did I get here?"

"I don't know. Perhaps there is a scientific explanation. I still wonder if you are real or a ghost." Paula touched his face, then quickly withdrew her hand and looked away.

"But if this is real, where have I been for 66 years?"

"Perhaps nowhere," she said. "Maybe you just jumped from one time into another. Perhaps somewhere, in another dimension, World War Two is still raging, but you're just not there any longer. You're here."

Sutton froze as the implications hit him.

"My grandparents must be dead. Guess I can't go home again."

Paula saw the tears well in his eyes. She took his hand.

"No, you can't go home again, Arthur."

Roth's kick handicapped them all. Holcombe stumbled along between Kemp and Loomis, each step sending surges of pain though his badly bruised abdomen. Twice he dropped to his knees on the pine needles to retch and curse Roth. Loomis offered to lighten Holcombe's load by carrying his twelve-pound submachine gun, but Roth forbade it because Holcombe needed "toughening up." Each of the privates

165

privately considered shooting Roth as they tramped through conifer forests and slogged across fields. None dared to do so, out of fear of him as well as their disorientation and concern that gunfire would draw enemy patrols.

They emerged from a plantation of pine seedlings onto a railway track. Roth checked that the others were still with him, then set off down the line, helmet pulled low to shield his eyes from sleet. The disgruntled privates followed, still unaware of their destination.

Lights appeared through the mist. Roth halted and motioned the others to join him in the lee of a railway tool shed.

"That will be Bodenmais. There is a Gestapo regional headquarters in the village police station. It is across the street from the railway station. We will kill the Nazis inside and set fire to the building. Holcombe will stand watch from the train station. When we leave, we follow the railway tracks so no footprints are left behind. Questions?"

The three blackened faces under the dripping helmets were silent.

The former Bodenmais police station - a two-story stone building with a steep tiled roof - was built in 1853 after completion of the railway line through Bavaria. As crime in the popular holiday village was almost nonexistent, the municipality sold the structure in 1985 to a retired Munich businessman named Karl Wachsmüth and his wife Helga. The Wachsmüths converted the old police station into a cozy home.

From 1936 to 1945, the building had been used by the Nazi *Geheimstaatspolizei* - the Gestapo - as a regional headquarters. The old Gestapo cells in the basement were nearly forgotten, hidden behind empty boxes and sacks of coal.

Helga was a Tyrolean whom some villagers said had the gift of second sight. She claimed that spirits of Gestapo victims haunted the basement. Her jowly husband scoffed and said rats caused the occasional noises coming from there.

For the past week, Helga had been troubled by dreams – disordered images of death, blood, and endless gray boxcars that echoed with cries like the lowing of cattle en route to an abattoir. When she told Karl about the visions, he snorted and told her she was watching too much television. But Helga had a growing premonition that death was imminent.

At three minutes to ten that night, Karl sat in the ground floor living room with his slippered feet propped on the coffee table and his buttocks in a cushioned chair. The top button of his trousers was undone, showing his white belly. He sipped from a beer stein and gazed through bifocals at the 107 centimeter flat screen Phillips television on the wall. The set had been purchased two years earlier when the viewing tastes of Karl and Helga diverged. Since then, he watched the TV downstairs every night to enjoy his sports in peace while Helga watched her sitcoms and Reality TV programs in the bedroom upstairs.

As he waited for the 10:00 PM news broadcast, Karl ran his eyes over the neatly ordered living room with the ubiquitous crucifix between photos of his grandchildren. Life in Bodenmais had been pleasant since he arrived with Helga after retiring as the sales manager of an Audi dealership in the Munich suburb of Trudering. He had enjoyed the life of a Bavarian pensioner – puttering in the garden, tippling with the *Herren* in the Gasthaus, seeing the grand-children on Sundays, and taking an annual ten-day pack-aged holiday to the Costa del Sol.

As he looked at the photos of his grandchildren, he thanked God for the thousandth time that he was in Germany instead of someplace like Argentina where many of his SS *kameraden* had ended up. After the war, a former *Hauptsturmführer* whom he had served under in the Ukraine ensured that Karl's SS file in Berlin was destroyed and helped him find a job. At the age of 86, Karl was content, confident that no one would ever know about his service with the SS *Einsatzgruppen* when he had killed such a mul-titude of *Juden.*

Karl belched contentedly and quaffed his beer. The ten o'clock RTL news came on, read by the pretty Annett Möller. *There was a time not long ago when I wouldn't have minded a roll in the hay with her,* Karl thought wistfully. His spirits brightened as various German citizens were asked their opinions about the terrorists who had wreaked havoc in the *Bäyerischer Wald* the previous night. Many angrily called for their summary execution. The segment contin-ued with an interview of the heroic General Hanno Kasper, who was advising the counter-terror operation as the Chancellor's personal representative.

Karl raised his stein to toast the screen image. "Good for you, Herr General!" *Deutschland* needed more tough guys like him.

The people of Bodenmais were proud that no one had to lock their doors at night. The custom was observed by the Wachsmüths. Karl did not hear the front door open or stealthy footsteps approach. He felt an eddy of cold air on the back of his bald head as the living room door swung open. He blinked in surprise as he heard a sharp intake of breath behind him.

"Gestapo butcher," a voice snarled in a Berlin accent.

"*What?*" Karl gasped, face slack with astonishment as he began swiveling his head.

He never managed to view the source of the voice. As Karl's face came into profile, Roth fired a three-shot burst from his Thompson submachine gun. The first .45 caliber bullet tore off Karl's jaw. The second and third 230-grain lead projectiles smashed into his skull. Karl's head exploded in a cloud of brain matter, blood, and bone chips that spattered the television screen. Hanno Kasper railed against immigrant terrorists from behind a dripping red curtain.

Roth quickly scanned the room, pausing as he noticed the unfamiliar television set. He raced out as Karl's body tumbled to the floor.

Upstairs in the bedroom, Helga Wachsmüth had been watching *Mein großer dicker peinlicher Verlobter*, the German version of the American reality surprise show *My Big Fat Obnoxious Fiancé*. The volume was turned high to compensate for her deafness.

When the gunshots exploded downstairs, she knew her end was near. She calmly made the sign of the cross and began reciting the Pater Noster.

In the room below her, Private Kemp heard the televised German shouts and clapping and assumed them to be the alarmed cries of Gestapo officers in their quarters. He pointed the muzzle of his Thompson at the ceiling and screamed at Loomis: "Krauts upstairs! Hit the ceiling!"

Plaster dust coated them like snow as they riddled the stucco ceiling with long bursts. They fired until the German shouts were replaced by electronic crackling. Bright drops of blood dripped through the bullet holes onto their white-dusted helmets.

"Cease fire!" Roth boomed from the doorway. He gestured for them to leave, then unclipped a grenade from his chest harness.

Holcombe had waited across the street in the empty railroad station's entrance. He nervously chewed his lip, bruised midriff almost forgotten, brooding about his conversation with von Scheller. The old Kraut had really shaken him up, even though he had pretended to agree with the other guys that the German was nuts.

Dan Holcombe knew he wasn't a dummy despite having only a fifth grade education. Just an ordinary Joe with no ambition beyond surviving this fucking war and getting home to Alabama. But he *knew* that von Scheller was neither fibbing nor loony. Back home, Dan was a hunter, and he had learned to notice things in the woods, signs of game, or people up to no good. So how could he help but notice so many things here that just didn't seem right?

Such as lights glowing through the mist from houses on the surrounding mountains – just like that Panzer base they had attacked. No blackout. And down the street he could make out a couple of parked cars like nothing he had ever seen. He walked towards the nearest – a strange, humpbacked little automobile - and bent down to squint at the logo and nameplate. He recognized the Mercedes logo, but puzzled over the name "Smart."

Something was seriously out of whack here.

170

He caressed his submachine gun and turned around to watch the police station, tensing as he heard the clatter of automatic weapons fire.

A vehicle's headlights took him by surprise. Shielded by the village's winding streets, the car turned a corner a hundred yards from Holcombe's post. Light beams hit his eyes, illuminated him like a deer in the flashlight he had held when he hunted with his daddy back in Alabama.

He shrank back inside the doorway, but the car slowed as its passengers spotted him. Holcombe had never seen a vehicle like it – big and shiny black. He wondered if it was some new type of Nazi scout car.

Holcombe fired from the hip. His first burst missed and shattered the windows of an Aldi market. The car's driver reacted quickly and accelerated. The automobile passed Holcombe as his bullets chipped the pavement behind it. He held the trigger down and let the Thompson spew lead at the taillights. One winked out and the car skidded as a rear tire blew, but it kept going until the darkness swallowed it.

A hand tugged Holcombe's sleeve. "Come on, Dan!" Loomis cried.

A grenade exploded in the police station and flames danced behind its shattered windows. The Rangers pounded back down the railroad tracks like the hounds of hell were after them.

16

Eddie Cassera's Blackberry pinged as his flight landed at West Palm Beach airport, alerting him to a text message from Bill Miller: the declassified Bandstand Operation file had arrived at the DPMO office along with the DNA profile on the cadaver in Germany.

Eddie rented a car and called Louise Jablonski to let her know that he was on his way. He entered her address into the car's GPS, following its directions through Palm Beach to the A1A coastal road where he turned south as darkness was falling.

As he drove he thought about the DNA analysis. Because the body in the Landstuhl mortuary was fresh, the lab technicians would have created a nuclear DNA (nucDNA) profile. The encrypted sets of numbers would serve as a "genetic fingerprint," a unique identifier for the donor. Unfortunately, unless a close relative of the deceased could be found who was willing to provide a DNA sample the profile was useless for his investigation. Of course, the best way of identifying unknown remains was matching the DNA with genetic

173

material such as blood or hair known to be from a certain person. But such a bonanza was extremely rare.

He passed ostentatious seaside mansions – closed up after their wealthy owners returned north at the end of the Palm Beach "season." The GPS alerted him that he was approaching his destination. He drove past a trailer court set incongruously amidst the expensive residences; the electronic navigator ordered him to turn around.

Cassera pulled into a narrow lane skirting the Briny Butterfly Garden, passing 1950s and '60s mobile homes packed sardine-like into a parcel of land adjacent to the Atlantic. He parked next to a weather-beaten single-wide, edged past a collection of tinkling wind chimes, and knocked loudly.

The door swung open, wafting the smells of sandalwood incense and feline urine, with the cat piss predominating. A very pale old face peered at him. Heavily wrinkled, its salient feature was an aquiline nose that nearly met a pointed chin. Faded blue eyes blinked behind cheap glasses. Wisps of fine white hair escaped from a red polyester turban.

"Mrs. Jablonski?"

The old woman gave a quick, birdlike nod. "You the man from Washington? Mr. Casova?"

"Cassera." Cassera edged past her into the cluttered living room.

"Casova," she muttered as she closed the door. "Any relation to Father Casova at St. Mary's in Cherry Hill?"

"No ma'am."

She waved a mottled hand. "Never mind. I don't get many visitors these days. Please sit on the divan, Mr. Casova. I'll make us some tea."

Cassera shooed away a cat and sank deeply into a musty sofa. He observed his hostess and surroundings while the old woman selected tea cups and saucers from a glass-fronted cabinet. Although bent by the weight of eighty-five years, Louise Jablonski carried herself regally – head high, thrusting indomitably forward.

The furnishings looked like they had been gleaned from thrift shops. Rickety chairs, yellowed doilies, and stained cushions with faded motifs of Atlantic City and Niagara Falls. Old paperback books and magazines in dusty piles surrounded a vintage 1970s television.

The walls were covered with cheaply framed photographs of children, grandchildren and great-grandchildren. There was a large black and white wedding picture of a somber Louise Jablonski in her youth with a blonde man in a dress Marine Corps uniform of the World War II era. The same man appeared in many other photos, progressively aging through the decades. He obviously wasn't the dead man in Germany.

"You like my pictures, Mr. Casova?"

Louise Jablonski stood in the doorway of her tiny kitchen holding a teapot in one hand and a milk carton in the other. A fat yellow cat rubbed against her legs, eyeing the milk.

Cassera smiled. "Nice family."

She hobbled across the room to place the teapot and milk on a coffee table, then sat heavily in a chair. Cassera watched her arthritic hands slosh tea into a pair of cups.

"Help yourself to milk and sugar." She nestled the cup and saucer in her lap and brooded over them until Eddie tasted the brew. He looked up to find her rheumy eyes gazing at him.

175

"I saw you looking at my wedding photo. That was my second husband, Mike Jablonski. He was a good man. Died 15 years ago."

She fell silent for several minutes.

"So," she said hoarsely, "did you find Nicky, Mr. Casova?"

Cassera swallowed and set his teacup on the table. "To be honest with you, ma'am, it's too early to say for sure. What we've found are some remains in association with Nicholas Sarnoff's military identification."

The old woman smiled, eyes unfocused as she gazed into the past.

"You know that saying about 'love of your life,' Mr. Casova? Well, that was my Nicky. Sounds silly, but it's true. We were high school sweethearts. He was two years older, but we were together from the time we were just kids.

"Nicky always acted like he was a tough guy, but he was good to me. We got married just before he shipped out in '43. I was at the pier in New York with thousands of other sweethearts. You should've seen it, Mr. Casova, all those waving handkerchiefs and tears. That was the last time I saw him."

She sniffled, fumbled in the pocket of her floral print pants suit to find a tissue. She blew her nose, dabbed at her eyes, then squared her shoulders.

"Excuse me. Long time ago but I still get emotional thinking about it."

Cassera cleared his throat, opened his briefcase and took out a notebook and pen. "I have a list of questions here to ask you about Nicholas that may help us positively identify these remains"

"Funny thing is," the old woman continued, ignoring him, "I never felt he was dead after they said he was missing in action. We were so close, and I thought I would *know* if he got killed.

"I didn't want to get married again after the Army said he was dead, didn't even want the money they paid me for his insurance. But I was just a young girl and my family talked me into marrying Mike when he came courting after he got home from the War."

She suddenly turned to him, face desolate, eyes haunted.

"I dreamed about Nicky last night! First time in many years. He was dead, Mr. Casova, really dead! Killed by the Germans!"

The old woman began sobbing. She got up and hurried into her bedroom as fast as her arthritic legs would carry her. Cassera fidgeted uncomfortably, wondering if he should leave.

She returned ten minutes later, composed, and laid a battered shoe box on the coffee table.

"Guess you want to see pictures of my Nicky, Mr. Casova? All these years I kept these – just couldn't get rid of them."

She handed him a yellowing envelope containing a few black and white photographs.

"These are all I got left. They were taken on his final leave before he shipped out for England."

The photos were smudged and grainy. Cassera used a magnifying glass to examine the features of a wolfish young GI in a garrison cap and walking out uniform. His pulse quickened. Without the animating life force, a dead person could appear unlike a photo taken while alive. But Cassera's trained eye immediately spotted the similarities to the photographs of the dead man in Germany. He wished that he dared take out the Landstuhl Mortuary pictures for a direct comparison, but the old woman was watching him like a hawk.

He tried to keep excitement from showing in his voice.

"Mrs. Jablonski, the government would be very grateful if we could borrow a few of these pictures for a day or two. I'll give you a receipt and we'll return them to you after we copy them."

Louise Jablonski looked at him shrewdly. Cassera had the impression that, for someone of her advanced age, her mind was remarkably sharp.

"How come you want these pictures, Mr. Casova?" she said. "The remains you found must be a skeleton, aren't they?"

Cassera did a mental squirm, finally deciding to answer obliquely.

"We blow facial photographs up to the same size as pictures of the skull. Then we superimpose them and try to match physical features. It works pretty well."

She nodded, but didn't seem convinced.

"Please be careful with them," she said. "They're all I got left of him now. Except for his letters." She gestured to a sheaf of V-Mail forms held together by rubber bands. "You want to see these too?"

Cassera declined and gently began asking questions. These were answered to the best of the old woman's ability. There were some misses, but enough hits to ensure her credibility despite the passage of nearly seventy years. She knew of no living relatives of her former husband, so Eddie crossed "DNA?" off his list.

The final question on his list related to something that had bothered both him and Miller – the only major discrepancy between the old 293 File and the new autopsy reports from Landstuhl. That caused a problem because PFC Sarnoff's medical records stated that his last physical examination had been made in March 1945 just before his posting from an army base in southern England to the Bandstand commando training camp in Scotland. Any physical markings such as tattoos would have been noted at that time by the medic.

Again, he had to lie a little.

"Ma'am, an old army buddy of Nicholas said that he had a tattoo on his arm. Something that looked like this –" He sketched a crude skull and crossbones with the Or Glory motto scrawled beneath it, and held it up for her to see. "To your knowledge, did Nicholas have anything like that?"

She squinted at the drawing, face screwed up in concentration, then took out the collection of letters from the shoebox and removed the rubber bands. She riffled through them, reading passages before discarding one after another. Finally she found one that she read slowly before solemnly handing it to Cassera.

"I think this is what you want, Mr. Casova."

Eddie quickly scanned the letter dated March 26, 1945, reading about Sarnoff's long wait at Euston station in wartime London. His heart skipped a beat when he came to the missing soldier's next paragraph:

179

We got leave last night after some Army quack gave me the once over. He said I am in fine shape and will live to 100. A couple of buddies and me went to a place called Soho to have some fun before we shipped out to the training camp. There was a place there that said it could do tattoos of all the famous regiments in England, but they couldn't do the Rangers! Anyways, I got a real spiffy one on my shoulder of this Limey regiment called the 17 Lancers. Looks like a pirate flag. The motto is DEATH OR GLORY and the guys and me thought that was pretty swell.

Cassera took several deep breaths, staring at the fragile piece of paper for much longer than needed for mere reading. He felt the old lady watching him, but she was silent. They seemed to share some understanding, a glimpse of something beyond normal human experience.

At last he folded the letter and offered it to her, but she shook her head and told him to keep it. Cassera hurriedly filled out a receipt and gave the old woman his business card. He managed to slow his pace while she accompanied him to the front door. Louise Jablonski seemed lost in thought. Cassera guessed that she led a life as lonely as his, confined to her trailer home and the artificial world on the screen of her TV.

"You'll let me know, please, Mr. Casova, if you really found my Nicky?" Her voice broke and her eyes again shone with tears.

"Of course I will."

He had just started the rental car's engine when the trailer's door opened and the old woman's pale face peered out.

"Yoo-hoo! Mr. Casova!"

Cassera rolled down the window and forced a smile as Louise Jablonski gingerly stepped outside and came towards him.

"I forgot about this. It was in my jewelry box." She handed him a locket on a chain. On one side was a tiny facial photo of Nicholas Sarnoff; on the reverse was a lock of dark hair preserved under the glass.

"You can take this too," she told him, watching his face intently. "*CSI Miami* is my favorite TV show. The hair is his – I know what you need for a positive ID."

Cassera accepted the ornament with shaking fingers.

17

Joachim Friedhof kept the rattletrap old Ford Taunus at a steady 60 kilometers per hour as it tooled down the Lam-Brennes road. Beside him, Herta Pilz fiddled with the radio knobs, searching the airwaves for hip hop music.

"Nothing but news bulletins about those terrorists," she whined. "That's all people talked about today!"

"Maybe we'll meet some of them," Joachim joked. "They were supposed to have been in this area last night."

"*Ach*, do you really think so?" Herta looked out the window as if she expected a battalion of terrorists to appear. "M-maybe you'd better take me straight home!

"*Nein!*" Joachim was alarmed at the possibility of their evening ending before the real fun started. "I was only fooling. Those terrorists are probably in Iran by now. Besides" - he tried to inject a masculine tone into his reedy voice - "I would protect you. I learned hand-to-hand combat during my National Service."

What limited fighting skills Joachim may have acquired during his compulsory national service had been quickly forgotten. He had spent most of his fifteen months in the *Bundeswehr* as a storehouse keeper. But the well-upholstered Herta seemed reassured.

After a first date with Herta during which he'd only managed to bare her sizable breasts Joachim had drooled in anticipation all week. He had chosen the site for tonight's seduction with care, remembering it from his boyhood rambles through the ancient forests. Joachim stoked her passion with dinner at the Burger King in Deggendorf. Figuring that his dating dues were paid, Joachim pushed the old car as fast as it could go.

Herta sat up when the vehicles' worn brakes squealed. She squinted at the old stone gateposts as Joachim steered between them.

"Hey," she said. "You sure it's okay to go in here? Looks like it goes to some baron's *schloss* or something."

"Nothing to worry your pretty head about, *Spatzerl*. A crippled old man lives here in a big house, but it's at the end of the drive. We're not going that far."

He put the Taunus in low gear and climbed a stone bridge over a stream. As the front tires touched the opposite bank he turned sharply, leaving the main drive to creep down a track towards a ruined cottage. He parked near a mossy brick wall.

"Here we are, my dumpling," he announced, and fell on the squirming Herta. Ten minutes later they were in the back seat and Herta was enthusiastically demonstrating her control of the gag reflex.

Unfortunately for Joachim, the quantity of beer consumed earlier in the evening exerted pressure on his bladder . . . and Herta's facile lips exacerbated the situation.

With a groan and muttered apology, he extricated himself and tumbled out of the car's door, clutching his trousers to keep them from falling to his ankles. He ambled bow-legged to a nearby clump of bushes. With a sigh of relief he loosed a jet of urine into the shrubbery.

His piss hit something inside the bushes with a metallic plink. *Strange,* Joachim thought, as he heard his water running down a hidden artificial surface. He finished and zipped his trousers, then investigated the hidden object. A large bush came away easily in his hands. He cast it aside and peered at a license plate and pair of headlights.

"It's a car," he muttered. "What in blazes . . . ?"

He went back to the Taunus and felt under the front seat for a flashlight.

"Hey," Herta called languorously from the back seat. "What's keeping you, *Kuschelbär?*"

"Back in a moment," Joachim mumbled.

"Well close the damned door, for Christ sakes! You're letting the cold air in!"

Joachim flicked on the flashlight as he squelched back to the partially concealed vehicle. He removed more of the freshly cut bushes until the car was fully revealed. He recognized it as a Mercedes G-Wagen — evidently a police vehicle. *What the hell was a police car doing stashed out here in the middle of the woods?* Suddenly, the words of the news bulletins he had heard throughout the day came back in red letters ten meters high.

"*Allmächtiger!*" he whispered in Bavarian dialect.

He almost tripped over his feet in his haste to get back to the Taunus. Herta's head popped up in the back as he threw himself into the driver's seat and locked the doors.

She clutched her blouse to her naked chest and glared at him, moon face ugly in its petulance.

"What the fuck's going on? You gone crazy?"

Joachim ground the ignition praying the recalcitrant old Ford engine would turn over. "Got to get out of here!" he gasped.

His apparent spurning had stung Herta's pride.

"You scared of a real woman," she taunted as the car jerked into reverse. "You some kind of homosexual?"

"Shut up, hag! That car the terrorists used is right in front of us!"

"*Terrorists!* Jesus, Mary and Joseph save me!" Herta wedged herself in the narrow floor space between the front and back seats, gabbling prayers for salvation from terrorists and forgiveness for fornication. Her wide white bottom jounced like jelly as Joachim reversed the car over the rutted track. She moaned when the Taunus sideswiped a gatepost before careering out onto the main road.

Six kilometers up the road Joachim spotted a *gasthaus* with a public telephone outside it. He was so agitated that the operator made him repeat himself three times before she understood that he wanted to be connected to the police. As he waited for his call to go through his eyes darted around the menacing night, expecting a hail of terrorist bullets. The only sign of Herta was one gibbous buttock quivering behind the front seat and her plaintive wail, "I promise to be good from now on, God!"

". . . so that's how it ended," Colonel von Scheller said. "The surviving top Nazis were tried at Nuremberg for war crimes. Many were sentenced to death but a few – such as

186

Goering – managed to commit suicide before they could be executed. All the rest who were convicted were released or died in prison, like Rudolf Hess."

"Mindboggling," Sutton remarked huskily.

Sutton and Paula flanked von Scheller's wheelchair as they sat around the freshly stoked fire. A Bach concerto flowed from the radio, heightening the charged emotional atmosphere.

"And to think," Paula added, "that if this time warp or miracle hadn't happened, my grandfather might have been killed by your men in 1945. God! My father would never have been born, and neither would I!"

Sutton felt a rise of anger, with an undercurrent of shame. "I was opposed to all of those damned assassinations on the Bandstand target list. Soldiers shouldn't go around murdering people in cold blood even if they're Nazi politicians or senior officers. I gave clear orders to my men to forget about those assassinations."

"I believe you," Von Scheller said tightly, "but obviously your Sergeant Roth disagreed. Roth would have killed me if he believed I was the same man in that wartime photo."

"The man seemed demented!" said Paula. "I know he thought he was still fighting in World War Two, but at least the other men behaved like human beings!"

Sutton sighed. "We've got to try and understand him." He sketched Roth's background as related to him by the Jewish sergeant's former commanding officer and the intelligence staffers who kept tabs on German exiles serving in the armed forces. As he spoke he remembered scenes from the pictorial history — skeletal figures in striped pajamas, hills of desiccated corpses awaiting crematoriums, warehouses of human hair, *Arbeit Mach Frei.*

"I guess those pictures in the book prove it's all true," Sutton finished. "I heard stories about those concentration camps, but I guess like most guys in the Army I found it hard to believe the Germans really killed people like that."

"It's true," von Scheller said harshly. "But it is incorrect to say 'the Germans'. It was the *Nazis* who exterminated millions — a tiny segment of the German population who tried to keep their hideous crimes a secret from the German people!"

"Weren't you a Nazi? How could that be when you were a Major in the Luftwaffe?"

Von Scheller gripped the arms of his wheelchair. Paula covered one of his hands with hers and squeezed comfortingly. She turned to Sutton as the old man struggled to contain his ire.

"My grandfather was never a member of the Nazi Party," she snapped. "In fact, he was interrogated by the Gestapo because the Nazis suspected that he was involved in the plot to kill Hitler in July 1944. My father's uncle Manfred was one of the main conspirators. He was a *Wehrmacht* general, a close friend of Rommel. The SS strangled him with piano wire hung from meat hooks. They filmed it for Hitler's amusement. Rommel was also part of the conspiracy, but he was too great a hero to be executed — it would have embarrassed the Nazis. So they made a deal with him: commit suicide or his family would be murdered. Rommel chose the poison. The Nazis said that he died of wounds and gave him a state funeral."

"Jesus Christ." Sutton looked at von Scheller. "I didn't know that."

"Few people did," von Scheller replied. "I was not a Nazi, but my brother officers and I were nonetheless guilty for not acting sooner to prevent Hitler from destroying so many millions of lives and ruining our Fatherland.

"We Germans hated the terrible chaos and depression after the First World War, and we admired Hitler for dragging us out of that quagmire and restoring our pride and strength. Oh, we members of the old ruling class considered the Nazis common buffoons and thugs, but we let them take over. I was aware of the persecution of the Jews; I heard whispers about death camps, but I did not *know* then about the mass murder. Perhaps I – and my countrymen – did not *want* to know. The Nazis tried to keep their crimes hidden from us. I did not involve myself in politics – I was a soldier and devoted myself to my duty and looking after my men. My uncle was closer to the Nazi filth. He and his comrades decided to take action. Think of the multitude that would have been saved if they had succeeded!"

Tears welled at the corners of his eyes, and he angrily dashed them away with his fingers. "I was not part of the conspiracy to assassinate Hitler, but I wish I *had* been. My uncle was the *true* hero, not I!"

"*Ach*, Opa!" Paula hugged him, kissed his cheek.

Sutton changed the subject with youthful impatience. "Okay, if that's history now then we've got to think about the present. What's going to happen to Roth and the other men in my team?"

"They won't get far if they try to cross the Czech border," von Scheller replied. "Actually, there is no real border these days as both the Czech Republic and Germany are members of the European Union."

189

Sutton looked puzzled and opened his mouth to ask a question, but von Scheller warded it off with a raised hand.

"Later. Now, the tragic thing is that your men believe they are isolated in enemy territory. The KSK – the German army's special force – is searching for them along with hundreds of policemen. If they find your men I would hope that they surrender. I pray there will be no more bloodshed."

"What am I going to do?" Sutton grimaced. "I'm so confused that it feels like a tornado's loose in my head!"

"We can discuss that in the morning," Paula said, yawning. "Why don't we all try to get some sleep? This has been one of the longest days of my life."

"I agree," von Scheller said. "My dear, please turn off the radio for me and then you can show Herr Sutton to a guest room."

Paula stood and walked towards the radio. Her hand froze inches from the dial as an announcer's voice cut into the Baroque music:

"We interrupt this program with a special news bulletin. Word had just been received of a terrorist attack in Bodenmais. Eyewitnesses report that black-faced men dressed as American soldiers attacked a private home with machine guns and grenades, killing an elderly married couple. A passing motorist was also fired upon but escaped unharmed. Authorities believe the culprits to be the same band of terrorists responsible for last night's attacks. Stay tuned for further details."

"Oh no," Paula whispered. "You don't think . . . ?

Sutton was ashen-faced. "It has to be Roth and the others," he declared grimly. "Bodenmais was on our target list.

We were to attack a Gestapo headquarters in the police station there."

Von Scheller closed his eyes and shook his head in sorrow.

"*Gott im Himmel.* Of course – I remember when that building was used by the Gestapo during the war. Everyone feared even looking at it. It became a private home some years ago.

"Bodenmais is several kilometers southwest of here," he continued. "In the opposite direction one would travel to reach the Czech border. Your men must have changed their minds about joining forces with partisans or the Red Army."

"*Damn Roth!*" Sutton trembled in anger. "His hatred for Germans is so bad that he would sacrifice the whole team to satisfy his thirst for revenge. We've got to stop him! He'll never let those poor guys surrender!"

"You're right," said von Scheller. "The population is so inflamed over the planned terrorist attacks on children, and now your team's murder of the couple on Bodenmais, that Hanno Kasper's force will almost certainly shoot your men down like mad dogs even if they surrender — which they probably won't do, judging by what we know about your Sergeant Roth."

Sutton rose and stood in front of the fireplace with his hands gripping the mantel.

"There are several dozen other targets on our operations list. Factories and radio stations in addition to military and Gestapo installations. My men must be stopped before they attack other places and kill more people!"

"But how can they be found?" asked Paula.

Sutton pivoted. "Roth must have taken the operations plan, my maps and the target list when I was unconscious. I memorized the places I had chosen to attack and can probably remember most of the others if I can get a good map of this area. My guess is that Roth will hit other places that will lead to the greatest number of German casualties. If I can meet my guys at one of those targets I'll order them to surrender."

"And what if Roth disobeys you?" asked von Scheller.

Sutton glanced at his holstered Colt .45 hung on a webbing belt over a bedpost. "If it means saving my other men, then I'll shoot him."

Paula's eyes widened at the grim determination in his voice.

"Do you think they will attack more places tonight?" she asked.

"Most likely. Our operations plan was based on night attacks while remaining hidden during the day. My bet is that Roth will keep punching until he's stopped."

"I'll get a survey map." Von Scheller wheeled towards the door.

It opened as he was halfway across the room. Maria, the housekeeper, came inside. She wrung her hands and looked fearfully at Sutton.

"What is it, Maria?" von Scheller asked. "You and Sepp should be in bed this late at night."

"Sepp saw lights by the old cottage, *Mein Herr*," she explained. "He went down there to see what they were."

"Lights?" Von Scheller frowned. "What were they?"

"Policemen. Sepp thinks they will come here next."

18

Hanno Kasper was a blood sports man. He received countless invitations to hunt on corporate and private game reserves; gentlemanly requests to shoot grouse in Scotland, stalk elk in Norway or lance wild boar in Spain's Las Marismas swamp. To Hanno, such sport was just a substitute for his real passion — hunting human beings who threatened the Fatherland.

The bloodlust was upon him now, a powerful tonic that sprang from his loins and suffused his heart and mind. He stood by the ruined cottage with sleet wetting his black beret and slicking his leather jacket, flexing his fingers to keep them warm and supple. The policemen around him wore gloves on this cold night, but Hanno preferred to keep his hands free for rapid drawing and firing of his pistol.

"Well?" He swished his flashlight across the men who poked and prodded at the freshly exposed Mercedes G-Wagen.

The Provincial Police *Hauptwachtmeister* whose patrol car had been first on the scene turned and trudged up to him.

"No doubt about it, Herr General. That paint job was sloppy enough to leave some of the original civilian body color exposed in spots."

"So? Footprints?'

"*Ja.* Many. Seem to go in and out several times along the track. No sign of them entering the forest along here."

"Come with me." Kasper trotted towards the dark shape of his personal CLS 550 that was blocking the main drive in front of the rustic bridge. The Mercedes had been flown to the *Bäyerischer Wald* with other specialized vehicles and equipment.

Kasper's driver snapped to attention and opened the car's rear door. The interior lights were synchronized to work in reverse when the one-way windows were up, extinguishing when a door opened to foil snipers.

"Get in," Kasper ordered the local policeman.

The *Hauptwachtmeister* slid across the leather seat away from Kasper. The policeman blinked as the dome lights came on, his eyes bloodshot after thirty hours of duty. A KSK *leutnant* sat in the front passenger seat tapping the keyboard of the dashboard computer terminal. He turned towards Kasper.

"Sir, no license plate numbers correspond to those on the G-Wagen. They are forgeries."

"*Danke*, Manfred," Kasper told him. "That settles it then." He faced the Bavarian policemen. "Do you know who owns this estate?"

"Yes, sir. It belongs to Major von Scheller. His house is at the end of the lane."

"Von Scheller, eh?" Kasper pursed his lips, wondering why the name was familiar to him. He smiled. "Hans-Ülrich von Scheller, the Luftwaffe hero?"

"*Jawohl, Herr General.* He is well known in this area, but keeps to himself these days. I heard that he is ill."

"He was one of my heroes when I was young," Kasper said briskly. "Von Scheller and Otto Skorzeny were my favorites. One of our most decorated fliers. But his uncle was a traitor and I heard rumors that ...."

He looked thoughtful, then shook his head. "Let's hope those terrorist swine haven't taken the major hostage and holed up there. Are you familiar with the house?"

"Yes, sir. Sometimes we drop by for coffee with von Scheller's servants. Decent folks. I've only met the old man twice though."

"You wouldn't happen to know von Scheller's telephone number, would you?"

The policeman shook his head. "*Nein.*"

"Manfred!" Kasper barked. "Get the number of Hans-Ülrich von Scheller and call him for me. You, *Herr Hauptwachtmeister*, will describe the house in detail."

The tired policeman sketched the layout and surroundings of the von Scheller mansion while Manfred spoke on the Mercedes' telephone. After several minutes, the lieutenant interrupted the men in the rear seat. He wore a look of concern.

"Sir, there is no reply. The operator says the line appears to be out of order."

195

"Cut, most likely." Kasper's eyes narrowed. "Tell General Michalke to get the company here as fast as possible. In the meantime deploy a cordon around the house with the platoon we've got here. Night order, snipers and an infrared video cameraman front and rear. *We* shall go in for a closer look." He smiled mockingly at the provincial policeman. "You don't mind accompanying us, do you *Herr Hauptwachtmeister?*"

Actually, the policeman *did* mind. He was a keeper of the peace, not a member of a counterterrorist assault team. But there was no denying Hanno Kasper. Although he wished he were safely back in his patrol car, the *Hauptwachtmeister* was fascinated by the KSK's calm efficiency as it went into action. He accepted a flak jacket from the lieutenant, noting that Kasper refused to wear body armor.

While waiting for the platoon to encircle the house, Kasper checked the magazine of his pistol and slipped a high fidelity digital recorder into his pocket. Besides their value as evidence in criminal cases, recorded conversations could be added to a library of voiceprints.

A light pulsated on the radio console. "We are in position," the KSK platoon leader's voice said over the car's speaker.

"Forward, Gerhard," Kasper lolled in the luxurious seat, seemingly unconcerned as the Mercedes rolled up the driveway. The *Hauptwachtmeister* tried to swallow the lump in his throat and wondered if he would see his *frau* and children again. He glanced at Kasper's calm profile, admiring the former *Hitler Jugend's* composure. *God in heaven*, the policeman thought, *that fellow really is one of those old-time Nazi supermen.*

Hanno may have appeared relaxed, but he was like a coiled spring. He knew it was possible that he was driving into an ambush. Boldness had always paid off for him, and he preferred to literally march up to the enemy's door rather than engage in a siege or lengthy negotiations. The Mercedes approached the von Scheller house and stopped outside the porte-cochere. Kasper eyed the Porsche and Volkswagen parked under it.

"Run their license numbers," he snapped to Manfred. "Stick GPS trackers on them, too. Right, let's go *Herr Hauptwachtmeister.*"

The driver and lieutenant exited the car and crouched behind it. Their eyes began a constant sweep of the mansion's windows and roof as they hefted their submachine guns. The policeman followed Kasper up to the front door, where Hanno tugged at the bell pull.

"I've always wanted to meet Major von Scheller," Kasper said conversationally. "During the war I used to read of his exploits in *Hör Mit Mir* magazine and the old *Völkischer Beobachter.*"

A light went on behind the door. One of its panels opened and a young woman in a dressing gown looked at them in annoyance.

"What is it, gentlemen? It's past midnight!"

Hanno observed her closely. Her haughty voice fitted her appearance — good breeding, quality education, old Junker stock.

"*Grüss Gott, Fraulein.* I am General Hanno Kasper, the Chancellor's National Security Advisor. We would like to ask you some questions."

"Yes ... yes, of course."

She introduced herself and invited them inside. Kasper removed his beret as he followed her through the entrance hall into the landing. His eyes darted everywhere, appraising details. The black and white marble floor tiles had been recently mopped, judging by the tiny puddles still dotting the floor and the tinge of ammonia in the air.

Why would the floor be cleaned this late at night? He moved slowly to get a closer look as Fraulein von Scheller led them across the landing. His scrutiny was rewarded as he spied half a muddy footprint under the overhang of the staircase's bottom tread. He paused to examine it. The print was of a cleated paratrooper boot, similar to many he had seen that day.

"Herr Kasper?" Paula could not conceal an anxious catch to her voice.

Kasper took his time to catch up with her. He smiled. "I was admiring your house, Fraulein. Lovely old place."

"Yes. It's been in the family for many years." She opened the door into a paneled library. A split log burned in the marble fireplace. The newly laid fire had not yet dispelled the room's clamminess.

An old man in a plum velvet smoking jacket sat in a wheelchair with a blanket across his knees. He held a leather-bound copy of Goethe's *Faust* as if he had been disturbed in the act of reading. Kasper wondered if this sad old wreck could be his dashing hero of seven decades years ago. He thought it odd for the elderly man to be up so late at night.

"Herr Kasper," Paula said, "permit me to introduce my grandfather, Major Hans-Ülrich von Scheller."

"*Gruss Gott,*" Kasper said before clicking his heels and saluting. The older warrior sat up straighter, squared his emaciated shoulders, and invited Kasper and the policeman to sit. Kasper stroked von Scheller's ego for several minutes, relating his boyhood adulation and describing a scrapbook he had filled with clippings of the Luftwaffe hero's victories against the Russians on the Eastern Front. Still wearing his smile, he abruptly shifted the conversation.

"*Mein Herr*, are you aware of the terrorist outrages that have taken place in this area over the past two days?"

"Of course," von Scheller said, scowling fiercely. "We heard just a short while ago about those killings over in Bodenmais. Disgusting!"

Kasper leaned forward.

"*Herr Major*, an ersatz vehicle used by the terrorists was discovered on your property. When the *Hauptwachtmeister* told me that you lived alone here except for an elderly servant couple" - he glanced quizzically at Paula - "we wanted to check on your safety via telephone. We became concerned when it appeared that your line was out of order. We thought it best to come here to see if you were safe. As you know, these terrorist swine are prone to hostage-taking."

"You found the vehicle on my property? Where exactly?"

Kasper told him, and the old man looked concerned. "Thank God they didn't come here!'

"So, you did not see or hear anything suspicious today?"

When the older man shook his head, Kasper turned to Paula.

"Did *you*, *Fraulein*? But perhaps you've just arrived here. Visiting your grandfather for the long weekend?"

"I drove from Regensburg last night," Paula said. "I saw nothing unusual. I've been inside all day. The weather has been miserable."

"I see. Did you realize your telephone was out of order, *Herr Major?*

"*Nein.* I use it very little these days. Thank you for telling me. I'll have it repaired."

"Allow me to see to that. It's the least I can do for someone who inspired so many of us during the war years. Besides, it is essential for you to have a means of communication with the outside world with all this terrorist activity locally."

Kasper stood. "Well, we must continue the hunt. Tell me, would you care to have one of my men stay here with you until the emergency is over?"

"No thank you," von Scheller replied a fraction too quickly. "Most thoughtful of you, but I enjoy my solitude and hardly think it would be necessary."

Gute Nachts were said. Kasper lingered as he retraced his steps. He toyed with Paula, watching her bite her lower lip as she waited by the front door for him. Kasper paused to fix the beret on his head. He faced Paula, making his eyes and voice as cold as possible as he leaned close.

"Don't fear, Fraulein. We'll catch these Muslim *untermenschen* soon, and when we do I guarantee they'll never again desecrate our Fatherland. Extermination is the only cure for their foul disease."

Paula caught her breath, and Kasper showed his teeth in a knowing smile. He clicked his heels, swung around, and strode to his Mercedes.

Paula bolted the door, then ran into the landing. Her grandfather waited in his wheelchair at the foot of the stairs.

"They suspect something, Opa! I could tell by the way Kasper looked at me!"

"Possibly. But they'll have to get a warrant to search the house. You'd better fetch Herr Sutton."

Paula raced up two flights of stairs to a cramped room under the eaves where Sutton had been hiding. He left his military equipment behind and accompanied her to von Scheller's bedroom. The drapes were drawn.

"I watched from the window," Sutton said as he entered the room, "but I couldn't see the guys who got out of the car. Who were they, police?"

Von Scheller told him about the KSK and related Kasper's career and reputation. "The Third Reich is *kaput*," he ended, "but unfortunately we still have people like Kasper who remain Nazis at heart."

Sutton paced around the room. "Hell, maybe I should have surrendered to them instead of hiding! If they come back and find me it's just going to complicate matters!

"Under different circumstances that would have been the wisest course," said von Scheller. "But Kasper would probably just execute you, convinced you were a terrorist, then claim you were shot while trying to escape. Even if you survived, the authorities wouldn't believe your incredible story until you had been thoroughly interrogated and investigated – or maybe never. They would probably lock you up in an insane asylum. Meanwhile, your men will continue their attacks, killing innocent people until they are stopped. Kasper and the KSK must be hot on their trail!"

"Grandfather is right!" Paula cried. "Roth and the others won't stand a chance with General Kasper. He told me he will take no prisoners!"

"Lieutenant Sutton, you are the only one who can stop this," said von Scheller. "You must find your 'Fox' team before the KSK does and make them surrender openly and without a fight so Kasper has no excuse to execute them."

Sutton was pensive. Finally he nodded, jaw set in determination. "Okay, I can see that's the way it has to be. I'll need that map and a pencil and paper. A cup of coffee would be good, too. Black."

19

Someone tapped on the window of the big Mercedes. The *leutnant* aide peered through the one-way glass, then interrupted Kasper's perusal of boot print photos on an electronic tablet with special analytical software.

"Here is General Michalke, sir."

Kasper opened the rear door to admit the KSK commander. "So, Baldur, it appears we have found our quarry's safe house."

"Indeed, sir. Our first real break. What a pity the swine have already fled."

"You're sure?"

Michalke nodded and consulted a notepad. "We found four sets of footprints identical to those at Höhenbogen and the other sites. Outdated US Army Corcoran pattern paratroop boots. The same as the ones in those photos you've got there." He gestured to the tablet that Kasper held.

"I spotted a clear portion of one of these inside the house," Kasper said. "Luckily, they missed it when they swabbed the others away. Please continue."

"*Danke.* The ground is soft here and the footprints are well preserved despite the rain. The four individuals wearing those boots left the G-Wagen by the cottage, came up the lane and circled the house – probably to see if it was staked out. That series of prints stops at a terrace on the west side, where a pane was freshly broken in the French doors. That seems to be the way they entered the house."

"Seems odd for them to have broken in," Kasper mused, "especially since I suspect the *fraulein* must be their accomplice. Why else would the von Schellers pretend they had no contact with the terrorists?"

"Three of the suspects later left the house by the front door and went to the scout car. They returned to the house carrying something heavy between them."

"Probably weapons and explosives," said Kasper.

"*Ja.* Finally, the same four suspects leave the house for the last time by the front door and go directly into the forest on a southerly heading – towards Bodenmais. One of our platoons is on their trail now."

Kasper tossed the tablet onto the seat. "As I said, this von Scheller woman appears to be one of them." He sighed loudly. "Treason must run in the family."

"Sir?"

"Her grandfather's uncle was a ringleader in the plot to kill Hitler during the war. Major von Scheller was a suspect as well, but nothing was ever proved."

"Does Paula von Scheller have a record?" asked Michalke.

"None. Manfred checked with the *Bundeskriminalamt* and tapped the Social Services Ministry database. We have accessed her Facebook page and Linked-In profile. She lives in Regensburg and is a medical student. The 2009 Porsche with the Regensburg plates belongs to her and the VW is registered to her grandfather. That's it. If she's a terrorist or an Al-Qaeda agent, she's under deep cover."

"What about her grandfather?"

Kasper looked pained. "Von Scheller lied to me about the use of his house by the terrorists. He is a sick old man. My guess is that his granddaughter took advantage of his age and infirmities to make him harbor those swine. We shall soon find out the truth, one way or another!"

"Shall we place Fraulein von Scheller under arrest?" Michalke asked. "The Justice Minister has been granted special emergency powers under the Antiterrorist Act. We could get a warrant issued almost immediately. They may be harboring other terrorists."

Kasper fingered the Iron Cross on his jacket, then shook his head.

"You know how badly our hands are tied when it comes to interrogation these days. The moment that bitch is arrested, she'll scream for one of those liberal lawyers and never open her mouth again except to say, 'Fuck you, pig!' No, Baldur, this time we shall be more subtle. I suspect the traitorous slut will try to contact her comrades soon to tell them we've discovered the G-Wagen and that their safe house is compromised. We'll make a show of finishing our detective work and pulling out of here, but we'll leave a team to stake out the house. The Porsche is bugged and we can track Fraulein von Scheller's cell phone, so we'll be able to follow her wherever she goes. She may lead us to the terrorists. We shall only use the Federal Search and Arrest warrant if that bitch remains holed up in there for another twenty-four hours."

Sutton frowned at the Bavarian State Forestry survey map.

"It's hard, damned hard," he muttered. "Some of the targets I remember aren't even on here."

"How many have you been able to come up with?" asked von Scheller.

"Only five. An autobahn bridge north of Zweisel, a railway trestle over the Regen river near Viechtach, a radio station and Völksturm arsenal in Petersdorf, and the home of some Nazi bigwig outside a village called Lam. There was at least one other military camp and an airfield, but I just can't place them on this map!"

"They probably no longer exist," Paula said. "Well, Zweisel and Petersdorf are not far from Bodenmais. Which place do you think Roth would be most likely to attack?"

"Probably Petersdorf. It would take too much time and be too dangerous to plant explosives on those bridges. Roth likes human targets, not structures. He wants to kill Germans. The radio station and arsenal would attract him. The problem is that Roth may strike what we call 'targets of opportunity' – anything that tempts him."

"My God," said von Scheller. "Some schools and hospitals were taken over by the military during the war. He could hit those!"

"Then we must move quickly," Paula said. "We'll start with Petersdorf." She ran an appraising eye down Sutton's lean frame. "We'd better see if any of Opa's clothes fit you. You can't go out in your uniform. They would arrest you for sure if we were stopped by the police because they are looking for 'terrorists' in old American uniforms."

"'*We?*'" asked Sutton. "You mean you're coming with me?"

"How else do you think you'd accomplish this? Do you expect us to just say '*Auf Wiedersehen* and good luck, Arthur?'"

"Don't you realize the danger? Both of you are extremely lucky to have escaped this morning. Roth is a killer and it sounds like that Kasper guy is no better. And now he apparently suspects that you are involved with terrorists!"

Paula looked with determination at her grandfather. It was a long moment before the old Luftwaffe officer nodded his blessing. Paula swung back to Sutton, defiant. "Arthur, as my grandfather said earlier, we are now part of this incredible experience. I could not live with myself if I didn't help you. I accept the danger. Admit it, you need me!"

Sutton cleared his throat and nodded. "You're right. And I'm grateful."

He changed into a plain shirt, Loden jacket, and pair of flannel trousers provided by von Scheller. The German was a smaller man and the clothes fit Sutton snugly. Shoes were a problem – the one-legged Luftwaffe veteran had only single shoes for his left foot. Paula fretted about this, but finally agreed that Sutton's heavy paratroop boots were his only option. She frowned as he tucked the Colt .45 into his waistband.

"I hate guns," she said. "You have no need for that."

"I told you that I'm prepared to shoot Roth if that's what it takes to save my other men. Regardless of what has

207

happened, I'm still a serving officer in the US Army, and I have every right to carry a weapon."

Paula turned away and gathered up his discarded clothing. They hid Sutton's helmet, M43 uniform, and equipment in a trunk in the attic. Sutton fingered the blue Ranger patch on the sleeve of his khaki jacket. He took only his US Army identification and the Roosevelt campaign button.

At the last moment, he bent to retrieve Elaine's letter from the pocket of his uniform. He paused, closed his eyes, trying to recall Elaine's image as he had last seen her. Curiously, his memory could only conjure a featureless picture of a young woman with too bright lipstick in a yellow gingham dress.

She'd be in her late eighties ... if she's still alive. Older than grandma.

His knees nearly buckled under him. Aching sadness suffused every atom of his body.

"Arthur?" called Paula, waiting for him at the attic door.

Sutton's shaking hands shut the trunk's lid.

Like closing a coffin with my old life buried inside.

He stood erect and squared his shoulders before striding to the door.

After Paula and Sutton rejoined Von Scheller, the latter roused Sepp and sent him to the ruined cottage. Twenty minutes later, the old servant shuffled into the room rubbing his hands, face scarlet from cold and glasses fogged by the bedroom's warmth. He blinked at von Scheller over the rims.

"The police have gone, *Mein Herr,*" he reported. "Took the G-Wagen with them."

Paula buttoned her Barbour quilted jacket. She kissed her grandfather's forehead and squeezed his hand. As Sutton approached she stood aside.

Sutton awkwardly extended his hand. Von Scheller gripped it with surprising strength and drew the young American closer. The elderly man's eyes seemed to probe Sutton's soul, shining as if drawing strength from the young soldier.

"I shall pray for you," he said hoarsely.

Sutton and Paula exited the front door of the von Scheller house at 02:53 on Saturday, April 23, 2011. From the moment they became visible, their movements were recorded digitally by an infrared camera hidden in a blind 150 meters from the mansion's front door.

The blind was manned by a pair of KSK troopers. One soldier operated the camera while the other used night vision binoculars to watch the couple enter the silver Porsche. Both men wore modified helmet mounted SEM52/SL radios with throat mikes. The *unteroffizier* watching through the binoculars reported the suspects' movements from the time they appeared until the Porsche's taillights vanished down the driveway.

A little over two kilometers away, at a rest stop on the Lam-Brennes road, Kasper thanked the *unteroffizier* and leaned back in the seat of his command car.

"So, the *fraulein* has a young male companion," he said. "If I were a betting man, I would wager he is one of the terrorists."

"We don't know that for sure, Herr General," said the lieutenant. "He may be a boyfriend spending the weekend with her."

Kasper shook his head and smiled smugly. "You have much to learn, Manfred. Activate the homing device. As the English say when the fox is in sight, tallyho!"

20

After leaving Briny Breezes Caserra used his Blackberry to check return flights. He drove south to Fort Lauderdale airport and caught a red-eye via Atlanta to Washington National, arriving at 06:55. A text appeared as he landed: *"In office. See me when you get here. Miller."*

He took the metro from the airport one stop to Crystal City, rode the escalator to the station entrance and walked towards his building as quickly as his aching hip would allow. He flashed his ID card at the sleepy security guard in the lobby and swept past him to the elevator bank. At the end of the eighth floor corridor, he managed to reign in his impatience long enough to knock on the director's door.

"Come in."

Miller's bloodshot eyes were expectant.

"Okay, Eddie, let's hear it."

Cassera's meeting with Louise Jablonski tumbled out of him, an electrifying torrent of words that had Miller on the edge of his seat. When Cassera finished, the director shot questions at him, scribbling notes as Cassera elaborated on points of the interview.

Cassera removed the Sarnoff materials from his briefcase while Miller cleared his desk of everything but a stack of folders covered by a thick manila envelope. Miller tenderly handled the locket in its plastic evidence bag and promised to send the hair sample for DNA analysis. Together they went through Cassera's collection of papers and pictures, comparing the brittle old photos of Nicholas Sarnoff with the face of the cadaver in the Frankfurt mortuary. Forty minutes later Cassera sat back, waiting for Miller to read for the third time what they had dubbed the "tattoo letter."

Miller let the yellowed V-mail form drop from his fingers. He ran a hand over his thinning hair. Cassera had never seen his boss so grim.

"This is overwhelming, Eddie. The implications are staggering."

"I've been thinking about those implications all the way back from Florida," answered Cassera. "I mean, hell, if that autopsy report is valid, Private Sarnoff was alive yesterday!"

"You don't know the half of it." Miller took off his glasses and closed his eyes. When he opened them again they held a look of mingled awe and fear, as if the usually imperturbable government bureaucrat had seen a ghost.

"I really hoped you'd draw a blank in Florida. But you confirmed something that is going to have titanic implications if it's not handled right. Eddie, we've got the most important verifiable paranormal event ever. It could also turn out to be one of the greatest tragedies of all time if we don't act quickly!"

"What do you mean?" Cassera asked.

Miller took a large manila envelope from the stack on the corner of his desk. Cassera saw that the pile was composed of black War Department folders identical to Sarnoff's dossier from the old 293 File.

"The World War Two Special Missions records have been declassified." He pulled a sheaf of about fifty photocopied pages from the envelope. "The Military History Center sent this over. It's the official record of the Bandstand operation that Sarnoff was on when he went MIA."

Miller handed the report across the desk. Cassera glanced at the title page, then back at Miller as he continued speaking.

"Only a hundred and twenty-two men took part in Bandstand, so there's a lot of information relating to individuals in that report. The reference to Private Sarnoff starts on page eighteen. He was part of a six-man Rangers team dropped from an aircraft over Germany near the village of Kötzting in the Bäyerischer Wald – the Bavarian Forest. Their mission was to 'deceive and harass the enemy through sabotage, raids and assassinations.' Not one of those six men was ever accounted for after they parachuted out of that C-47."

"Until now."

"Until now," Miller agreed. "Eddie, after I read the Bandstand operation report, I decided to dig deeper into the circumstances involving the finding of Sarnoff's body. I was intrigued by the fact that it was found with a group of dead terrorists disguised as German special ops police. So I had a long chat with General Forbes who heads Army CID in Germany. He filled me in on the details."

The DPMO Director took a yellow legal pad from a desk drawer and reviewed his notes.

"There's been a rash of terrorist activity in the *Bäyerischer Wald* during the past thirty-six hours. Our CID is working with the Germans on this case because one of our bases was infiltrated and badly damaged by saboteurs last night."

"I saw an article about that in the *Post*," Cassera said.

"The evidence shows that two terrorist units were involved – a 24-man Islamic unit disguised as German special ops police, and a 6-man team dressed like World War II American paratroops. Forbes said investigators are baffled as to why the unit in antique US uniforms attacked and nearly wiped out the other group. The action took place at a former SS camp near the Czech border where the Muslim terrorists were staging for a massacre attack on a youth convention. That's where Sarnoff's body was found."

Cassera whistled. Miller grimaced and loosened his tie, then wiped his sweating face with a handkerchief.

"Here are some more facts," he said. "As you know, Sarnoff was killed by rounds fired from a modern MP5 submachine gun. The terrorists were equipped with such weapons and used them in the firefight at the old SS camp. A quantity of shell casings identified as World War II vintage American .45 caliber ammunition was collected from the scene. CID is still waiting for ballistics reports, but they're sure that several of the terrorists were killed by those .45 rounds and they think Sarnoff was killed by an MP5 used by a dead terrorist in civilian clothing.

"In addition to the Thompson submachine gun found with Sarnoff's body, a second M1A1 weapon manufactured in 1944 was discovered at the scene. After analyzing footprints found there and two of the other places attacked, the investigators confirmed that six men wearing American World War II Corcoran type jump boots were the perpetrators. Sarnoff's boots matched one set of those prints at each location."

Cassera's jaw hung slack, breath coming in gasps like a man who had climbed a long staircase. He started to say something, but Miller held up his hand.

"Wait, I haven't finished. The Bandstand operations report lists major targets assigned to each of the twenty teams on the mission. Sarnoff's unit - Fox team - planned to attack a panzer depot called Höhenbogen Kaserne, a Luftwaffe base at Mühldorf, and an SS Werewolf training camp."

Cassera knew what was coming. His body was as taut as a bow with an arrow nocked for release.

"The US Army post attacked on the night of April 21st occupies the former German panzer depot. The second place the saboteurs struck was a private flying club at the old Luftwaffe base." Miller heaved a deep sigh and pushed the notepad aside. He looked at Cassera with haunted eyes.

"I can see you've already guessed that Sarnoff's body was found at the same old SS camp that was on the Bandstand target list."

Cassera felt as if an icicle had replaced his spine. He suppressed a shudder.

"Bill," he said carefully, "you used the word 'paranormal'. Are you ..." Cassera paused, suddenly aware of the unreality of such a discussion within the sterile bureaucratic enclave of a Defense Department office in Crystal City, Virginia.

"… are you saying that this MIA Ranger team has popped up again, right on target, only sixty-odd years too late?"

Miller smiled humorlessly. "Real *Twilight Zone* stuff. Sounds like I should've been retired years ago, doesn't it?" Cassera shook his head. "And I was afraid you'd think *I* was a nut case!"

He looked at Miller with a penetrating gaze. "Give it to me straight. What do you think is going on?"

Miller removed his glasses again and rubbed the indentations left on the bridge of his nose.

"I'm going to answer that in a roundabout way, Eddie. Despite outward appearances, we both know that because DPMO deals with the dead and missing it is not your average government organization. I've been keeping my eyes and ears open for a long time, and I've come to the conclusion that there's a hell of a lot more to this old universe than we can even guess at right now. Most people – especially the Congress – don't realize that there's still a unit in Defense Research and Engineering that's as heavily involved in paranormal or psychic research as it was during the Cold War. And I've personally experienced some things that were so far out - yet authenticated - that even the White House took notice.

"The weirdest example took place in 'Nam back in 1971. I was hitching a ride on the lead Huey of a three-ship flight going upcountry from Phan Thiet. It was just before the monsoon season and the air held that tense feeling that you must remember. The only unusual thing going on that day was that all the commo people were bitching about heavy static on their radio gear, blaming it on sunspots or gook jamming. The sky was blue and nearly cloudless. You could see the rice paddies stretching all the way to the mountains.

"About twenty minutes out, the formation went into a weird-looking cloud bank – purplish and boiling vapor around the edges - that cut off visibility for less than a minute. Temperature dropped about 30 degrees as soon as we went in. When we came out the other side, there were only two aircraft. The flight leader figured the other Huey might have gone off course, so he radioed them. We circled for fifteen minutes while he tried to raise them. We then figured they might have gone down, because they carried main and back-up radios and would have answered us otherwise.

"The next thing that happened was McComas Air Base - which was only a couple of miles away – called to see if we needed assistance or an air strike on an enemy position. They'd been tracking us on their radar and saw our missing bird vanish off the screen. We were cruising at six thousand feet, so McComas would have noticed if it had fallen out of the sky. The McComas controllers thought the Huey might have taken a direct hit from a SAM and disintegrated. But that was impossible because we were flying such a tight formation that a missile would have blown us all out of the sky. And we would have seen or heard an explosion.

"Of course there was an investigation, but not a scrap of wreckage was ever found. I found out later that we'd been flying right over a column of the 25th Armored Division when that Huey went off the screen. Some of those guys testified that they saw three choppers go into the cloud and two come out. They were watching because a lot of people on the ground noticed that weird cloud.

"The closed door inquiry into this thing went on for months. Even had a White House aide sitting in as an observer. But nothing ever turned up, and those five crewmen joined the MIA list. You know, Eddie, I've always wondered if those guys are really dead or just caught in some other dimension that is still in the metaphysical realm - an area of science that we're not sophisticated enough to understand yet. This Bandstand case has some disturbing parallels."

"A time warp, you mean?"

Miller shrugged. "For want of a better term I guess you could call it that. But, yes, I'd say we've got compelling evidence that a missing World War Two GI named Sarnoff jumped out of a plane in 1945 and landed in 2011. And I think that five other guys landed with him. What makes me sick is that I believe those other poor bastards have no idea that they're not still in the middle of the Second World War. They're carrying out the objectives of Operation Bandstand at this very moment!"

Cassera had a sudden image of Louise Jablonski's worn face, remembered her words that were so like Miller's: *"All these years, I never felt my Nicky was really dead."* The tragedy overwhelmed him for a moment. He looked away, struggling for control, then turned back to Miller.

"You're saying that those so-called terrorists over there are actually World War Two Rangers blowing things up and shooting people?"

Miller's face hardened. "It sure looks that way. Although how long those poor bastards are going to last before they end up like Sarnoff is anybody's guess. The Krauts think they're modern terrorists and are going after them tooth and nail!"

"But certainly if this is true, those Bandstand guys can't go on thinking this is 1945! I mean, they've got to realize something pretty weird has happened to them and surrender to the authorities!"

Miller's expression remained grave.

"I hope so, Eddie, I really hope so." He slid the stack of 293 Files across the desk. "These are the files of the five other Rangers on Sarnoff's team, along with their finger-prints. A lieutenant, a sergeant, and three privates. Five young soldiers who grew up during the Great Depression. Our parents' generation. What a fucking tragedy if they survived World War Two by a metaphysical fluke only to be killed like Sarnoff."

"What are we going to do?"

Miller slapped the desk in frustration.

"I've got a raging headache trying to decide how to deal with this! I was just dictating a report on our investiga-tion when you showed up. But damn it, there's just no way to make a case like this sound plausible. Think about it – the red-taped Defense Department weenies who'd read the report as it's passed up the chain of command over a period of weeks would pigeonhole it along with the Bermuda Triangle and the UFOs in Operation Blue Book. This mat-ter is so incredibly sensitive that there's no way I'm gonna let those bureaucratic buffoons fuck up what could be a scientific breakthrough into the paranormal. No – we're going to approach this in an unorthodox way. And that means using the old rubber stamp that says Secret."

"You mean CIA?"

Miller grimaced. "No, I mean DIA, the Defense Intelligence Agency. They're the ones who are really behind DoD's paranormal research. I have enough faith in their abilities to think that they are the only government agency that could handle this right."

"What will you tell them?"

"The truth. Present 'em with the evidence and let them reach their own conclusions. I'm friendly with the senior brass at DIA because I allowed some of their guys to use our MIA search teams as cover to infiltrate Cambodia and North Korea. They'll know that I wouldn't bother them with this incredible case unless I believed it was worth checking into. I'm going to work the phones this morning and call in some favors even if it's a Saturday."

Cassera shook his head. "Those bureaucratic wheels turn too slowly, Bill, even if you light a fire under your DIA buddies. It may be too late for the Bandstand guys if something isn't done immediately!"

"My thoughts exactly." Miller smiled ruefully and looked at his wall clock. "Eddie, I've cut some travel orders for you. There's an Air Mobility Command C-40 leaving from Andrews for Ramstein this evening. You've got a seat aboard it."

"Germany?" Cassera brightened. "You bet!"

"I had to come up with a cover story to get you over there. So when you arrive, go to the Landstühl Mortuary and have Samoff's body checked again from toenails to tonsils. Go through his personal effects with a fine-tooth comb. We've got to be one hundred percent correct on everything if we're going to stick our necks out. Also make sure they do a dental chart on the cadaver. On your way over you should familiarize yourself with those other files and the Bandstand operation report."

"And after that?"

"Hang loose until we can pull the right strings to ensure that the surviving Bandstand guys are captured instead of killed. It's going to be crucial to have someone on the spot who's an expert on the case when we bring them in. And Eddie."

"Yeah?"

"I'm assigning a Secret classification. This is just between us for now, okay?

When Cassera nodded, Miller smiled tightly.

"Now," he said briskly, "Go home and catch some sleep before you head out to Andrews."

21

"Cold?"

Sutton nodded, betrayed by his chattering teeth. He hugged von Scheller's thin jacket to his body.

"Let's go back to the car," Paula suggested. "I'll turn on the heater and warm our blood."

Reluctantly, Sutton agreed. An hour's exposure to the cold night was his limit, even though he hated to admit it. And the fruitless wait had lowered his sprits.

Petersdorf was a medium-sized village on Bundesstrasse 85, the main artery from Passau to Cham. Sutton and Paula had left the Porsche in a parking lot and wandered the empty streets. Knowing that their presence so late at night would be suspicious, they slipped into alleys when an occasional car passed. Twice they saw police cruisers.

There was no sign of the World War II-era radio tower, and the site where Sutton thought the *Völksturm* arsenal had been was now a gasoline station. They stood in a doorway across the street from it anyway, watching for Roth and the other Rangers while Paula snuggled close to Sutton for warmth.

"I don't think they'll come here," Sutton said as he slumped into the Porsche's passenger seat. "Even if they'd planned to, my guys would've been spooked by the bright lights and that highway over there."

"We shouldn't give up on them so soon. We'll park by the service station and give it another half hour. That way we'll be able to keep warm while we wait."

She parked the car across the street and turned to Sutton, feeling his tension as his eyes roved over the streets and buildings around them.

"You can relax a bit," she told him gently. "The war is over, you know."

"Yeah, I guess it's hard to break the habit. After being in combat for so long I can't stop thinking I'm behind enemy lines."

He grinned at her, a boyish smile that unexpectedly squeezed her heart.

"This seems like a crazy dream. Like Dorothy had in *The Wizard of Oz*." His voice grew dreamy. "That was such a swell movie. Judy Garland's a great kid. One of my favorite stars, along with Clark Gable and Humphrey Bogart."

"They're dead."

"*What?* "

"Garland and Gable and Bogart. They've all been dead for many years."

Sutton fell silent. Paula heard him choke back a sob. She regretted her comment about the movie stars as she saw the grief that had replaced his smile.

"Forgive me, Arthur. I didn't mean to upset you."

He turned away, eyes blinking as a single tear rolled down his cheek. "I guess ... I guess it's going to take me a while to realize how much things must have changed in 66 years. I ... I was just thinking about my folks back in Missouri. It must have nearly killed them when I didn't come home. They're long gone now."

She reached for his hand, feeling a wave of compassion. "I understand how you must be feeling," she whispered.

"I had no parents," he mused. "They were killed by a tornado in 1926. So was my brother. I was six years old. My grandparents raised me after that. They were getting pretty feeble last time I saw them."

"I'm sorry." Paula's words caught in her throat.

She wanted to hold him, ease the shock and sadness, the terrible dislocation. But her intuition told her Sutton wasn't ready for consolation. He was proud, an old-fashioned man who couldn't expose his churning emotions because he thought doing so was a sign of weakness.

The silence inside the car became oppressive. Paula plugged her iPhone into a jack in the center console and switched on the Bose surround sound system. The music distracted Sutton. He cocked his head to listen.

"You like it?" Paula asked.

Sutton shrugged. "Don't know if I do. What is it?'

"An American singer called Lady Gaga."

"Oh. Well, I guess Harry James and Artie Shaw are more my style. I could listen to them for hours. Say, do you like Benny Goodman?"

"I'm afraid I don't know him."

"He's a clarinet player. The greatest!" His smile was back. "When I was a senior in high school, our Glee Club took a train trip to Chicago to see Benny Goodman play. January of '38, it was. There were dozens of kids dancing in the aisles. Best swing in the land!"

Paula smiled back at him. "They still dance in the aisles. I suppose young people really haven't changed that much." An idea occurred to her. She took out her iPad, touched the YouTube app, searched for Benny Goodman, and chose a performance of "Sing, Sing, Sing (with a Swing)" from the 1937 film *Hollywood Hotel*.

Sutton's jaw fell open in amazement then slowly closed.

"Ronald Reagan was in that film too," she said mischievously. "He became the US president in the 1980s. Many Americans think he was one of your greatest leaders."

Sutton shook his head and grinned.

"Now I *know* you're joshing me. Next thing you'll be telling me that Mickey Mouse was his vice president."

Paula showed him how to search for other music from his era, her soft fingers guiding his clumsy ones on the tablet's screen. They reverently watched Judy Garland sing "Over the Rainbow." Sutton turned away again and looked at his dim reflection in the car's window. He cleared his throat noisily. Paula gripped his wrist.

"Time's up, Arthur. We'd better get on to the next target."

Sutton sat straighter, again the tough Ranger officer.

"Okay. That will be the highway bridge north of Zweisel."

The engine fired and the Porsche roared up the cobbled street and entered the on-ramp of Federal Highway 85. Within sixty seconds, Paula had the car up to 160 kilometers per hour.

Half a minute later a large black Mercedes pulled out of a churchyard on the outskirts of Petersdorf. The CLS 550 stopped to pick up a chilled KSK *gefreiter* who had kept surveillance on Paula's Porsche from a doorway. The Mercedes left Petersdorf and sped southeast on Bundesstrasse 85, following an electronic dot on its dash-mounted GPS screen.

"You're sure they didn't make contact with anyone?" Kasper said.

The shivering young private nodded. "I am positive, *Herr General*. They appeared to be waiting for something or someone."

"Sir," the *leutnant* called, keeping his eyes on the screen, "they're heading straight for the roadblock outside Regen. Shall we arrest them?"

"No. Alert all roadblock units to let them through. I think the rats will lead us to their nest."

At the junction of Bundesstrasse 85 and Federal Highway 11, Paula's Porsche burst upon the police roadblock. She rapidly decelerated down a funnel of flashing lights leading to the barrier.

"*Scheisse!*" she cursed. "I should have taken another route!"

"What should we do?" Sutton eyed the green and white police vans and signs reading *Halt - Besichtigung von Polizie!*

"Play it by ear," Paula answered glumly. "They always ask to see identity papers. But once they get a look at your antique military ID and find your gun, it's going to be good-bye freedom, hello police station!"

She was wrong. A squad of courteous Bavarian policemen ran the Porsche's license plates on a tablet database, asked a few perfunctory questions, and opened the barrier for them. Sutton expelled his breath in a shuddering sigh of relief. The proximity of German policemen in uniforms not unlike those of the Third Reich had unnerved him. It had taken strong willpower not to reach for his pistol.

"That was a real stroke of luck!" Paula breathed as she sped away. "Maybe those police were just looking for stolen cars instead of terrorists."

"Weren't those Kasper's men?" asked Sutton.

"No. The KSK are German Army. Real stormtrooper types. Those were Bavarian police"

She looked in the rearview mirror and slowed to a more sedate 70 kilometers per hour. "You must get rid of your gun, Arthur. Carrying a concealed weapon is a very serious offense at any time, and Kasper's men may shoot you if they find you with it."

"How would I stop Roth?"

"You'll have to find another way if he disobeys your orders."

"Look, you don't know him. I need–"

"I do know him!" she said fiercely. "I've seen what he is capable of. But you are risking my life as well as yours if you keep it!"

Sutton bit back a retort, then nodded in resignation.

They exited the autobahn and drove along a country lane until they found a mill pond. Sutton left the car and walked to the water's edge. As his fingers curled around the .45's familiar fretted grip, he remembered how it had saved his life in Normandy when his submachine gun had jammed during a German counterattack. Later, he'd used the weapon's barrel to twist a tourniquet around the stump of a screaming Ranger's leg after the man's foot was severed by a mine.

Sutton swung back his arm and threw the pistol and its spare magazine into the middle of the dark pond. He plodded back to the car feeling naked and vulnerable — a soldier without his weapon, a man lost in an alien world.

Twelve minutes later they came to Zweisel. The concrete bridge traversed by Bundestrasse 11 was still there, unchanged since 1945. Another police unit blocked traffic on it. Once more Paula and Sutton prepared for the worst, but were again waved on after a cursory check. They continued north for another eight kilometers before pulling into a rest area outside the border village of Bayerischer Eisenstein. Sutton voiced both their thoughts.

"Roth and my guys wouldn't go anywhere near that bridge with those police vehicles on it."

Paula slumped over the steering wheel. She stifled a yawn.

"Do you think it's worth going to those other places tonight?" she said. "What were they now? Sorry, I'm so sleepy I can't remember the names."

"It doesn't matter. Those other potential targets were too far from Bodenmais for Roth to hit them before dawn."

Sutton felt his headache returning. The Porsche's digital clock said 4:39 A.M. He was tired, hungry, and depressed. He touched the bruised flesh on the back of his head, wincing. Paula noticed.

"Is your head bothering you?"

"Yeah." His eyelids drooped shut and he struggled to open them.

"That's it then." Paula put the car in gear and swung back onto the highway.

"Where we going?" Sutton mumbled.

"We are both badly in need of rest. We'll start looking for your men again in the morning. Maybe you'll come up with some other possibilities when your mind is fresher."

Sutton blearily gazed at the black pine forests streaming past at 145 kilometers an hour.

"We going back to your grandfather's house?"

"No. It's not too far from here but we really can't risk it. The safest place will be my flat in Regensburg."

"Far?"

Paula made a face. "About a hundred kilometers. I can do it in forty minutes. Why don't you try to get some sleep? I'll wake you when we arrive."

She showed him how to recline the seat. Sutton drifted off with an image of Roth's bitter, mocking face floating away down a dark tunnel.

"Where are you, you son of a bitch?" he muttered before lapsing into snores.

At that moment, Hugo Roth was a mile and a half away, squatting on a hillside overlooking a winding *Nebenstrasse* or secondary road between Zwiesel and Frauenau. A railway ran beside the road, the same tracks the Rangers had used to escape from Bodenmais, bypassing police roadblocks and patrols.

Roth used his binoculars to study a fuel storage complex at the end of a short rail spur. A pair of large steel storage tanks stood in a wire mesh enclosure. On the tracks outside the fence sat three railway tank cars marked with the name of the ARAL gasoline brand.

"Completely unguarded!" Roth said. "Not even barbed wire on the fence. Easy pickings, yes?"

There was no acknowledgment from the other men, not even a grunt. Roth turned. "You hear me?"

The three privates were spectral shapes in the pre-dawn gloom. Holcombe sat with head bowed, hugging his knees. Loomis hunkered beside him while Kemp squatted under his poncho.

"I hear you, Sarge," Kemp answered, breath misting in the frigid air.

The men's apathy triggered Roth's temper. They had traveled more than five miles since the attack on the Bodenmais Gestapo station – a punishing hike for men who had already made a six-mile forced march through unfamiliar country. Although Roth was just as exhausted as the others, he knew that his determination would keep him going. The Americans were weaklings, but he realized that their physical endurance was worn to the breaking point. And dawn was getting close.

"Kemp, you come with me." Roth unbuckled his harness and set it aside with his submachine gun.

"Oh shit," Kemp spat. "What the fuck are you gonna do?"

"I have explosives left. You watch my back while I place them. That will be all for tonight. When we finish, we find a place to rest. Okay?"

"You're the boss," Kemp said sullenly.

They stumbled down the hillside and followed the railroad spur. Roth warily approached the ARAL tank cars, hissing at the shambling Kemp whose weary legs threatened to collapse under him. Roth placed Kemp in the shadow of the last tanker and crept towards the storage compound's gate. He was sure that the place was unguarded, but kept his silenced pistol ready.

The gate was secured by a metal bar that had been recently oiled. It made only a tiny squeak when Roth lifted it. He had three charges of plastic explosive left. Each had a set of twenty-minute and one-hour acid-pencil detonators. Roth chose the latter to give them time to get clear before the charges blew.

He stuck explosives on each storage tank. As he worked, he wondered why the Bandstand planners hadn't included such juicy targets on their operations list. If these tanks were full, they contained enough fuel to run a panzer division for a thousand kilometers or supply a Luftwaffe fighter wing for weeks. And the facility wasn't even camouflaged against Allied photo reconnaissance planes or bombers! Those college boys in US Army Intelligence were really a bunch of fools!

Roth's fatigue allowed doubts to enter chinks in the armor of his resolve. This part of Germany seemed nothing like the reports he had read of a disintegrating Third Reich. There were no refugee hordes, no signs of war damage. Unlike the Britain he had left two days earlier, there was no blackout. The Germans seemed to have an abundance of electrical power and appeared unconcerned about attracting the British bombers that swarmed over Germany each night. Come to think about it, he had not heard the omnipresent drone of heavy bombers at any time since his landing. Of course, this was an isolated part of Bavaria, and cloud cover had been unremitting, but the Allied air forces supposedly ruled the Fatherland's skies. And where was the distant artillery thunder of the approaching Red Army? Shaking off the disturbing thoughts, he concentrated on his work.

He fixed the final explosive charge against the curved belly of the middle tank car. Roth pressed the detonator plunger, noted the time, then roused Kemp. The private was noticeably lighter on his feet as they moved back up the hill.

"Now," Roth said as Holcombe and Loomis stood up. "We'll find a place to hide."

The *Bundesamt für Verfassungsschutz (BfV)* forensics van arrived at the mill pond minutes after Kasper's Mercedes. Its team efficiently swept the ground, placing little flags on the footprints and snapping photos. Kasper leaned over and shone a flashlight on a clear impression of Sutton's paratroop boot.

"No doubt about it," said the BfV detective in charge of the forensics team. "Perfect matches with the prints at all the other sites."

"Just as I thought," Kasper said. "Fraulein von Scheller is one of them. She will pay the same price for her treason."

22

The radio speaker crackled inside the warm cocoon of the Mercedes.

"They've entered an apartment house," reported the surveillance team leader. "The Porsche's parked outside."

"Give me the address," Kasper snapped.

"Einen Augenblick, bitte."

The *unteroffizier's* voice returned a moment later.

"Hohenzollernplatz 7 is the address of the apartment house, Herr General."

Kasper turned quizzically to his aide. The lieutenant nodded.

"That's it. Apartment 3b, Hohenzollernplatz 7, 3000 Regensburg 41, Mein Herr."

Kasper swore an old Bavarian curse concerning gypsies and bestiality. The speaker squawked a question.

"Maintain position until further orders," the lieutenant answered.

There was a long stretch of silence while Kasper pondered his quarry's behavior, stroking his chin to speed the mental processes. The young driver – a civilian employee of Kasper's DSH security company who wore a uniform almost identical to the KSK troopers - hummed a few bars of Rihanna's new song "S & M." He terminated the performance as he caught Hanno in the rearview mirror glaring at him. Kasper squinted at his GMT-Master Rolex. It told him the time was eight minutes past six on a cold Saturday morning.

"So," he said, "Fraulein von Scheller and her terrorist boyfriend must have gone to rendezvous points near Bodenmais to meet their comrades. The swine didn't show, and now the bitch has decided to—"

The Mercedes' ringing telephone interrupted. The lieutenant answered and quickly handed the handset to Kasper.

Kasper's face twisted as he listened. He asked several questions before issuing a string of orders. When the conversation ended, he pounded the receiver on the leather seat.

"They've struck again!" he yelled. "Blew up a fuel storage site near Frauenau. There'll be no rest for any of us until those filthy swine are liquidated!"

His chest heaved and nostrils flared as he planned his strategy. After a few minutes, he nodded emphatically. "Manfred, what's the closest Luftwaffe base to Regensburg?"

Manfred had been appointed Kasper's aide for more than his Aryan looks. His mind was like a computer. "That would be Flughafen Walhalla, Herr Oberst. Joint civil and military use. The Luftwaffe's Jagdgeschwader 73 is based there."

Sometimes Kasper wondered if Manfred wasn't a little too bright for his own good. There were times when the young *leutnant's* quick answers bordered on the impertinent. But Kasper had more important things to think about than a possibly insubordinate aide.

"How far is Walhalla?" he asked, relishing the way his lips curled to form the name of the paradise for Nordic warriors.

"18 kilometers north on Bundesstrasse 16."

"Good. Proceed there now and have a helicopter waiting for me. I must go to the *Bäyerischer Wald* immediately. You will then return here with the car and take command of the surveillance team. Follow the von Scheller whore and report to me every hour."

Roth led Fox team's survivors on a southeasterly course through the primeval forests of fir and spruce that covered the Bavarian mountains and lapped far across the Czech border into Bohemia. Their trek was hard and the rest stops became more frequent as the men's last reserves of energy were burned by the steeply scarped slopes and numbing cold.

Roth checked his luminous watch frequently. He halted the team nearly an hour after setting the charges on the fuel tanks. The privates sprawled on the wet pine needles under the trees. All three instantly dozed. Roth took out his compass and aligned it in the direction of the ARAL fuel storage complex. He cursed the tall conifers that limited visibility.

The explosions were muted by the trees and distance — three thumps that could have been missed if he wasn't listening for them. The charcoal clouds over the rail spur turned crimson as if the sun were rising in the west that day. Roth felt a wave of satisfaction that dispelled his fatigue.

The other Rangers didn't stir.

Roth had no set destination or plan. The team had used its explosives but still had plenty of ammunition and K-rations. Rangers were experts at escape and evasion, and Fox team could probably elude the enemy and link up with partisans. But he was unwilling to seek haven in Czechoslovakia. The war would be over soon and this mission was probably his last opportunity to legally kill Germans.

His primary concern was to get as deeply into the wilderness as possible before dawn broke. He kicked the men awake and got them moving again. Forty minutes later, Private Holcombe collapsed from exhaustion.

They were at the base of one of the foothills crowding the western face of Grosser Rachel, a mountain whose eastern slopes overlooked the Bohemian forest in the Czech republic. Roth wanted to push on, but Kemp and Loomis stubbornly wrapped themselves in their ponchos and crawled beneath a ledge, dragging Holcombe with them.

Roth's need for rest was as great as the others'. Ever cautious, he climbed to a rocky outcropping on the crest of the hill. Wedging his body between two boulders, he listened to the wind keen overhead while rain pattered on his helmet.

He dozed fitfully. When he awoke, the rain had ended and watery sunlight leaked through cracks in the clouds. He hobbled out, flexing his stiff muscles, and swept the landscape with his eyes. To the east was the towering mass of Grosser Rachel; on the north and west were forested hills with small fields and houses tucked into their folds. His gaze shifted north, catching the glimmer of water. He took out his binoculars for a closer look.

Less than a mile away was a glacial lake, scarcely bigger than a pond, one of many in the area probably stocked with fish for weekend anglers. A dirt track paralleled its left bank and twisted uphill to a cabin set in a clearing hewn from the forest. The log house was shuttered.

Roth watched the cabin and its surroundings for twenty minutes before slipping down the hill to the sleeping privates. Kemp awakened instantly, but Roth had to kick and threaten the other two men to get them on their feet. They stood around, eyes resentful in stubbled faces on which the camouflage paint remained in patches.

"We can't stay out here," Roth told them. "We've got to get under cover for the day. There's a cabin over there that looks deserted, but we need to scout it."

He flushed in anger as the men's apathetic expressions didn't change. "Pull yourselves together! I'm not going to keep wet nursing you sorry excuses for soldiers much longer!"

Roth's drill instructor snarl had little effect. The men were still too numbed with tiredness and cold to do more than watch the track leading to the cabin while the sergeant reconnoitered it.

The cabin was old, probably constructed for one of the King's *Jägers* or foresters when the *Bäyerischer Wald* was a royal hunting preserve. Solidly built of pine logs, it could have been an American pioneer house except for the ubiquitous Bavarian crucifix nailed above the door. Roth shattered a windowpane, unlatched and raised the window, then wriggled through it.

The interior was as he expected – fireplace, small kitchen, living room, and bedroom with a pair of bunks. A ladder led to a sleeping loft. The cabin appeared to have been unused for months. Mice skittered away from him and cobwebs flourished.

Roth unlocked the door, stepped outside, and sniffed the fresh mountain air. He made an "all clear" hand signal to the watching men. They joined him, spirits brighter after they inspected the cabin.

"Jesus, a real bed," Loomis cried, falling onto one of the dusty bunks. "Just what the doctor ordered."

"Hey, and there's canned food in here," Holcombe called from the kitchen. "No more K-rations for a while!"

"Don't get too comfortable," Roth said. "Tonight we move out again."

"Yeah." Kemp glared at him. "Across the border into Czechoslovakia. With or without you, Roth."

"He's right," said Loomis. "Our mission is finished. We're going home."

Roth turned away and began field stripping his submachine gun on the dining table.

Sutton awoke with a start, disoriented by the unfamiliar surroundings. He sat up, surveying the small living-cum-dining room with a kitchenette tucked into one corner. Daylight filtered through floor-length curtains drawn across a sliding glass door, illuminating bookshelves, paintings, and the sofa on which he lay covered by an eiderdown. His eyes caught a decorative wall calendar, focusing on the month and year at the top. *April 2011.*

He lay down, careful of the sore spot on the back of his head. *So it wasn't a dream! Jesus, just wait 'til I get back home and tell Elaine about this! Wow, she'll really flip when—*

Forget it, he reminded himself savagely. *Elaine was 89 years old now. 89 . . . if she was still alive. . . . Which meant that he would be 91 next month!*

In irrational alarm he bolted upright, felt his face for wrinkles, combed fingers through his hair in fear that the terrible time change might have aged him overnight into an old man, like Major von Scheller.

He padded across the carpet to the bathroom Paula had shown him after their arrival at her apartment. He fumbled for the light switch and thrust his face close to the mirror over the basin. The image reassured him, reflecting the familiar, clean-cut features of his twenty-four-year-old self.

He shaved and showered, movements mechanical while he thought about why and how Fox team had been projected 66 years into the future. He remembered jumping from the troop transport, the wrenching vortex like being sucked into a tornado. Those strange blue flames around the aircraft before he jumped. Textbook landing, some dizziness and disorientation, but nothing climactic, nothing to indicate the moment when he and his men had spanned the chasm of seven decades.

After toweling himself dry and dressing, he peeked into the small bedroom. Paula slept peacefully, her unbound hair fanning over the pillow. He studied her calm, fine-boned face. *Gutsy babe. Not a bad looker, either.*

He roamed the living room. Paula's eclectic tastes were evident. Bright abstract paintings confronted a nineteenth-century landscape of the Bavarian Alps. The coffee table held unfamiliar magazines – the German edition of *Cosmopolitan, Stern* and *The Economist* in English. A bookshelf sat beneath a flat rectangular object with a glassy face and the word *Sony* on it.

On the bookshelf were novels in German and English by unfamiliar authors like Christa Wolf and Stephen King, old friends such as Hemingway and Kafka, and medical texts. One shelf held a few volumes of poetry – Rilke, Dickinson, Whitman. He pulled out *Leaves of Grass*. Sutton had carried a dog-eared copy of the work with him throughout his military service but left it behind with other personal effects before embarking on the Bandstand operation. He opened the book to "On the Beach Alone" and read the last four lines:

All identities that have existed or may exist on this globe,
or any globe,
All lives and deaths, all of the past, present, future,
This vast similitude spans them, and always has spann'd,
And shall forever span them and compactly hold and enclose them.

One sideboard held a few framed photographs. A teen-age Paula with a middle-aged couple who must have been her parents and a scowling, bearded young man. A picture of her grandfather with a sweet-faced woman of his generation, obviously taken decades earlier. Another, more recent, of Hans-Ulrich von Scheller alone in his wheelchair with his dog Loki on his lap. Paula at a sidewalk cafe gazing coquettishly at the camera. The silhouette of the photographer was visible, and Sutton felt a twinge of jealousy as he wondered who the man was.

One frame lay face down, back gaping. He turned it over. The frame was empty, glass cracked. He replaced it as it was, wondering.

He was ravenous. He poked around in the kitchenette, opening cupboards and investigating a small refrigerator overlooked at first because it was unlike those he knew back home. He wolfed down a sandwich of rye bread, cheese, and sausage, followed by a liter of milk. He found some apples and munched one as he pulled aside the curtain over the glass door and went out onto the balcony.

Below was a square paved with bricks in a herringbone pattern, surrounded on three sides by modern buildings. Paula had told him that she lived south of the medieval city center, near the university.

So this was modern Regensburg. He had seen photographs of the city during his intelligence briefings. Allied bombers had struck Regensburg while attacking a Messerschmitt aircraft factory and an oil refinery, reducing parts of it to rubble. *And now look at it!* Sutton was struck by the obvious prosperity, contrasting so sharply with the austerity of the America he had known as it emerged from the Great Depression. Sleek automobiles jammed the streets. Pedestrians window shopped. Mothers pushed red-cheeked babies in strollers. A white-hatted traffic warden scribbled a ticket for a time-expired BMW.

A fresh wave of sadness washed over him. Where had he been for 66 years? Paula had said *nowhere* . . . but his years had vanished while his contemporaries were getting married, raising families, building careers. He had missed entire generations. Now he was adrift in a frightening new world in which his country was fighting other wars in places he had barely heard of, a world where Nazis still lurked, and America's old enemies Germany and Japan were economic powers producing more cars and other manufactured goods than the United States.

The panic he'd felt earlier came upon him again, with more force this time. Sutton had to grip the balcony's railing to control his trembling.

He heard Paula's footsteps behind him. She came onto the balcony wearing a silk bathrobe and pink slippers.

"Good morning," she said, stretching her arms. "Checking out Regensburg?"

He shook his head, no longer able to conceal his anguish. "I don't think I can deal with this, Paula," he said bitterly. "My whole world is gone. Everything! My friends are all old or dead now. They've all gone ahead with their lives and left me behind. I feel like a sideshow freak!"

"But you're the lucky one! You're still young and healthy and handsome while they've grown old and fat and bald."

"I'm 90 years old. A 90-year-old freak!"

"You're not. It's going to be all right, Arthur. Trust me, just trust me."

She led him like a child into the living room. He sat on the sofa, burying his face in his hands, fighting unmanly tears.

"You know what the worst part of it is?" he rasped. "I'm sitting here worrying about this, while my men are out there thinking it's still World War Two, risking their lives for a country that doesn't even know they still exist. How the hell am I going to save them?"

Sutton's shoulders shook as sorrow and frustration finally overwhelmed him. He felt Paula sit next to him, then she was hugging him, her head on his shoulder. Her body felt warm and soft against his, and for some reason that made the tears come harder. She drew away from him.

"Sorry," she said softly.

"No," he said. "It felt good. Better than I've felt in a long time."

He looked at her. There was an awkward silence until she smiled affectionately at him. Suddenly they were kissing. Sutton didn't know how, or who'd started it, just that he didn't want it to stop.

Paula's kisses were different from Elaine's — less lip sticky, more aggressive. Her desire seemed to match his hunger. His hand crept down, finding a smooth thigh beneath the folds of her robe and nightgown.

He couldn't believe it, but he was the one who had to put a stop to it. If they didn't get going soon, Roth would lead the men - his men - to their deaths.

Heart pounding, he pulled away. "We must—"

She touched his lips with her fingertips, stilling him.

"I understand." She stood, smoothing her robe. "We need to get back to looking for your men."

He nodded. "I can't relax until I've found them."

He looked up at her. Her hair was messy from sleep, something a girl like Elaine would have never let him see, but he thought she looked beautiful. He stood and, impulsively, leaned in for another kiss.

She smiled when he pulled away again. "I've always preferred older men," she teased. "You're not bad for a 90-year-old!"

Sutton couldn't help smiling.

"Hey, bet you can't dance the Lindy Hop like this old fart."

"I can learn."

She switched on the wall-mounted flat screen Sony television, then went to dress. Sutton watched with regret as she disappeared into the bedroom. He hoped he'd have the chance to see her in her robe again.

And bare-assed without it.

He turned to the TV, soon entranced by the color images. Television was not unknown to him. Like most Americans of his day, he had heard and read of it as early as the mid-1930s, but had never actually seen a TV broadcast before. A biopic of Shirley Temple was being aired, showing the actress being sworn in at a 1989 White House ceremony as US ambassador to Czechoslovakia and being honored by President Obama as a spokesperson for Breast Cancer awareness. The scene suddenly cut to a clip from the 1934 film *Bright Eyes*, showing the future ambassador as a child dancing and singing "Good Ship Lollipop."

Sutton sat down heavily.

Paula came back into the living room, brushing her hair. She wore jeans and a black sweater that accentuated her slim figure and blonde hair.

"So what do you think of television?" she asked.

Sutton shook his head in wonder. "Shirley Temple was an ambassador and a Negro is president. Who would've believed it!"

A news bulletin broke into the program: "Terrorists struck again in the *Bäyerischer Wald* early this morning," the grim-faced anchorman said, "destroying an ARAL fuel storage complex worth an estimated 1.5 million Euros. Now we go to Jutta Hofnagel, reporting live from the scene."

The camera cut to a bespectacled woman holding a microphone. In the background, firemen hosed down the gutted shells of fuel storage tanks.

"Targets of opportunity," Sutton said hollowly.

"I'll get the car keys," said Paula. "Time is running out."

23

The US Air Mobility Command C-40 touched its tires to the north runway of Ramstein Air Base at 09:04 hours on Saturday, April 23rd. The eight-hour transatlantic flight from Andrews Air Force Base outside of Washington DC had been uneventful. The transport carried twenty aluminum coffins and 100 body bags (officially called "Human Remains Pouches" or HFPs) to replenish the storeroom at the Landstühl Regional Medical Center. The aircraft also carried a civilian named Edward G. Cassera.

Cassera disembarked onto the runway carrying his briefcase and a flight bag. He trudged through the drizzle towards a door marked Arrivals - All United States Military Personnel. An umbrella-shielded figure detached from the doorway.

"Mr. Cassera?"

"Yeah?"

The umbrella tilted to reveal a woman's face with short brown hair and glasses. Raindrops marred the lenses.

She held up a laminated card bearing her photo and the US Defense Intelligence Agency logo.

"Debbie Lueckenhoff, DIA."

So, Eddie thought, *Miller managed to pull some official strings after all.* He introduced himself and the DIA agent held the umbrella over them as they continued toward Arrivals.

"Okay, Cassera," she said. "Our station got a flash signal telling us to meet you. I'm your liaison officer, aide, or whatever."

"Have they told you why I'm here?"

"Not really. All I know is you're working on some hush-hush project involving a body belonging to DPMO that my bosses back in Washington are taking a big interest in. 'Ours is not to reason why,' as the saying goes, but I can sure help you cut the red tape and shovel the bullshit over here."

"That's great, 'cause there sure might be some shit to shovel."

Debbie held out an arm to restrain him before entering the terminal.

"Just a second. I've gotta warn you that we'll have a German detective from the *Bundesamt für Verfassungsschutz* – the Federal Office for the Protection of the Constitution, their version of the FBI - working with us. He's waiting in the car. My boss said the corpse in RMC Mortuary is connected to that terrorist activity in the Bavarian Forest, and by law, that's BfV's responsibility. Really, the BfV is being very generous about our participation in this business because a lot of German bigwigs are opposed to what they consider American interference in their internal affairs. This detective is a good guy. I've worked with him before."

She strode along in front of him as they entered the Arrivals hall, flashing her ID at the sleepy USAF warrant officers behind the customs and immigration counters. She nodded, they nodded back, and Cassera followed her through the barriers and down a corridor to the exit. As he did so, his Blackberry connected with the Ramstein AB WiFi and a text message appeared from Miller: *"DNA perfect match. Got you some help. Good luck."*

A blue Audi S5 slid up to the sidewalk as they stepped outside. A muscular man in his late twenties emerged from the driver's door and approached Cassera with a warm smile and extended hand.

"Christoph Veditz," he said in flawless English. He grinned. "I'm sure Debbie has told you who I am and why I'm here."

Cassera shook hands and introduced himself while appraising Veditz. The German didn't look like a cop – spiked short black hair, Tommy Bahama shirt, leather bomber jacket over frayed jeans. His handshake was strong.

"So, Herr Cassera," he said after locking Cassera's luggage in the trunk. "I place myself under your command. Where do you wish to go?"

"The US Army Regional Medical Center."

On the short drive to Landstuhl, Veditz updated them on the search for the terrorist gang that continued its attacks in eastern Bavaria. "We have dog teams hunting them but they've lost the scent several times. Whoever the terrorists are they are very good – professionally trained in escape and evasion I would say. Cloud cover has been too low for aircraft but that is predicted to clear today. General Kasper is confident that they will be apprehended soon."

The Regional Medical Center looked like a modern stateside hospital, except that the security guards were US Army MPs armed with submachine guns. Cassera and his companions showed their credentials to a uniformed receptionist. Two minutes later, a paunchy little man bounced into the waiting room. He beamed at Cassera, pumping his hand like a small-town mayoral candidate.

"Eddie Cassera! Hey, great to see you again, man!"

Cassera turned to the others. "This is Nestor Sanchez, Chief Mortuary Officer here. We worked together a few years ago."

The others murmured names and greetings. Cassera looked at Sanchez. "Sorry to drag you into work on a Saturday, Nestor. It's important."

"No problem, bud. No rest for the wicked, ya know. Hey, Bill Miller was on the blower to me at eight this morning. That's two A.M. in Washington! This thing must be important, Eddie. I never heard Miller so hyped before!"

"Time is really of the essence, Nestor," Cassera said. He addressed Debbie and Christoph: "Would you both please wait out here until I've finished my business with Nestor? It may take a while."

Debbie nodded. The German detective glanced at her, then gave Cassera a quizzical look. "Of course. Is there anything I can do while we wait?"

Cassera thought for a minute. "There just may be. I understand that two World War Two vintage Thompson submachine guns were found at the old SS camp. One was discovered in context with the body we've got here and the other on its own. I know that the first weapon is with our CID, but wonder if you know who's got the other?"

"Yes. That weapon is now in the BfV headquarters in Cologne."

"Dusted for fingerprints?"

"Of course. We've already lifted and filed them. A complete set of clear prints belonging to a single individual."

"Have you been able to match them with any in your database?"

When Veditz shook his head, Cassera unlatched his briefcase and delved among the files inside. He extracted an envelope containing five FBI fingerprint cards and handed them to the BfV detective.

"Could you please have these checked against those prints you took from the Thompson?"

Veditz scanned the cards, eyes narrowing as he noted the names and dates when the fingerprints had been taken. He looked at Cassera as if waiting for an explanation, bur Eddie pretended not to notice. Veditz started towards the door. He paused, raised an eyebrow at Debbie.

"Perhaps you would care to accompany me, Debbie?"

"No thanks," she answered. "I'd better stick around here in case Cassera needs me."

Cassera wondered if she had been ordered to stay close to him.

"You ready?" Sanchez asked, rubbing his hands.

Cassera followed him into his office. Sanchez closed the door and looked at Eddie grimly, his ebullience gone.

"I got a dentist in to do that dental chart Miller wanted for body XI-04-2011, that stiff from the Bavarian Forest." He handed Cassera a printed dental chart marked with notations and sketches. "I've assigned it an 'X' for 'Unknown,' even though it's got dog tags and ID with the name of Private Sarnoff. Did you bring some positive ID over for us, Eddie?"

Cassera hadn't been listening. He was comparing the new dental chart with the one on Sarnoff's 293 File. He already knew what the outcome would be – the match was perfect. He looked up.

"Sorry, Nestor. Didn't catch what you were saying."

Cassera had kept the charts behind the lid of his brief-case on his lap, but Sanchez had clearly caught the look on his face as the comparison was completed.

"You got a positive ID on that boy, don't you?" Sanchez asked quietly, his eyes troubled.

Cassera liked Sanchez, and he felt the need to tell others about his stunning discovery. But Miller's orders had been unequivocal.

"This case has a security tag on it, Nestor. You know what that means."

Sanchez looked hurt, but only briefly. Cassera had often wondered how a mortuary officer could be so unfailingly cheerful.

"Okey-doke," he said. "What's next on your agenda?"

"I want to see Sarnoff's personal effects."

"You mean the effects of cadaver number XI-04-2011," Sanchez said reprovingly, slipping on a lab coat. "No names without proof, that's DPMO policy, Eddie."

"Yeah sure," Cassera said.

Sarnoff's possessions were laid out on a formica table in a storeroom. 62 items including blood-stained clothing and grenades. A clipboard with three pages attached lay on a corner of the table.

"This a complete list?" asked Cassera as he picked it up.

"Yep. 'Items of clothing and equipment found with remains.' Same as the list we sent to Washington."

Cassera moved slowly down the table, pausing to pick up an opened D-Ration packet containing Wrigley's PK chewing gum and tiny envelopes of Jack Frost sugar.

"Like a museum display," Sanchez said. "Every item is one hundred percent genuine World War Two equipment. Just can't figure it out."

Sarnoff's personal effects were in a tray at the end of the table. Dog tags, the high school ring, a cheap wristwatch, pencil stub, pocket knife and cigarette lighter. The tray also held his Army pay book, identity card, and the three letters, all spotted with brown stains. Cassera knew the contents of the letters by heart, having read their copies several times on the transatlantic flight. He nonetheless felt a lump in his throat as he opened one of the originals and read:

"Missing you heaps, Baby. Don't go getting no ideas about those French madomaselles cause what I got waiting for you is better than anything they got (as you know from our last night before you shipped out!!!).

I love you forever & ever, Louise"

Cassera placed the letter back in the tray and braced himself for what he had to do next.

"I want to see him now, Nestor."

Sanchez led him through a tiled room where the reek of chemicals was almost overpowering. They passed a series of steel tables holding corpses of young soldiers, many horribly disfigured. Mortuary technicians were working on them despite the weekend.

"Constant crop of them from Afghanistan," Sanchez said sadly. "We try to fix 'em up before we ship 'em home, but most gotta be closed casket funerals.

The next room was well lighted and spacious with a pile of aluminum coffins stacked against one wall. A large steel refrigerator door was set in an adjacent wall. Sanchez swung the door open, and Cassera shivered as cold air rolled out and engulfed him.

The interior was crowded with more sheet-draped bodies on gurneys. Sanchez moved among them, whistling as he checked tags looped to the cadavers' big toes. He found the one he sought and pushed other gurneys aside so he could pull it out into the room. Cassera closed the heavy door and followed Sanchez to a spot beneath a fluorescent light.

"XI-04-2011," Sanchez said.

"Leave me, Nestor," said Cassera.

"What?"

"I'm asking you to leave me alone here for a while, please."

"You sure? I mean, maybe I can tell you somethi–"

"Orders," Cassera snapped. "Don't make it hard on me, Nestor."

Sanchez threw up his hands. "Okay. You can call an orderly when you want to put your stiff back in the cooler. I'll be in my office."

Cassera waited for Sanchez to leave, then laid his briefcase on a surgical instrument stand and opened it. He took out the photographs borrowed from Louise Jablonski along with the medical records from Nicholas Sarnoff's 293 File.

He had not been entirely truthful with Sanchez. It wasn't just "orders" that made him want to be alone. The investigation had become a lot more personal than any other case he had investigated. But then it was unlike anything he had ever encountered. Cassera steeled himself before pulling back the green sheet that covered the body.

"You poor bastard," he whispered, gazing into the pale face of Nicholas Sarnoff.

24

Hugo Roth wolfed down a bowl of canned *Kümmel Suppe* from the cabin's pantry. The caraway seed soup had been a childhood favorite of his. The canned variety couldn't compare to that made by his family's cook in Berlin, but it was still a treat. He had never relished the traditional Yiddish matzah and gefilte fish that his aunt in New Jersey had served. Although all things German were anathema to him, it was hard to deny one's appetites, and he often hungered for the dishes of his youth.

Kemp and Loomis snored in the bunk beds, catching up on sleep before Fox team embarked on their trek into Czechoslovakia that night. Roth hated to leave Germany while his desire for revenge was unsatiated, but he knew the Bäyerischer Wald region was alarmed now and potential enemy targets would be on full alert. That part of Czechoslovakia not yet overrun by the Russians was German-occupied territory, and there would be plenty of Nazi patrols to ambush and officials to assassinate. The Czech partisans would undoubtedly have more stomach for killing Germans than the three Rangers under his command.

Roth poured a cup of coffee made from D-Ration Nescafe packs. Now that he'd had a few hours rest, he was able to think more clearly, but his mind remained troubled. Although Fox team had kept clear of cities and large towns, he had seen their lights glowing in the distance. These should have been beacons for the Allied bomber fleets that pounded Germany night and day. The lack of blackouts seemed flagrantly suicidal, yet there had been no sign of bombers since the start of their mission. Their absence could not be due to the bad weather, as he knew that heavy bombers flew high above the cloud cover.

The intelligence officers back in England had told the Bandstand teams that Germany was a ruined nation on the verge of collapse. Roth wondered if this was Allied propaganda. Perhaps, in truth, the Third Reich was nowhere near its death throes. Were Hitler's mythical secret weapons a reality? Could Messerschmitt jets and *Vergeltungswaffen* missiles have turned the tide of war in Germany's favor?

And that device in the Gestapo beast's office in Bodenmais. The box with moving pictures on the screen. Roth had seen something like that in a display at the 1939 New York World's fair. It was called a television. But this one was different. Flat and streamlined with amazingly clear pictures. *Color* pictures. The World's Fair exhibit had a sign saying every American family would have a television in their homes by 1960, but if the Nazis already had such things then it was possible that–."

"Sarge?"

Roth's head snapped up, combat alertness restored. Holcombe stood in the kitchen doorway.

"You're supposed to be standing watch, Holcombe. What the hell is it?"

"I spotted smoke, Sarge. Five or six columns like campfires. Not too far away, neither."

Roth picked up his binoculars and followed Holcombe outside. The private pointed. "Over there."

Five thin pillars of smoke rose from the forest about a mile away, spiraling towards the gray afternoon sky. Roth focused the field glasses.

"What do you think, Sarge?"

"I think they're campfires. Perhaps an enemy patrol."

He went back inside the cabin and returned with his weapons.

"I'll check it out. You rouse the others and be ready to move out as soon as I return. And I want all sides of the cabin watched."

It took Roth half an hour to slip through the woods towards the presumed enemy bivouac. The hike brought bittersweet memories of summer visits to the Roth family's *Ferienhaus*, their holiday retreat on the Selchower See southeast of Berlin. He and his brothers would wear *lederhosen* and join their father for hikes through the peaceful woods and fields, the three Roth boys bronzed and proud as they waved to the peasants and foresters like Junkers.

Roth halted when the wind wafted the smell of wood smoke and the sound of voices. He was close. Crouching, he crept towards a clearing visible between the trunks of tall pines. He crawled the last twenty yards on his belly.

They were children. Adolescent boys to be exact. About thirty of them accompanied by two adult men wearing Tyrolean dress under green quilted waistcoats. The boys were in uniforms – *bergmütze* caps, blue neckerchiefs, khaki shirts, *lederhosen*, and hiking boots.

Roth knew immediately what they were.

Hitler Youth! Dirty little Aryan Reichskinder like the ones who had beat him. He clenched his jaw, running his eyes over the campsite on the bank of a stream. The boys huddled around the campfires, roasting sausages on long sticks while loudly talking and laughing. The two men - the *Hitlerjugendführers* - sat together on a log sharing a thermos bottle. The older red-faced one whooped and slapped his leg at something funny the younger man said.

It would be so easy, Roth thought. One grenade and a few well-placed bursts from his Thompson, with the pistol to finish off survivors. But there could be a *Wehrmacht or Waffen-SS* patrol nearby and the sound of gunfire would draw them like flies to a pile of shit. Much as he would have enjoyed depriving the Fatherland of these young *Übermenschen*, it would be foolhardy.

At some great distance he seemed to hear his gentle mother saying, *"What has happened to you, Hugo? How could you even think of killing children? You are no better than they are!"*

You're right, Muti, he thought fiercely, imagining, like he had countless times, the horrors of his beloved family's final moments. It was true – he was no better than the Nazis in *that* regard. His mother's goodness had not spared her from their evil. The children were not just children, they were future SS, Gestapo, camp guards.

Maybe tonight. He could slip down here before they left for Czechoslovakia. A few slices with the razor edge of his commando knife while the piglets slept.

He inhaled deeply, then elbowed backwards until he could safely rise and return to the cabin.

The boys and men Roth had observed were members of a Boy Scout troop from Salzburg, Austria, on a weekend camping trip to the Bäyerischer Wald National Park. Three boys were absent from the camp during Roth's surveillance. One was behind a bush in the forest with a roll of toilet paper and a bad case of diarrhea. The other two youths lay on their stomachs atop a boulder overlooking a clearing. They shared a cigarette and told lies about school girls.

They heard blueberry bushes rustle at the edge of the clearing as something pushed through them. Thinking it was Herr Grieger, their scoutmaster, they stubbed out the cigarette and flattened themselves so just their eyes showed above the rock.

It wasn't their scoutmaster who stepped into the clearing, looked furtively from side to side, and hurried across. It was an American soldier with leaves in the netting of his helmet and grenades jouncing on his chest. He carried a tommy gun like the boys had seen in films about World War II and Chicago gangsters.

The boys were intrigued. They slid off the boulder and stealthily followed the man, hiding behind trees when the wary soldier pivoted to check the woods behind him.

They trailed the soldier until the forest ended at a small lake, where they stayed inside the trees and watched him go up a track to a cabin. There the man stopped as three more soldiers came around the corners and joined him. After a couple of minutes they all went inside.

"I wonder what those American soldiers are doing out here?" one boy asked.

His more precocious and media-conscious friend frowned in concentration. He remembered a news broadcast seen that morning on Austrian television before leaving for the bus ride to Bavaria. He hadn't paid much attention, but his parents were concerned by it and had debated letting him go on the camping trip.

"I don't think those are real American soldiers," he whispered. "I think those are terrorists!"

"Really?" The first youth was delighted. "Let's go tell Herr Grieger!"

"Race you!"

When Cassera returned to the Mortuary waiting room, it was nearly one o'clock. He was haggard from jet lag and felt grungy, but his eyes blazed with zeal.

Debbie Lueckenhoff and the German detective greeted him between mouthfuls of hamburger and French fries. Debbie held up a McDonald's bag.

"Want some lunch? Got an extra burger and fries for you."

"No thanks," Cassera answered. "I'm not really hungry."

There's nothing like examining the cadaver of someone you feel you know to ruin your appetite.

Christoph Veditz wiped his hands on a paper napkin. "I think you are really Sherlock Holmes, Mr. Cassera." The German detective grinned at his clumsy joke, but his tone was respectful.

"Oh? How so?"

"Well, the fingerprints you gave me proved most valuable. One set was a perfect match for those found on that other Thompson submachine gun. The BfV are grateful."

Cassera leaned forward, face taut with anticipation. "Which one matched?" he demanded. "Tell me which one?"

Veditz raised his eyebrows and cleared his throat, wondering why the American DPMO investigator was so agitated.

"The name was Sutton. Arthur J. Sutton, US Army."

"Sutton," whispered Cassera. "The lieutenant."

"Lieutenant?" Veditz said. "You know this man? If so, it is imperative that we are told—"

"Forget it. Your superiors will be told when my superiors decide to tell 'em. Those fingerprints belong to American citizens who are also US Army personnel. Could I have those cards back?"

Veditz scowled as he gave Cassera the cards. Cassera knew that the German would have copied the cards and dispatched them to BfV headquarters, but he had expected that.

Cassera went to sit across the room and rummage in his briefcase until he found the black 293 File affixed with the name and serial number of Arthur J. Sutton. He had read each of the files during the flight to Germany, but the identification of the fingerprints on the submachine gun gave him a tangible connection to the long missing Ranger lieutenant. *This guy is probably still alive! Wounded, perhaps, but over there in the Bavarian Forest thinking he's still fighting World War II!*

Unlike the other Bandstand MIA files, Sutton's included a photograph, probably because he was an officer.

Cassera thought Sutton looked like a clean-cut, all-American college boy from the 1930s, a character from an old Andy Hardy movie. *Christ almighty.* Sutton was the same age as his dad would have been - 90 - and yet physically he must be as young as that poor pitiful kid in the icebox.

Inside Sutton's 293 File was a copy of the lieutenant's citation for the Silver Star medal. Eddie read the first line: "For conspicuous gallantry in the field."

Early on the morning of June 6, 1944 - D-Day - Sutton's unit had assaulted Pointe du Hoc, a natural fortress that dominated Omaha and Utah beaches. The Rangers scaled the steep cliffs and captured the German positions at a cost of more than half their force. Then Second Lieutenant Arthur Sutton had been one of the first men to the top. Although wounded, he destroyed a German pillbox with grenades. Under heavy fire, he returned to the cliff and rescued three badly wounded men who were snarled in barbed wire.

Sutton was a hero, Cassera realized, like that kid in 'Nam who'd saved his ass when he was bleeding to death in that fucking rice paddy.

The black kid with his name on the Wall.

Goddamit! He could find Sutton! Track down him and the other Bandstand survivors before the DIA or the Germans did. What a thing. He could really help those guys. Save their lives. To hell with pussyfooting Miller and the other fucking bureaucrats!

Barely able to contain his excitement, he looked at Debbie Lueckenhoff. "I've got to get to the *Bäyerischer Wald* as quickly as possible! What kind of transportation can you lay on for me aside from that car?"

266

As Debbie thought about this, Veditz's mind raced. *Something big was going on here, something involving the terrorism case in Bavaria. If he could break that case, the laurels would be his! Christoph Veditz, the toast of TV interviewers, newspaper reporters, and sexy actresses. He'd probably never get another stab at something with as much career potential as this case.*

Debbie's mouth opened to reply, but the BfV detective beat her to it. "I can have a helicopter here in fifteen minutes," he said. "We can meet it on the hospital's helipad."

Veditz's offer of a helicopter was a gamble for him. He was a very junior detective in the great *Bundesamt für Verfassungsschutz*, and very junior detectives did not usually have the authority to conjure up official aircraft at short notice. However, he had a letter signed by the Federal Minister of the Interior that granted him extraordinary powers. Veditz hoped that the invocation of this, plus a judicious mixture of lying and bullying, would secure the promised helicopter.

He glanced at Debbie to see if the American Defense Intelligence Agency had other plans, but her bespectacled face gave nothing away.

"You've got a deal, buddy," said Cassera.

The German nodded and took out his iPhone.

Kommando Spezialkräfte

25

Franz Grieger, Boy Scout troop leader, tapped the German police emergency number 110 on his cell phone at 3:36 PM. The watch officer at Klingenbrunn police station recorded the Austrian's message and immediately relayed it to the regional headquarters in Straubing. From there, a dispatcher broadcast it to all police and military units in the *Bäyerischer Wald*.

At 3:49 PM, a *Bundeswehr* Eurocopter EC635 helicopter responded that it was half a kilometer due north of the village of Neuhütte and six kilometers south of Grosser Rachel mountain. The aircraft was ordered to the rough map coordinates derived from Herr Grieger's report.

Crewed by a pilot and observer, the helicopter had been aloft since dawn, landing only for refueling and rest breaks. The crew was thoroughly briefed on their quarry and given hourly updates on the hunt for the terrorists. The aerial search had been hampered by low cloud cover, while the ground patrols with tracker dogs were frustrated by wet weather that washed away scent.

The Eurocopter's pilot swung its nose north and dropped to tree-top height, skimming the folds of terrain. Throttled back to one hundred kilometers per hour, the aircraft arrived at the map coordinates relayed by the Passau dispatcher. Seeing nothing but forest at that location, the pilot took the helicopter up to five hundred feet and hovered while he rotated 360 degrees. The observer spotted a small lake to the northwest. They dropped down to the tops of the pines again.

The aircraft broke from the forest with its rotor wash buffeting the calm lake. Both crewmen saw the log cabin. The pilot opened the throttle and hurtled towards it. Before they swept over the roof, the observer glimpsed a helmeted man at the front door wearing a khaki uniform with a firearm slung over his shoulder.

Private Dan Holcombe sat in the open door of the cabin, looking at the peaceful mountain lake below and wondering how much longer he had to wait until Loomis relieved him. Holcombe had lost his watch in a crap game with British commandos; ever since, he seemed to have got the short end of the stick time-wise.

Holcombe was glad that Hebe son of a bitch Roth had decided they could safely stay at the cabin until night. He'd breath a lot easier once they got out of Germany and over into Czechoslovakia. He was mighty proud to be a Ranger but sick to death of this fucking war and more homesick than he could ever let on to the other guys. It would have been swell if what that crazy old Kraut had said was true and the war was over ... but that *had* to be impossible!

His thoughts wandered to the hunting rifle he had found in a closet that Kemp had jimmied open. Nice piece, sporterized 7.92-mm Mauser with a telescopic sight. Holcombe had hunted since the age of seven, bagging squirrels and rabbits in the Alabama woods to help keep his big family from starving. He had qualified as a marksman during basic training, and he wished he could try out the Mauser. Maybe he would bring it along as a war souvenir.

When Holcombe first heard the noise he wasn't alarmed. It was a faint throbbing somewhere in the forest to the southwest. The sound grew louder as it came closer. He stood up and craned his neck. Suddenly a fantastic machine like a giant cricket zoomed over the lake at the foot of the knoll, making a thrumming noise as it charged towards him.

His jaw hung loose, muscles frozen. The hellish thing whipped overhead, going like the dickens, shaking branches and churning up loose pine needles. There were people in it! *Son of a gun, must be some newfangled airplane!*

"Holy Moses!" he yelled, and started to step outside for a closer look.

Someone caught the back of his jacket and roughly jerked him inside the cabin. He stumbled and nearly fell.

"Dummkopf!" Roth was livid. "Stupid fucking hayseed!"

Holcombe felt a cold despair. He knew he had made a terrible mistake. "I-I don't think they saw me, Sarge. I was just—"

"Hillbilly fool! I should have shot you!" Roth kicked the door shut. The shouting and aircraft's noise had roused Kemp and Loomis, who ran into the room with their weapons.

"What's going on?" Kemp cried.

273

Roth crouched below the windowsill, and the other men huddled behind him. They watched the sky below the eaves as the thrumming sound of the strange aircraft returned. The machine came back into view, turned, and hovered. Roth's stomach knotted as he saw the black iron crosses on the aircraft's fuselage.

"Get down!" he snarled.

The three privates dropped to their knees and continued to look fearfully through the window.

"What the fuck is that thing?" said Holcombe.

Loomis's brow furrowed. "It's a, uh, a helo-... helo-... "

"Helicopter!" Kemp shouted. "Read about 'em in *Life*. Didn't know the Krauts had 'em!"

"They know we're in here," Roth said. "Can't see any guns on the thing, though. We're going to have to make a run for it!"

Aboard the helicopter, the observer finished his radio conversation and made a hand signal to the pilot, who had listened on his own headset to the orders given directly by the KSK commander General Michalke. The pilot hovered above the cabin's weathered shingle roof to maintain unobstructed surveillance over all sides of the building. The observer quickly slid back the door on his side, swung up and locked a pylon into position, then leaned out to open a plastic case alongside the fuselage. Inside was a 7.62-mm Rheinmetall MG3 machine gun. The observer snapped the weapon onto its mounting and reached for a drum magazine.

"Can't see him," said Holcombe. "Damn son of a bitch is hanging up there over the roof!"

Roth checked the load of his submachine gun clip, then snapped it back into his weapon. "It's about sixty yards to the forest. I'll go first. Each man will wait until the one in front makes it to the trees. Kemp next, then Loomis. Holcombe last. I will lay down covering fire for you."

"Good luck," Kemp said.

"I make my own luck," Roth snapped. He gripped the Thompson so hard that his knuckles stood out like white pebbles.

He opened the door, listening to the rotors beat the air over the cabin. The eaves overhung the doorway by several feet, sheltering him as he edged outside and sidled along the wall. He sucked a deep breath, expelled it, and pushed off, sprinting for the nearest large pine tree.

The helicopter crew spotted him before he covered six yards. The pilot swung the tail boom around and tilted the EC635 to give the observer a clear field of fire.

The observer obeyed the *Bundeswehr* Rules of Engagement and fired a carefully aimed burst that tore up the ground around Roth. The sergeant pivoted and ran towards another tree. Machine gun fire again barred his path. Then the 7.62-mm slugs moved closer, herding him back towards the cabin.

Roth realized the gunner's ploy. He halted outside the cabin door and raised his Thompson.

"Break left!" yelled the Eurocopter's observer. The pilot flung the aircraft in a violent bank, narrowly avoiding Roth's stream of .45 caliber bullets. The observer snugged his machine gun's plastic butt into his shoulder as the helicopter righted itself. He aligned the weapon's sights on the figure in the old American uniform, who was trying to aim at the bucketing helicopter.

"Shall I shoot him?" the observer shouted. "We've taken fire and can legally return it!"

"*Nein!* Just drive him back inside. I don't think he'll try to escape again."

The observer dropped the MG3's muzzle a fraction and chewed the ground at Roth's feet into stinging clods. Roth jumped back into the doorway as a round creased his boot. He scrambled inside and slammed the door.

"Good shooting, Theo!" The pilot touched the transmit button on his helmet radio. "Tango-Alpha-Drei to base."

"Base receiving you loud and clear." A voice crackled in his earphones.

"We've got definite hostiles up here," the pilot said. "Just fired on us. Tell General Kasper that we'll hold them for him until he gets here."

Michalke brought the news to Kasper. He found the National Security Advisor inside a *Bundeswehr Wiesel* command post vehicle parked near the steaming ARAL fuel storage complex. Kasper sipped a cup of coffee while studying a map.

"We've found them, *Mein Herr.*" He handed Kasper a message slip.

Kasper read it, then sprang to his feet. His eyes gleamed.

"*Wunderbar!* Get another helicopter gunship up there immediately. Do you know if any of this has leaked to the news hounds yet?"

"Most likely," Michalke answered. "You know they monitor all the police radio channels even though ours are secure."

"Then I want the entire area sealed. No reporters, TV cameramen, or other bleeding heart witnesses. We'll finish off those Muslim monsters as soon as the area is secured. You know the drill."

"*Klar*. The company is already on its way, Herr General."

"Good. I will go ahead by helicopter and meet you there. Carry on."

Michalke saluted and hastened out. Kasper pulled on his beret and unclipped an HK MP7A1 submachine gun from the CP vehicle's wall. The weapon fired 4.6x30mm all-steel rounds from a 40-round magazine that could penetrate the best body armor at a distance of 200 meters. Just as he was about to exit the vehicle, one of the communications specialists called to him.

"Sir, Lieutenant Gershner has another surveillance report. Do you wish to speak with him?"

"Ask if they have anything significant to report," growled Kasper.

The private repeated the question into his telephone, listened to the response, and turned back to his leader.

"Fraulein von Scheller and her companion stopped at a news agent shop in Frauenau. Nothing else to report."

"Tell Manfred to maintain surveillance," Kasper snapped, impatient. "We have more important fish to fry."

In the village of Frauenau, the KSK lieutenant named Manfred made a face as he acknowledged the message. "And I thought I'd get to see a lot of action as old *Mord und Totschlag* Kasper's aide-de-camp," he said. "So while the big show is going on at Grosser Rachel mountain we've got to keep an eye on some rich liberal *hure* having a weekend fling with that American!"

"You're right, sir," a private agreed. "Well, maybe they'll get a room at a *Gasthaus* for some screwing, then we can at least get some sleep."

"The exciting life of the dashing young KSK commandos," The *leutnant* mocked one of the many tabloid articles written about their unit. "Hah!"

Sutton and Paula stood in line at the shop. After rushing out of Paula's apartment, they realized that they had no idea where to begin looking for the Rangers. "This area is vast," Sutton had said. "It's going to be harder than finding that old needle in the haystack!"

They decided that the best strategy would be to get as close to the last reported "terrorist" attack and monitor the news bulletins.

Paula, remembering her grandfather's frustration when trying to convert the monolingual Bandstand privates, had suggested that they buy newspapers and magazines printed in English. When they got to the newsagent's, she selected the *International Herald Tribune* and two magazines. As they stood in line to pay, Sutton flipped through *Time*. Marvelous new world indeed!

"Jesus," he said. "Nuclear radiation leaks, American soldiers fighting and dying in Afghanistan, high school kids hooked on drugs and a madman murders hundreds of students in Norway." He frowned. "And we really thought we were fighting for a better world! If I showed these stories to my guys, they'd probably think they would've been better off if they hadn't survived the war!"

"Don't say that. It's not as bad as the media says. And it could be much worse. If you and your team had not stopped those real terrorists hundreds of children would have died! You're here for a reason – you must believe that! And now you've got to save your men."

Sutton reached for her hand. "I was just thinking of that line from Shakespeare, you know where Hamlet's telling his buddy that there's more to the universe than meets the eye."

"'There are more things in heaven and earth, Horatio,'" Paula quoted, "'than are dreamt of in your philosophy.'"

"That's it!"

She gripped his hand. "It's true, Arthur."

On impulse, Sutton reached into his pocket and took out the Roosevelt button. He opened her hand and placed it on her palm. She squinted at the lettering encircling a stalwart face. "Carry On With Roosevelt," she read. "Why do you have this? I noticed the way you touched it when you woke up at Opa's house."

Sutton explained the button's significance, omitting certain details of his subsequent good luck he'd told to Bouncing Betty's flight engineer. Paula started to hand it back to him.

"No," he said. "You keep it."

"You're sure? What about the good luck?"

"It seems like you're my good luck now."

Paula bit her lip, smiling, and slipped the button into the pocket of her jeans.

The shop clerk had the radio tuned to a rock station, and she turned it up louder when a man's voice interrupted the song. Sutton and Paula froze, unable to clearly hear the announcer.

"What did the radio just say?" Paula called to the female clerk, talking over the shoulder of the man in front of them who had just finished paying.

"They found those terrorists who've been pretending to be American soldiers. "Got them surrounded in a cabin." She began ringing up their purchases.

Paula drew in her breath. Sutton gripped the counter-top. "Where?" he demanded. "Did the radio say where?"

The shopkeeper seemed flustered by Sutton's strained face and American-accented German. She handed Paula the newspaper and magazines and backed away from the counter. "Well, I believe they said it was on the south side of Grosser Rachel mountain."

"Do you know how to get there?" asked Paula.

"I have no idea," said the clerk warily.

"There's a road leading out of the village to the east," said a clean-cut young man behind them in line. "It's marked *Nationalpark Bäyerischer Wald*. You have to cross the railway tracks."

Paula and Sutton bolted for the door oblivious to the clerk yelling after them for not paying. They also failed to notice that the helpful young man behind them in line didn't buy anything, but left the shop immediately after they did.

Manfred, the KSK *leutnant*, saw the signpost pointing the way to the Bäyerischer Wald National Park as the Mercedes followed the speeding silver Porsche. When the towering mass of Grosser Rachel mountain came into view, he grinned.

"So, Gerhard," he said to the driver, "maybe we'll see some action after all, *ja?*"

In the rear seat, the two surveillance team members were changing from civilian clothes into combat gear.

Hanno Kasper's helicopter carried him to the besieged cabin in less than 20 minutes. The original Eurocopter aircraft still orbited the cabin in company with another helicopter that Kasper recognized as one of the German Army's Tiger gunships. It was armed with a 30-mm cannon in a chin turret and thirty-four 68 mm SNEB rockets in a pods. Kasper would have enjoyed seeing what such an arsenal could do to an old log cabin, but knew that he had to forego that pleasure today. Noting the registration number of the Eurocopter, he keyed the radio and called the aircraft.

"We read you," came the reply. "Glad to see you up here, General."

"Have you seen the terrorists since their attempt to break out of the cabin?" asked Kasper.

"Negative. Theo put the fear of God into them with his fancy shooting."

A movement on the dirt track at the far end of the lake caught Kasper's eye. He twisted his head to see a pair of LGS *Fennek* reconnaissance vehicles emerge from the forest, followed by a column of armored personnel carriers. He looked back at the Bundeswehr helicopters, sorry that he must issue his next order. But regardless of the other forces' dedication, they might still talk. This time there must be no witnesses beyond the trusted ranks of the KSK.

"*Achtung* helicopters," he broadcast. "This is General Kasper. You are ordered to leave immediately and establish an orbiting perimeter two kilometers from here. Ensure that no civilians are allowed to approach this spot. You may use force if necessary, particularly for personnel belonging to the news media."

The two helicopter pilots acknowledged the order with disappointment weighting their voices. They separated and flew away to take up their new positions.

After familiarizing himself with the terrain around the cabin, Kasper radioed Michalke and began deploying the KSK company as it disembarked from the armored vehicles. Two teams of three men each began assembling 120-mm mortars as other troopers surrounded the building at a distance of five hundred meters.

The unit's ten snipers calmly unpacked their Mauser 86 SR rifles. The marksmen wriggled up the knoll and settled behind logs and in shallow depressions approximately three hundred meters from the cabin. The troop movements generated a response from the log building. A pair of submachine guns fired short bursts from the two front windows with as little effect on the Germans as tossing a handful of pebbles.

Kasper smiled from his helicopter seat as he watched the muzzle flashes at the windows. The terrorists were apparently armed only with clumsy, antiquated submachine guns that were inaccurate at ranges greater than 50 meters. His force's HK416 assault rifles had an effective range of 400 meters, and any of the KSK snipers could shoot the eye out of a liberal or a Muslim at twice that distance. This was going to be the easiest operation he'd ever commanded. The only way they could suffer casualties would be from carelessness, and his men weren't careless.

He tapped the pilot on the arm and asked to be dropped near the collection of military vehicles at the far end of the lake. He jumped out of the helicopter before its skids touched the ground and strode casually towards General Michalke, in full view of the cabin. He sneered at the burst of .45 caliber gunfire aroused by his presence.

Michalke, not to be outdone by his former commander's display of courage under fire, left the cover of a Dingo armored transporter. He stamped his foot and saluted.

"Requesting permission to return fire, *Mein Herr!*" he boomed.

"Permission granted, Baldur. Light arms only. We'll have to hold off on the mortars until we have confirmation that the perimeter is secured against those bleeding heart reporters."

"*Jawoh!*" Michalke saluted again and raised a radio to his lips. "All rifle teams, commence firing at will."

So let the battle be joined, Kasper told himself. He flicked a pine needle off his leather sleeve and smiled as his men went to work.

26

The road condition worsened, deteriorating to a potholed track that shook the Porsche's passengers and scraped its suspension. Paula fought the wheel, cursing the deep ruts that forced her to drive at a crawl.

"Up ahead!" Sutton yelled. "There's a bunch of cars stopped."

Paula squinted at the collection of vehicles parked haphazardly under the trees. People milled about, some with television cameras on their shoulders.

"Reporters and TV crews," Paula said.

She pulled the Porsche off the road and stopped behind a van with an extended satellite dish on its roof and ZDF painted on its sides. As they got out of the car, they heard the distant stutter of automatic weapons fire.

"We must hurry!" Paula gasped. "Oh God, I hope it's not too late!"

They ran towards a knot of shouting, gesticulating reporters surrounding a trio of Bavarian police in full

SWAT gear who were erecting a portable aluminum barrier at the mouth of a side road.

"This is an outrage!" a scruffy reporter shouted. "The public has a right to know what's going on up there!"

"It's against the law!" a young woman wearing a *Süddeutsche Zeitung* press badge added. "The constitution guarantees freedom of the press, you know!"

A *Polizeikommissar* shook his head. "It's for your own safety, *fraulein*. Bullets are flying all over the place up there."

"Rubbish," a *Deutsche Welle* newscaster snorted. "The Army threatened to shoot down our helicopter if it came too close!"

Paula turned to Sutton, face grim. "We'll never get past."

"We'll try going through the woods," Sutton said tightly as the gunfire increased in intensity.

They left the hornet's nest of reporters and camera crews and walked farther up the track. One of the police sentries noticed them. Thinking they were reporters trying to sneak up to the besieged cabin, he called out to them.

"If you two are trying to be clever and go up there through the forest, you'd better forget about it. We've got hundreds of police and soldiers patrolling these woods to make sure nobody gets in or out. They're all pretty trigger-happy right now, so I wouldn't risk it if I were you."

"*Scheisse,*" said Paula through clenched teeth.

At that moment several of the reporters recognized the Mercedes CLS 550 Coupe rolling up the track as Hanno Kasper's personal command vehicle. When it halted they swooped down on it with pens and cameras poised, hoping to get a statement from the renowned national security advisor. They were disappointed to discover that its passengers were a KSK lieutenant and three other men. The passengers ignored the reporters' questions, and after a few minutes they lost interest and drifted away.

The driver turned the car's phone to speaker mode and turned to the *leutnant*. "He's coming now, sir."

All four men in the Mercedes sat up straighter as Kasper's clipped voice roared from the speaker.

"So, Manfred, I understand they are trying to reach their comrades in the cabin."

"It appears so, *Herr General*. The guards down here turned them back and I believe they are planning to seek another way in."

There was a brief silence. Kasper's returning voice was harsh.

"Arrest them and bring them up here. We will deal with them after we finish this business."

Manfred acknowledged the order and loosened the flap on his holster. "I wonder what he means by 'deal with them after we finish this business,'" he said.

The *unteroffizier* in the back seat chortled. "You ever hear of that old expression, 'shot while trying to escape,' *Herr Leutnant?*"

"I'm going to try to get past those patrols," Sutton whispered. "Rangers are trained for this."

Paula turned her back on a rotund reporter who eyed them with open curiosity. "Oh, Arthur, they might kill you. Can't we try to ...." Her voice trailed off as she noticed a KSK trooper pushing towards them through the swarm of news people.

"What's wrong?" Sutton asked.

"That soldier. I swear he was that man at the newsagent's who gave us directions. Only he was wearing civilian—"

Something round and metallic pressed against her spine as a strong hand gripped her left bicep. "You are under arrest," a voice hissed. "You will come with us now. Quietly. No trouble. No scenes."

Her head pivoted to see a blond officer beside her. The man's pale blue eyes flicked from the reporters to her face and back again.

"*Raus,*" the solder said. "Walk normally."

Sutton stepped along in front of her with his hands clenched at his sides, followed by another KSK trooper who dug a pistol into his lower back. The man she had seen in the restaurant flanked them with a submachine gun. He tried to shield them from the view of the news personnel.

"*Schnell,*" growled the blond officer. "Move quickly!"

A couple of the reporters called out to their colleagues and converged on the soldiers and their captives. The news people shouted questions and frantically began training cameras. But the troopers outdistanced them and hustled Sutton and Paula into the Mercedes. The doors slammed shut before the frantic reporters could get a clear look at the detainees.

Paula clasped Sutton's hand while the troopers patted them down for weapons. The *unteroffizier* removed Sutton's US Army ID and handed it up to the KSK lieutenant. Manfred frowned at the identity papers, then showed them his own warrant card in a leather wallet.

"You are under arrest under the Prevention of Terrorism Act," he said. "Now we shall go to meet General Kasper."

Paula's shaking hand tightened its grip on Sutton's.

Private Loomis crawled across the floor to where Roth crouched beneath a window.

"You're supposed to be watching the back, soldier!" Roth said.

Loomis's eyes shone with fear. "Sarge, I'm down to—"

A fusillade of enemy gunfire drowned his words, flailing the cabin's exterior and knocking chunks of plaster from the gaps between the logs. Bullets hummed through the shattered windows and drilled into the opposite wall. Holcombe fired an answering burst from his position at the other window in the living room.

Loomis cleared his throat as the firing subsided. "I was saying that I've only got one full Thompson magazine left and the fourteen rounds from my pistol clips. Kemp and I were talking and we think we're gonna be finished if we don't surrender."

"You're finished for sure *if* you surrender," Roth said. "Those are SS out there and they are not interested in taking prisoners. Remember what they did to the GIs who were captured at Malmedy?"

"We want to take our chances with 'em," Loomis said. "We ain't got a snowball's chance in hell of ever getting out of here alive otherwise!"

Roth punched the top of Loomis's helmet, harder than he meant to, so that his chin hit the floor. For a moment Loomis lay still, and Roth thought he'd knocked him unconscious. When Loomis looked up again, breathing hard, Roth turned away from his glare.

"Get back to your post, now," he said. "Save your ammo for when they rush us."

Loomis wormed back to the bedroom. Kemp looked up from feeding .45 rounds into a Thompson clip.

"So what'd Little Mr. Hitler say?" he asked.

"He's dead set on going down with the ship," Loomis said. "Fucking damned nut hit me." He began lashing a pillowcase to the barrel of his submachine gun using an extra pair of bootlaces. "Well, buddy, I'm taking my chances with the Krauts. That crazy kike wants to get his balls shot off, it's okay by me."

"I'll be right behind you, Tom," Kemp told him.

Loomis slowly raised the white flag in the bedroom window. A rifle cracked instantly, punching a hole through the cloth. "Damn," Loomis swore, then waved the flag back and forth for several minutes. There were no more shots from the Germans.

"You think it's safe now?" asked Kemp.

"Sure. The Krauts are civilized. They belong to the Geneva Convention. They know what a white flag means."

He looked at Kemp, chin quivering. Tearing a strip off the pillowcase, he clutched it and slowly rose to his feet.

When the white flag appeared at the cabin's rear window, the Non-Commissioned Officer commanding the rifle team nearest to it ordered a cease-fire, then reached for his radio. He called Hanno Kasper and conversed for less than a minute before relaying the National Security Advisor's orders to the men in his squad.

Eleven pairs of narrowed eyes lined their laser sights on the wobbling green helmet that rose above the windowsill. A pale, pathetically smiling face followed between a pair of raised hands that fluttered a white strip of cloth.

"*Feuer Frei!*" the NCO barked.

The frightened young face in the window exploded into fragments of scarlet jelly.

When Roth crawled into the bedroom, he found Kemp weeping over his friend's headless body. The sergeant watched the scene for a long moment, then picked up the dead man's ammunition.

"He didn't believe me," Roth said. "Now, you, Kemp, will get back to your post and behave like a man. I hope your friend's stupidity has taught you something about the Nazis."

"Fuck off," Kemp sobbed.

"Well, we're being taken where we wanted to go," Sutton said as the Mercedes ground up the track passing heavily armed police and Bundeswehr infantrymen.

"I hope we can get General Kasper to believe us and stop this terrible thing!" Paula whispered. "It was a mistake to lie to him earlier. He admired my grandfather and might have believed him. Now, no matter what, we must tell him the truth."

"No talking, you!" the lieutenant said.

As the Mercedes emerged from the forest onto the lakeshore, its passengers craned forward to see the besieged cabin. Sutton counted eight military vehicles emblazoned with Iron Crosses parked under the trees. The driver nosed behind the *ATF Dingo* vehicle serving as a Command Post.

291

"Get out." The *leutnant* held open the car's door while the *unteroffizier* covered Paula and Sutton with his submachine gun.

Kasper stepped from the CP vehicle and waited for the prisoners to be brought to him. He gave Sutton a baleful look that the American officer returned stoically, even though his stomach knotted when he saw the swastika-embossed Iron Cross on the old German's black leather tunic.

"So, Fraulein von Scheller, we meet again," said Kasper. "I am pleased to return your hospitality. And I see that you have brought your friend."

The KSK lieutenant handed Sutton's papers to Kasper and stood at attention while he perused them.

"Herr Kasper," said Paula, "I want to tell you the truth now. I lied to you at my father's house, but there was a very important reason for doing so. You see, this man and the ones in that cabin are—"

"Silence!" Kasper looked up from the papers, peering at Sutton with a puzzled expression. "Who are you?"

Sutton drew himself up as if he were on a parade ground.

"First Lieutenant Arthur Sutton, Second Ranger Battalion, United States Army. Serial number 18265451. Just like it says on my ID there, Sir."

Kasper froze, face mottled with rage. He waved the World War II ID at Sutton.

"Listen, you filthy swine, how dare you insult my intelligence by claiming this is your identification! Your Al-Qaeda controllers have let you down badly this time, *Scheisskerl!* Instead of giving you modern forgeries like your dead terrorist comrades, *you* were issued with false papers dating from the Second World War!"

"They're not false. I'm exactly who those papers say I am."

Kasper strode closer, so that his face was right in Sutton's. "You confirm what I have suspected for a long time, namely that you terrorists are criminally deranged. We knew what to do with people like you when I was young!"

He turned to the KSK *leutnant*.

"Manfred, I don't want these swine underfoot. Have them kept under close guard until we have finished with the business at hand."

"*Jawohl, Herr General!*" Manfred shouted and gave the stiff-armed Fascist salute.

Paula gasped. "My God," she whispered as they were marched away at gunpoint, "this is unreal. These men are acting like old-time storm troopers."

27

At 16:21, the copilot of the *BfV* helicopter picked up news of the siege during a routine sweep of military and police band radio traffic. He told the pilot about it but neglected to mention it to any of his passengers until fourteen minutes later. Even then, he refused to announce it over the PA system because the two Americans on board had no right to know about the German Federal Republic's official business. He went aft to the passenger compartment and leaned close to Veditz to give him the update.

The BfV detective fought his disappointment as he watched the copilot return to the cockpit. He had missed his chance at breaking the big terrorism case and now there would be hell to pay with his superiors for commandeering the helicopter.

"We're too late, Mr. Cassera," he announced. "We must turn back."

"What?" Cassera was unable to hear him properly in the inadequately soundproofed cabin.

"The copilot told me that those terrorists disguised as American soldiers have been trapped in the *Bäyerischer Wald* and have no chance of escaping."

Cassera unbuckled and stood over the German, swaying as the helicopter bucked wind currents.

"What did you hear?"

Veditz repeated the sparse details provided by the copilot.

"A mountain cabin? You don't know where exactly?"

Veditz shook his head. "Didn't bother to ask. The situation is out of our hands now."

"The hell it is! There's a lot that I can still do about 'the situation.' Your job is to assist me over here, Veditz. Now I want you to find out where that cabin is and tell the pilots to get us there as fast as possible. And find out as much other information as you can!"

Veditz was incensed that this American as old as his father was giving him orders. Now that the terrorist case was close to resolution, he had lost interest in putting himself out to help the Amis. It was time for damage control. He struggled to dampen his temper.

"Mr. Cassera, it appears that my government's forces have control of the case. Both this helicopter and I must return to BfV headquarters immediately. From now on you must rely on your own country's resources."

He was about to tell the pilot to return to Wiesbaden, when Debbie Lueckenhoff called to him. "Christoph? May I speak with you, please?"

Scowling, Veditz edged past Cassera and sat beside her. He pointedly looked at his watch.

"Look, Chris," the DIA agent said in rapid German, "you and I are on the same side, *nicht wahr?* You know what kind of things my agency gets involved in. I don't know the full story about this Cassera guy's mission over here, but it's some project that has the Washington brass pretty agitated, and they don't usually get shaken up over domestic German terrorism. There's something much bigger going on. I'd play along with him if I were you. I'm pretty sure there'll be something worthwhile in it for you, if you know what I mean. And my outfit will cover the expenses for this aircraft and square it with your boss if necessary. *Klar?*"

Veditz's interest quickened. He knew the American intelligence officer meant what she said. He nodded. "*Ja, alles klar.*"

He left her and went to the cockpit, nodding respectfully at Cassera as he passed. Five minutes later he reemerged and gave Cassera a report on the siege at the cabin near Grosser Rachel mountain.

"How soon can we get there?" asked Cassera.

"I thought you'd want to know that. I've ordered the pilot to proceed there. He puts our ETA at 17:05, about fifteen minutes from now. Will that suit you?"

"Suits me," Cassera answered, his voice tight with tension.

The white-painted Eurocopter skimmed the underside of the darkening cloud canopy, racing against the approaching night as the sun descended on the western horizon.

Michalke ran to where Kasper was inspecting the positioning of the mortars. "Sir," he said breathlessly, "the police report the area completely sealed off. No chance of reporters getting through."

"In the nick of time, too," Kasper said. "It will be dark soon." He glanced at the waiting mortar crews. "All right, Baldur, you can pull the men back to a safe—"

The radio in Kasper's hand squawked. He answered it with a growl.

"Herr General," a communications *feldwebel* reported. "One of the patrol helicopters radioed that it is escorting a BfV aircraft into the restricted zone."

"*Zum Teufel!* Nobody was to be allowed in! The orders were explicit. Why wasn't it turned back?"

"They were ordered to turn back, *Mein Herr*," the *feldwebel* said. "But they refused. The pilot claims they are carrying an official representative of the Federal Interior Minister."

"Meddling bureaucrats can't leave us alone, can they!" Kasper shouted. "Well, I'll personally send them packing. *I* am in command here, not the fucking Minister of the Interior!"

The white *Bundesamt für Verfassungsschutz* helicopter came into view seconds later, accompanied by the heavily armed Tiger gunship. As the BfV aircraft alighted on the lakeshore the dying wash of its rotors buffeted a sullen cordon of KSK troopers.

The first person out was a young man in designer civilian clothes who immediately raised Kasper's hackles. The intruder took only four steps before Kasper barred his path.

"I have declared this a restricted zone," Kasper said. "The Antiterrorism Act gives me complete emergency jurisdiction. I order you to leave immediately!"

Veditz was daunted to find himself facing the wrath of the famous Hanno Kasper, but he had already risked too much to back down now. He took out his warrant card together with a letter and handed them to Kasper.

"*Mein Herr,*" he said, mind racing to come up with a credible explanation for his audacity, "I am aware of your emergency powers, but the Interior Minister is still your superior and has the right to overrule you as and when he sees fit. As you can see from this letter, I have been personally authorized by the Minister to investigate matters concerning the Federal Republic's role as a NATO partner. Because of the terrorist attack on Höhenbo-"

"*I* report directly to the *Chancellor!* And this operation has nothing to do with NATO! This is a case of internal subversion affecting the security of the Fatherland. Now, you will ... who the devil are *these* people?"

Debbie Lueckenhoff and Eddie Cassera had exited the helicopter. They introduced themselves, flashing US Defense Department ID cards at the enraged German security chief.

"*Americans!*" Kasper exploded. "You have absolutely no right to interfere in my operation here!"

A fusillade of shots broke out on the slope above them, answered by a brief stutter of fire from the cabin.

"These Americans are NATO representatives also," Veditz said, hoping it was true. "Herr Cassera has flown directly from Washington to investigate this incident."

"I don't care if he came *directly* from Mars! Now get back aboard your aircraft and get out of here or I'll have you handcuffed and thrown aboard!"

"That would create a nasty international incident," Debbie Lueckenhoff said in her flawless German. "I'm sure my government would be very displeased." Kasper looked close to apoplexy. "All right, we shall settle this through official channels. You come with me and I will call the Chancellor!"

They walked to the Command Post vehicle with Kasper and two KSK officers. Kasper motioned to the short officer who wore a general's rank badges. "Baldur, come inside with me. Manfred, you stay out here with our unwelcome guests until I call for them."

The *ATF Dingo's* door clanged shut. Kasper's aide looked at the female DIA agent. "You speak good German for an American," he sniffed. "A trace of a Swabian accent. Where did you learn it?"

"At my mother's knee in New Ulm, Texas," she replied. "German is our second language there."

"In Texas?" Manfred looked like he thought Lueckenhoff was baiting him.

While they talked, Cassera stepped a few feet away to get a better view of the besieged cabin. *He was so close. Soon the Germans' wrangling over authority would be resolved. Typical officious Krauts*! He willed the guys in the cabin to hang on, hoping he would be able to persuade them to surrender. *They had to respond to a fellow American, someone who understood what had happened to them (even if the "how" was inexplicable), and could ease their transition into the modern world. Eddie Cassera was going to take them home!*

A raw wind howled off Grosser Rachel's snow-capped peak, presaging a cold night. Cassera shivered and looked around him. He noticed a German soldier standing with his back to him about thirty yards away, partially obscured by a bush. The trooper moved aside, revealing a woman and man in civilian garb, leaning together against a tree trunk.

They were a fair distance away, and the light under the trees was dimming, but he had the feeling that he knew the young man. Unnoticed by the chattering KSK lieutenant, Cassera approached the people behind the bush. As he got closer he saw that the soldier was covering the couple with an assault rifle.

He took another few steps, and halted as the bareheaded young man in a green jacket looked towards him. Cassera felt a giddy rush of excitement as he realized why the fellow looked so familiar. The face was the same as that in the old 293 File photograph he had memorized just a few hours ago.

"*Sutton,*" he whispered.

The guard whirled as footsteps crackled on dry pine needles. He swung his carbine towards the trench-coated man who limped into the clearing.

"*Halt! Was wollen Sie?* Who are you?"

The civilian kept trudging toward the pair of terrorists the trooper was guarding. He raised his carbine, confused by the look of wonder on the intruder's face. "*Herr Leutnant!*" he shouted to Manfred. "*Kommen Sie her. Schnell!*"

The stranger seemed oblivious to both the guard and the female terrorist. He stopped in front of the male subversive, looked into his face, and smiled.

"Hello, Sutton."

Sutton flinched as if struck. "You know me?"

Cassera nodded. "First Lieutenant Arthur J. Sutton, Second Rangers. Born Lee's Summit, Missouri, May 18,

1920. Silver Star and Purple Heart on D-Day. Commanding officer of Fox team on Operation Bandstand, April 21, 1945."

"*How?*" Sutton gasped.

"I'm here to help you. Crazy as it sounds, you and your men have been caught in a time–"

"*He knows!*" interrupted Paula. "Arthur realizes what's happened. But the other Bandstand men up in the cabin *don't.* Kasper is convinced they are terrorists and is going to kill them without letting them surrender!"

There was an angry shout and the KSK lieutenant charged through the bushes. "This place is off limits!" he screamed at Cassera. "No communication with these prisoners!"

"Prisoners? What have they done?"

"They are members of the terrorist gang in the cabin. You must come–"

"The woman says you are going to murder the men in the cabin without giving them a chance to surrender," Cassera said. "Certainly that can't be true!"

"The scum fired on us first and now they must be exterminated. But that is no concern of yours, *Amerikaner.* Come with me!"

Rage ignited inside Cassera, exploding to incandescent fury as the German officer signaled to the trooper, who prodded Cassera in the ribs with the muzzle of his carbine. "*Weitergehen!* Move!"

Cassera had been an infantry officer in Vietnam, and he hadn't lost his combat skills despite the passage of over four decades. He grabbed the carbine barrel, swung the trooper off balance, kicked him in the kneecap with his good leg to drop him and then in the face as he went down. Eddie wrenched the rifle away as the man cried out and raised his hands to his broken nose. Reversing the weapon, Cassera aimed it at the stunned German officer and clicked off the safety. His damaged leg hurt like hell, but exultation dwarfed his pain.

"Take his pistol, Sutton."

Paula gazed at the writhing trooper on the ground. "What are you doing?" she cried.

"I'm going to force these assholes to let Sutton's men surrender. My two colleagues over there will guarantee they can get away from here safely. We'll escort them out."

"I'm the only one who can get my guys to surrender," Sutton said. "They'd never believe a stranger, especially when surrounded by these goons."

"How will you get to the cabin without being shot?" Paula asked. "It's surrounded by soldiers and they think you're a terrorist!"

Cassera eyed the rigid KSK lieutenant. He pointed to the radio on the officer's belt.

"Guess it's time for America to take a few hostages," he said. "This Kraut's going to call up his pals, tell 'em I'm holding them hostage, and order an immediate ceasefire. If they don't let Sutton through to the cabin, these two jokers are going to get blown away." He nodded grimly. "I mean it, too."

Paula looked at Manfred with open revulsion and repeated Cassera's instructions in German. The *leutnant* obviously didn't care for the murderous expression on Cassera's face.

He nodded and unclipped his radio.

303

"*Befehlsstelle*. Calling the Command Post. Urgent!"

Michalke's voice crackled a query. Manfred cleared his throat and gave him Cassera's demands.

"Repeat, please," Michalke said.

Manfred complied. Seconds later Cassera saw the CP vehicle's door open as Kasper and Michalke scrambled out to stand with Lueckenhoff and Veditz, who had mutely watched the entire action since the KSK lieutenant left them.

"I'll see that you get thirty years for this," Kasper hissed at Veditz.

The BfV detective was shaken. "I didn't know! I never suspected he'd–"

"Shut up, traitor!" Kasper snarled.

"We'll have to do as they say," Michalke said. "There's no doubt these monsters are mad enough to kill Manfred and our other man."

Kasper studied the quartet behind the bushes, contorted features relaxing as a plan came to him. "This may yet work to our advantage," he said. "Tell them we agree, and order a cease-fire."

He stroked his submachine gun. "You are in charge until I return," he told Michalke, and walked quickly away.

28

The radio Paula had taken from the KSK officer came back to life. She listened to Michalke, then turned to Cassera. "They've agreed to your demands. The cease-fire is in effect. They promise that Arthur can go to the cabin without danger from them."

Sutton touched Cassera's arm. "I don't know who you are, Mister, but you're sure a Godsend. You were a soldier, weren't you?"

"In another war long after yours. But, yeah. A soldier. Like you." The two veterans locked eyes for a moment. "Good luck, Lieutenant."

"I'll thank you properly when we're all safely out of here," Sutton said. He looked at the German officer's pistol in his hand, glanced at Paula, then tossed the weapon into the bushes. He tried to ignore the tears in Paula's worried eyes.

"Arthur?" she said.

"I'll be back." He turned away.

"Wait." She pressed something into his hand. He opened it to see Franklin Roosevelt's resolute features. "Your good luck charm. Take it with you."

"I'm no Indian giver," he said, dropping the button into his pocket. "I'll give it back to you soon as I return."

Then he strode purposefully up the slope towards the bullet-riddled cabin.

Private Dan Holcombe had expended the last of his .45 caliber ammunition a few minutes earlier after the fusillade that took Kemp's life. He had heard Kemp cry out in the bedroom and crawled in to check on him when the enemy gunfire subsided. Kemp had been hit in the eye and must have died instantly. When Holcombe told Roth about it, the sergeant curtly ordered him to go back and collect Kemp's ammunition.

Heartless son of a bitch, Holcombe thought. Panic squeezed his chest so he could hardly breath. He knew he wasn't going to get out of the cabin alive, would never again hunt coons with Pa in the Alabama backwoods. His fingers shook so badly that he had a hard time loading the Mauser hunting rifle from the box of 7.92-mm rounds. He climbed up to the loft and wriggled across the dusty floor. *Good thing he had remembered the rifle. Now he could try to pick off some of those goddam Krauts out there that the tommy guns hadn't been able to reach.*

He inched up to the small dormer window. Enemy bullets had shattered the glass, saving him the risk of opening the sash. He propped the rifle muzzle on the windowsill, far enough inside so the Krauts couldn't see it.

The loft was almost dark, but there was still enough light outside to get in some clear shots. Holcombe adjusted the focus of the telescopic sight, then lifted his head to seek a target. He spotted a man in civvy clothes marching up the hill towards the cabin as if he were unconcerned about getting plugged by one side or the other.

Holcombe dropped his eye to the telescopic sight and zeroed in on the man's face. *Glory be, it was Lieutenant Sutton!* But why the hell weren't the Germans shooting at him? Maybe, just maybe, they had killed poor Loomis and Kemp by mistake and the lieutenant was coming to tell Roth and him that it was okay to surrender after all!

Then he noticed something else — a black uniformed SS officer creeping along the edge of the woods behind Sutton. Holcombe focused on the enemy soldier, clearly seeing the Iron Cross on his jacket and the submachine gun in his hands. Better not take any chances in case that guy's fixing to shoot Lieutenant Sutton, he thought, centering the Mauser's crosshairs on the German's head.

Hanno Kasper slipped behind a tree with the submachine gun held close to his chest. *Yes,* he thought, *this will work out perfectly.* The insane terrorist who had arrived with the von Scheller bitch could be exterminated along with the others in the cabin. First, though, he would take care of the girl and the swarthy American holding Manfred and the trooper hostage. Poor Manfred – he probably wouldn't survive the spray of machine gun bullets at close range, but he would die for the Fatherland.

He slid off the MP7's safety catch and curled his hand around its pistol grip. He was close now, the unsuspecting American bureaucrat only ten meters away. The swine was talking to the von Scheller girl while covering Manfred and the injured trooper on the ground with a stolen carbine.

A twig snapped under Kasper's heel. He saw the girl turn her head, eyes widening at the sight of him. His finger took up the slack on the trigger. Paula von Scheller screamed a warning, her cry drowned by the roaring machine gun.

Kasper took the Semitic-looking American first, grinning as the bullets stitched a line of bloody holes across his back. He traversed the stream of hardened steel rounds towards the girl, flinging aside the stupefied Manfred. *Just another half meter and the girl would be–*

Something slapped his neck with sledgehammer force, boring through his throat in a split second before exiting in a geyser of blood and bone chips. Kasper dropped the gun as an irresistible weight forced him to his knees. He clawed at his gushing throat, fingers rapidly growing cold and unresponsive to his mental commands. He toppled onto his back.

Hanno Kasper's fading eyes stared into roiling black clouds that formed images from his past. For a moment he was a youth again, gazing into the *Führer's* hypnotic eyes. Far, far away he thought he heard a host of Valkyries coming to get him, but their singing was only the icy wind in the trees.

Eddie Cassera lay on the ground with arms splayed, looking at his twitching right hand as the final breath wafted from his shattered chest. He noticed someone approaching across a lush tropical landscape that had replaced the German forest. As the figure came near he saw with wonder that it was a skinny black kid, a teenager in an oversized helmet wearing a sleeveless green combat uniform. The kid was grinning widely, as was the group of young soldiers following. Eddie recognized them all with a joy beyond anything he had known.

The black kid squatted in front of Cassera.

"Now what you gone and done to yourself, 'Tenant?"

The kid took Eddie's hand as the lost men from his platoon gathered around.

"Time for us all to go home now, sir," he said gently, raising Cassera from the earth.

The *feldwebel* commanding an LGS *Fennek* twenty meters from Kasper's corpse screamed in sorrow and rage. He slapped the gunner on his shoulder.

"They've shot General Kasper!" he cried. "Sniper in the cabin's loft. I saw the muzzle flash. Get him!"

The gunner elevated the barrel of his GMG grenade machine gun and sighted at the dormer window on the cabin's roof. The weapon hurled 40-mm grenades straight into the opening until the window and much of the roof around it were blasted into kindling.

Through his ringing ears the gunner heard someone shout "cease fire!"

Sutton was less than fifty yards from the cabin when the submachine gun chattered at the base of the knoll. He threw himself flat, waiting for the bullets to find him. They didn't come, and he raised his head as a rifle cracked from the cabin's roof.

"It's me, Lieutenant," Holcombe called from the dormer window. "Come on in."

309

Sutton sprinted towards the cabin. He had almost made it when a heavy machine gun began pounding and rounds whistled overhead, striking the roof. He heard a strangled, bubbling scream from Holcombe amidst the explosions. The door opened and he fell inside, landing on his hands and knees on a floor covered with dozens of empty brass shell casings.

"Nice of you to join us," said Hugo Roth.

Paula confronted General Michalke, who stood horror-struck over Kasper's body. "Stop them!" she screamed as the armored reconnaissance vehicle shelled the cabin. "You promised! For God's sake stop the shooting!"

Michalke's head snapped up, regaining control as he realized that he was now in command. He looked at Paula, then at the cabin. The blood returned to his strained pale face.

"Cease firing!" he boomed. "Nobody gave those men permission to open up!"

The 40-mm GMG fell silent after four more shots. Debbie Lueckenhoff and Christoph Veditz left Cassera's body and joined Paula. Michalke glanced around him at the ring of stunned faces, some - his troopers' - hungry for revenge, the others' imploring. His decision was a compromise.

"We'll give them ten minutes to surrender. Let them know over the megaphone. If they ignore us, I'll wipe that cabin from the face of the earth!"

"You're wounded," said Sutton.

Roth was helmetless. He touched a furrow in his close-cropped blond hair. The fingers came away sticky with blood. "Just a crease. The Nazis have been going for head shots. That's what happened to Loomis and Kemp."

"Loomis and Kemp?"

"In there." Roth gestured towards the bedroom. Sutton checked the two sprawled corpses and returned, looking sick.

"Holcombe's dead too. Upstairs." Roth spat on the floor. "He's nothing but mincemeat. You and I are the only ones left."

A metallic voice blared outside, addressing them in German. "Attention the occupants of the cabin. You are called upon to surrender and be taken into custody for a fair trial. You have ten minutes from now to comply. If you fail to do so, your refuge will be destroyed. That is all."

The message was repeated in English.

"Fair trial my ass!" Roth sneered. "Since when are prisoners of war put on trial? That just proves they are trying to trick us into coming out in the open. Loomis tried to surrender under a white flag and they killed him. They'll do the same to us." He suddenly looked at Sutton with suspicion. "How'd you get here, and where's your uniform?"

"Paula von Scheller, the German woman, helped me. We heard about the siege and were arrested when we tried to get up here to you. I was able to escape from those German antiterrorist troops after they brought me here."

"Antiterrorist troops? Those are *SS* troops, Lieutenant!"

Roth wiped away a ribbon of blood that had run into his eye. Sutton took a deep breath.

"Sergeant Roth, as your commanding officer I order you to put down your weapons and surrender. Regardless of what happened to Loomis, I give you my word that you will not be harmed. I will walk out of here at your side."

Roth grinned crookedly, shaking his head as he wiped blood drops from the stock of his Thompson. "You can go back out there if you want, Lieutenant. I will stay here and watch the SS guns tear you to pieces."

"They are not SS. The SS no longer exists, Roth. Those men out there are security forces who believe we are terrorists."

"Terrorists?"

"Anarchists. People who wage an undeclared war during peacetime."

"Peacetime?"

"The war is over, Roth."

"Since when?"

"Since May 8, 1945."

Roth went rigid. He *knew* that something was wrong, had noticed too many anomalies since the parachute landing. *But this? No.* He shook his head in disbelief.

"I think that bump on your head made you *verrückt* – crazy – Lieutenant. You sound just like that old Junker and his granddaughter who tried to convince us that the war had been over for 66 years."

"It has."

Roth gave a bitter laugh. "Prove it, college boy."

Sutton pulled the newspaper and magazines from his pockets and handed them to Roth. "I didn't believe it either. I know it sounds impossible, but it's true. We were caught in some aberration of time."

Roth scanned the *International Herald Tribune*, then dropped it on the floor. He did the same with *Newsweek*. Sutton saw his hands trembling.

"No," Roth whispered as he turned the pages of *Time*. "This cannot be true, it cannot be true." An article riveted him. "*Israel*," he said wonderingly. "It says here that a German opera company from Berlin is touring Israel!"

"I was told that Israel has been an independent Jewish country since the year 1948," said Sutton.

Roth raised his bloody head, face twitching as he stared blindly at the bullet-chipped wall. "*Israel.* If only it were true …."

"*Funf minuten!*" said the loudspeaker outside. "You have five minutes to surrender!"

Roth's eyes returned to the magazine, brows knitting as he turned the page. His features hardened. The sergeant closed his eyes, shook his head, shaking fingers crumpling the magazine. Sutton stepped forward and gripped his wrist.

"Come with me, Roth," he said gently.

Roth was still for several seconds longer, then straightened and jerked his arm away.

"There are only two possible explanations," Roth said. "One is that what you say is true." He waved the *Time* magazine. "But the world I read about here is such a perversion that it is implausible. The other explanation," he whispered, "and the only one I can believe, is that you are a traitor."

"What?"

"Dirty lying turncoat!" Roth flung the magazine in Sutton's face, then hefted his submachine gun by the barrel and clubbed Sutton's shoulder with it. Sutton fell against the wall clutching his numbed arm.

"Roth!"

"They sent you here, didn't they?" Roth yelled. "The Nazis got you to come here and trick me into surrendering with their cleverly printed magazines. What did they offer you, your life in exchange for this subhuman Jew's?"

He cocked the Thompson, pointed its wavering barrel at Sutton's chest. Blood flowed freely now from Roth's head wound, his words slurred and accent thickened. "It didn't work, Lieutenant! I'm too smart for them! This Jew-boy's too smart for all of you! For Americans *and* for Nazis!"

Sutton saw Roth's forefinger tighten on the trigger. "Don't! There's no trick!"

Roth's chest heaved. He used his left hand to dash blood from his eyes.

"Believe me, Roth! For your family's sake, you've got to take this chance to go on living!"

"My family? *Meine Familie ist tot.* Dead." He lowered the submachine gun. "My world is gone!"

For the first time since he'd known him, Sutton saw Roth's face display an emotion other than bitterness. The sergeant's shoulders hunched, and his features seemed to shrivel like the dried apple dolls made by Sutton's grandmother. In the dim light, he appeared to age decades. Sutton had seen wounded men who simply gave up the will to live, and now he sensed Roth's spirit withering even though his body was whole. He had never witnessed such bleakness on a man's face.

"*Vergessen Sie nie,*" said Roth, looking past Sutton, as if talking to ghosts. He swayed, stumbling a little to recover his stance. His gaze shifted to Sutton. "That means—"

"Never forget," said Sutton. "I know."

Roth raised the gun again, pointing it at Sutton's head. Sutton tensed, but didn't turn away from the trembling barrel. Beyond it, he met Roth's eyes, which were as dim and cold as a dead man's. Then Roth lowered the gun and ran out the door.

Roth came out at a charge, blood like tendrils on his face. He shrieked curses as he ran down the hill, firing his Thompson from the hip at the encircling Germans.

General Michalke gave the command to fire. Roth was stopped mid-run, caught in the cross-fire of over 30 automatic weapons, his body held up by the force of striking bullets for several seconds. Finally, he collapsed and rolled to the foot of the knoll, so mutilated as to be unrecognizable.

Sutton heard the cacophony of automatic weapons as he reached for the *Time* magazine lying on the cabin floor. He had to know what terrible thing made Roth say that this world was a perversion.

The last article Roth read was titled "Iranian President Calls for Cleansing of Israel." The leader of Iran was quoted as saying that the Jewish state should "be wiped off the map," and that the Nazi Holocaust of European Jewry was a "myth."

Does anything really change? Sutton grimaced and crawled into the bedroom, blood drenching his clothes from the congealing pool around the cadavers of Loomis and Kemp. He peered through a chink in the log walls where the mortar had been shot out, straining to spot the German soldiers in the twilight. He saw the figures of armed men rise from their positions and flit back into the forest. The odds were slim, but no less than they had been since the start of Operation Bandstand. He crawled to an open window, sucked a deep breath, and rolled over the sill.

The KSK commander General Michalke neither knew nor cared how many, if any, terrorists were left alive in the cabin. It was time to end the siege that had taken his beloved leader's life. The troopers surrounding the building were given two minutes to withdraw to a safe distance so they would not be endangered by stray high explosive rounds. As night descended, Michalke ordered the mortar crews to commence firing.

Five minutes later, all that remained of the cabin was a blazing heap of lumber that threw ghostly shadows on the ancient Bavarian forest.

29

Paula von Scheller was cleared of all charges of conspiracy and subversion and allowed to return to her ailing grandfather's home in the Bäyerischer Wald. She refused to speak with reporters. In September 2011, she quit her medical school program and moved out of her apartment in Regensburg without leaving a forwarding address.

General Hanno Kasper was given a state funeral attended by the German Chancellor and most members of her cabinet. Former Chancellor Helmut Schmidt (who had served as a Wehrmacht officer during World War II) made a surprise appearance, and the Pope – an erstwhile member of the Hitler Youth like the deceased hero – sent his personal condolences.

Kasper was buried with full military honors in the churchyard of St. John the Baptist in Trostberg, Bavaria. A contingent of Waffen SS veterans sang the *Horst Wessel Lied*. The day after Kasper's interment, a magnificent floral wreath in the shape of an Iron Cross interwoven with edelweiss was discovered on his grave. Inside the wreath was a linen cloth embroidered with the design of a Phoenix rising from a bed of ashes. Below it was the Latin word *Resurgam* – I Shall Rise Again.

Edward Cassera was laid to rest in Arlington National Cemetery on a warm late spring day. DPMO Director Bill Miller hung around for a long time after the few other mourners had gone. He took the rest of the day off and went to a bar in Alexandria where he got drunk and wondered what arcane government office had confiscated the Bandstand case materials. All he knew was that it was out of his hands, classified with the highest code word clearance.

"Forget about it," a putty-faced little man had told him when his equally expressionless team finished carting away every scrap of material relating to the case. "It never happened. Got it?"

Three weeks after Cassera's burial a US Air Mobility Command C-17 Globemaster III landed at Dover Air Force Base in Delaware. Thirty-six aluminum coffins were unloaded from the aircraft – 31 holding KIAs from Afghanistan, and five officially declared to be the remains of men who had been missing since 1945. The latter caskets were trucked to the military mortuary at Arlington.

The discovery of MIA remains from the Second World War was a rarity these days. Because the World War II generation remained an important voting bloc, the Washington power elite extracted as much political mileage as possible from the Bandstand team's homecoming. The official circumstances of their finding were vague.

The group burial three days later was attended by over a hundred people, including a general, a brace of colonels, a senator, four congressmen, the VFW national commander, the Washington representative of B'nai B'rith, the Governor of Alabama, nine reporters, and a rabbi. Flowers were sent by the President and First Lady and several dozen other Washington luminaries. Thirty-seven relatives of the deceased also attended.

Among them was an old lady from Briny Breezes, Florida.

EPILOGUE

June 2012

James C. Ward (plain "Jim" to his friends) wanted to give his wife Lucy something special for their 60th wedding anniversary. So on the big day he took her out to dinner, plied her with California champagne, and presented her with tickets and a brochure for a "Remember the '40s Big Band Cruise" to the Caribbean. Lucy was so thrilled that Jim got lucky that night. They did things that had made Lucy blush when they were newlyweds.

The kids and grandkids gave them a big send off at the St. Louis airport. Even though he had been retired for many years as a Senior Vice President at American Airlines, Jim and Lucy were upgraded to first class on the flight to Fort Lauderdale. Midway through the flight the pilot came out to shake Jim's hand. After he returned to the cockpit, Jim turned to Lucy and said, "And to think if it hadn't been for the War, I might have stayed on the farm instead of getting that aeronautical engineering degree on the GI Bill."

Every night aboard the cruise ship they danced to the big band hits of their youth. Almost all the other passengers were from their generation, and the men were mostly World War II veterans like Jim. The music and conversations with other aging men brought back memories of harrowing flights abroad *Bouncing Betty* when he was a young flight engineer.

Jim and Lucy could still cut a pretty mean rug, especially when the band played "In the Mood" and "Little Brown Jug." But they couldn't hold a candle to a particularly good-looking young couple that could jitterbug like there was no tomorrow. The pair were the youngest passengers by a good 50 years. All the oldsters noticed them. Some commented on them with envy, others with warmth.

"It's nice to see young people enjoying our generation's music," said Lucy.

"Unusual," mumbled Jim, unable to take his eyes off the laughing young man.

"You old goat," she teased with a knowing smile. "That girl sure is pretty. Makes you forget you're a grandfather, eh?"

"No." Jim's eyes took on a distant look. "It's the fellow. Looks familiar. You know I never forget a face."

"Someone from the country club?"

"No. That boy's the spitting image of someone I knew a long time ago. In the War. Just can't place him now. It'll come back to me."

"Maybe it's his grandson."

"Maybe."

Jim and Lucy held each other close during the band's closing number, "Moonlight Serenade." They walked arm in arm to the elevator, a little breathless but happy. Just as the elevator door was closing, the young couple squeezed aboard, giggling.

"Which deck?" the girl asked in a German accent, her finger poised above the lighted panel buttons. "Oh, same as us," she said when Jim responded. Her companion shifted uncomfortably under the older man's rapt gaze as they rode down to C deck.

The couple bade them good night and strode ahead along the corridor. They stopped outside their cabin door and the man delved into a pocket of his tuxedo jacket for his key. Something fell to the deck as he took his hand out. Jim and Lucy were just passing, and Jim stooped to pick up the small object.

"Excuse me, you dropped someth—"

Jim slowly straightened, heart pounding. Even without his reading glasses, he could see the tiny face of Franklin Delano Roosevelt.

"What's wrong, honey?" Lucy's voice rose in alarm. "You look like you've seen a ghost."

The young man plucked the button from Jim's quivering palm.

"Hey thanks, pal," he said in a voice that Jim had last heard seven decades earlier. "Wouldn't want to lose my good luck charm."

Liked *Time Fall*? You'll love Tim Ashby's gripping historical thriller, *Devil's Den*. Fast-moving and compelling, *Devil's Den* features Ashby's always meticulously researched real-life characters such as J. Edgar Hoover and Charles Lindbergh. As young gumshoe Seth Armitage battles both corruption and his own demons to solve his complex crime, you'll experience a fascinating and emotionally rich period between WWI and WWII in America. For fans of Caleb Carr's *The Alienist*, and such nonfiction works as Erik Larson's *Devil in the White City*.

Timothy Ashby would love to hear from you! Contact him through his website: *www.timashby.com*, or on Twitter through @tfashby.com

Timothy Ashby worked in Washington DC as a counter-terrorism consultant, holding a Top Secret security clearance and working with the U.S. military's Joint Special Operations Command (JSOC). He also served as a senior official at the U.S. Commerce Department. A licensed attorney in Florida and the District of Columbia, he has a PhD degree from the University of Southern California, a JD from Seattle University Law School, and an MBA from the University of Edinburgh Scotland. Visit his author blog at www.timashby.com.

CPSIA information can be obtained at www.ICGtesting.com
Printed in the USA
BVOW00s2240300114

343578BV00010B/75/P

9 781939 990150